P9-CLO-924

M.M.CHOUINARD

THE
VACATION

Bookouture

Published by Bookouture in 2021

An imprint of Storyfire Ltd.
Carmelite House
50 Victoria Embankment
London EC4Y 0DZ

www.bookouture.com

Copyright © M.M. Chouinard, 2021

M.M. Chouinard has asserted her right to be identified
as the author of this work.

All rights reserved.
No part of this publication may be reproduced,
stored in any retrieval system, or transmitted, in any form or by
any means, electronic, mechanical, photocopying, recording or
otherwise, without the prior written permission of the publishers.

ISBN: 978-1-80019-364-2
eBook ISBN: 978-1-80019-363-5

This book is a work of fiction. Names, characters, businesses,
organizations, places and events other than those clearly in the
public domain, are either the product of the author's imagination
or are used fictitiously. Any resemblance to actual persons, living or
dead, events or locales is entirely coincidental.

For *the* Bionic Woman

CHAPTER ONE

Now

Rose Martin sips her drink and closes her eyes as the warm Jamaican breeze brushes her face, her legs, her bare shoulders. The humidity is lush and sensual and when the air wafts past her, carrying the scent of the distant ocean up the mountainside, every inch of her skin comes alive, transforming her into a goddess. She wants to dance, slowly and with abandon, to the steel-drum melodies coming from the villa's Bluetooth speakers. Wants to laugh and sing, and make love long into the night.

Finally, *finally*, she's managing to relax, despite how hard the last couple of days have been. Maybe Brandon was right, maybe the vacation was just what they needed—time with family and friends in paradise. She's been ridiculous to stress so much about it, and she really does need to get better at dealing with her anxieties. She makes a mental note to make an appointment with her therapist as soon as they get back to the States.

"Gin," Anabelle calls.

Rose reopens her eyes to watch Anabelle spread her cards out on the wooden table with a single, graceful, well-manicured gesture; the moonlight glints off the pool behind Anabelle, playing up the contrast between her pink French tips and her brown skin. Rose glances down at her own pale hand—a dash of red polish might be the perfect touch for their upcoming Thanksgiving dinner.

"Dammit," Brandon says, and throws his cards down. "Five in a row. I give up."

Anabelle's uncharacteristically sharp laugh cracks across the tiled courtyard and echoes off the three mustard-yellow houses that enclose it. "That's because I'm the only one not drunk."

A chorus of half-hearted denials ring out, and Rose examines the nearly empty pitcher of rum punch as she sets her own cards down. It's the second pitcher, but even so, is that really enough to get six adults drunk? She's tipsy, without a doubt. Not a problem, the children are asleep, but she probably shouldn't drink anymore regardless. Everyone has to be up early tomorrow morning, and her brother- and sister-in-law have already gone to bed.

The thought reminds her. "I should go check on the kids. Do you want me to look in on your boys, too?"

Anabelle starts to answer, but her husband Mateo interrupts. "Chill out, Rosie, Brandon just checked on them. You're gonna turn into one of those—what's it called—helicopter parents. Oh, wait—too late."

Rose winces at the nickname he knows she hates, and stands. "I don't like being out of earshot for too long when they aren't feeling well. And believe it or not, it's been well over an hour since he checked on them. Time flies when you're having fun."

Mateo throws up his hands, a wry grin on his face. "An hour, well, then! My bad."

Rose refuses to rise to the bait—let him vent any way he needs to—choosing instead to shake her head gently and smile. "I'll just be a minute."

Sauntering toward the south-most house in the villa, she tries to refocus on the caress of the warm breeze. She steps under the gorgeous Moroccan-scrolled overhang to the door and then into the bohemian living room, all wicker furniture and bright, happy prints that make her smile. The room is stuffy—only the ceiling fans propel the warm air inside—and already she misses the intoxicating breeze. She cracks open the door to the children's room, and peeks into Jackson's crib. He's sound asleep, and she smiles at the sight of his face, cherubic in the soft glow of the night light. Thank goodness he's sleeping soundly—it's hard enough to get him to sleep through the night even without the sniffles that have made him fussy all day.

The door swings open the rest of the way, and the hair on Rose's neck stands up in the breeze. Because it's organic again, natural and flowing, not the artificial swirl of the fans. The window shouldn't be open, but it is, curtains billowing out into the room, obscuring Lily's bed just underneath.

She rushes over and bats aside the curtains—the bed is flat, empty. Heart pounding in her throat, she pulls at the covers and sheets and pillows as though her daughter could be hiding underneath them, playing an impossible game of hide and seek.

"Lily?" She frantically dives to check under the bed, kicks away the wicker chairs, pushes aside the clothes in the tiny closet. "Lily, this isn't funny. Come out right now!"

But she knows this isn't a three-year-old's prank. Lily's not the sort of child who hides from her mother. And she's timid, anxious even—she'd never climb out a window on her own.

Rose clambers onto the bed and sticks her head out, glancing left and right, seeing nothing except the empty street that leads past the house through John's Hall and toward Montego Bay.

No Lily. No anybody.

Fueled by a last scrap of hope, she dashes back through the small house—master bedroom, kitchen, living room—calling Lily's name, louder now, any concern for waking Jackson gone.

No Lily.

She hurries back to the children's room and searches again, the bed, the closet, Jackson's crib, behind the chairs, refusing to admit what she won't find.

Then, she sinks to her knees, screaming.

CHAPTER TWO

One month before

Rose

"Oh, I forgot to tell you, I talked to Leo today." Brandon froze at the entrance to the living room and smiled down at her. "You always look so beautiful when you're in your happy place."

Rose glanced up from her fabric swatches, legs tucked up under her as she cuddled into the couch, and laughed. "I never thought of it that way, but I guess strolling through a new set of fabrics *is* my happy place, like my brain's version of running free through Disneyland. But I also got some really excellent news today. That boutique in Boston called and said my collection is selling so well they want everything from my spring/summer collection. I've been riding the adrenaline rush all evening, waiting for the kids to go to sleep so I can dive into these and start planning for next fall."

"Congratulations, hon. Next step: New York Fashion Week." Brandon gestured an imaginary marquee above his head.

She rolled her eyes. "Maybe a few more steps in between. But you were saying you talked to Leo today?"

"Right." He set his glass of wine on a coaster, grabbed the television remote, and dropped onto the sleek black sofa. "He called and invited us for Thanksgiving."

Rose turned cold. "In Jamaica?"

Brandon took a sip of the wine. "Where else?"

"I thought they might be coming back to the States for the holidays," she said, her design process forgotten. "He called you at work?"

Brandon cleared his throat. "He left a message while I was in surgery. For a really jacked-up facelift, by the way—the woman's third, because the guy who did the second one butchered her. Anyway. I called Leo back on my way home."

Of course Leo would try to convince Brandon first. He'd been trying to get them to visit for the last six months, and knew full well that Rose wouldn't want to go. "That's nice of them to invite us, but—"

"He's inviting Mateo and Anabelle, too, so we'll have the gang back together. And you were just saying how you weren't ready for another New England winter."

"But we were talking about Los Angeles or even Napa Valley. And sometime in January, not over Thanksgiving. My parents will have a fit."

"We'll see your parents over Christmas. But this is the only way we'll get to see my sister over the holidays."

Rose's chest tightened. "But they'll be moving back in the spring. That's not so long, and we'll see them then."

He clicked on the TV, but muted it as he surfed the channels. "That's just it. AmericAid needs him there for at least another year. I guess the hurricanes last year slowed things down, so his part of the project won't finish on time. And Bree has never met Jackson. They need to bond."

"We've talked about this." Her mind raced. She slid the swatches onto the glass coffee table and grabbed her computer. She typed and clicked, then swiveled the machine to show the screen to Brandon. "Look. Travel advisory. Avoid unnecessary travel to Jamaica."

He flicked his wrist toward her and reached for his wine. "They always say that."

"That's because it's always true. Look here." She pointed at the screen. "And I quote: 'Violent crimes such as home invasions, armed robberies, sexual assaults and homicides are common. Local police lack the resources to respond effectively to serious criminal incidents.' The kids are too young for us to take those risks."

"The crime isn't against tourists, it's outside those areas. You're buying into alarmist stereotypes." He settled on a twenty-four-hour news channel.

"It says incidents happen frequently even at all-inclusive resorts, and it lists Montego Bay specifically. And it goes on to say that even *government personnel* are prohibited from traveling outside prescribed areas and shouldn't use public transportation. And that you shouldn't drive or walk at night." She moved her pointed finger across the lines as she read the page.

"Rose. There are plenty of places in *Boston* that aren't safe to go to after dark. You find that everywhere."

"But we know Boston. We know where to go and where not to go."

He reached over and gently swatted the laptop closed. "And Leo and Bree know Jamaica. They've lived there for two and a half years, and other people in the organization have been there even longer. They know where it's safe and where it isn't. And Anabelle's father was born and raised in the Dominican Republic. She's spent time on every island in the Caribbean."

Her voice wavered as she struggled to stay calm. "I told you about that piece I saw on *The Global Daily Gazette* site, about the little girls getting kidnapped in Jamaica."

"And I told you to stop reading that gossip rag." He gestured toward the TV with the remote. "Stick with real news. Hundreds of kids are kidnapped all over the world every day. You only clicked on that particular article because Leo and Bree are in Jamaica."

Rose shifted in her seat and shot a glance upward, in the direction of the children's rooms. "Can't they just come back here instead? We can even host Thanksgiving dinner. You've always wanted to barbecue a turkey."

Brandon followed her glance. He clicked off the TV and turned to fully face her. "Did you talk to the doctor about a new prescription?"

"Not yet."

"Why not?"

"My body's still readjusting from Jackson's birth, and I don't want to mess with that balance."

He tilted his head at her. "It's been over a year."

The truth was she wanted to prove, mostly to herself, that she no longer needed the medication. She cleared her throat. "I've been fine day to day, and the doctor gave me some emergency Xanax if I have a panic attack or anything."

Brandon's expression was skeptical. "Good, bring it with you. But talk to your doctor about starting a new prescription before we go, because you shouldn't be this distressed by a possible trip to paradise. I know why you worry so much about them, but we can't let it rule our lives. You have to get past it, your therapist even said so. You know I'd never let anything happen to you or the kids, right?"

She nodded. She also knew that her own father never would have willingly let anything happen to her or her sister. And yet, Lillian Marie had drowned in Lake Merritt just the same.

"Okay, then. Talk to your therapist too, she'll help you feel better about it. But we need this trip. You've been working so hard between the kids and your design work, and after everything I've had to deal with to take over the new practice, I need a break." He gestured toward the swatches. "Think how amazing a little island inspiration will be. We'll come back refreshed and happy. You'll see. Trust me."

Trust. She trusted *him* just fine. He made her feel protected and secure—his confidence and strength were the main reasons she'd fallen in love with him. But the downside of the alpha-male energy, the flip side of the confidence-and-strength coin, was he could be stubborn. He had strong opinions about the world, and when he committed to some sort of action, there wasn't any changing his mind.

And her therapist would say he was right about this. It was far too easy for her to slip into her safe cocoon, and that wasn't good for her or the kids. The last thing she wanted was to pass her anxieties off on them; she knew too well how the neuroses of a parent could bleed into every aspect of a child's life.

So she might as well find a silver lining. "You always see those stunning resorts on the commercials. Beautiful spas and gorgeous restaurants, and I'm sure they're all very secure."

He waved the thought away. "You can spend your entire trip in one of those resorts and never even know what island you're on. Leo said he knows a little villa close to where he lives that we'll love. Three houses built around a shared courtyard, tall protective wall enclosing it all, with a view of the ocean. It even has a nice big pool. Sounds amazing."

The fear stabbed back through her. "Doesn't he live up in the mountains? They're doing something with windmills up there, right, or solar panels? The travel warning says you should keep to the tourist areas."

"Rose. Do you really think my sister would let her husband bring us someplace that wasn't safe? Me and you, maybe. But with the kids? She loves Lily like she's her own, and she'll love Jackson just the same."

Too much.

The thought came unbidden, and she chastised herself for having it. She pushed it down and nodded. "I'm sure you're right. I'm being silly."

He smiled and squeezed her hand, then clicked the TV back on and took a long sip of his wine.

She pulled the swatches back into her lap and stared down, not seeing them.

CHAPTER THREE

One month before

Anabelle

Anabelle turned at the door to her sons' bedroom and gazed back at the boys. She shook her head—they always looked so sweet and harmless when they slept, nothing like the rowdy Energizer bunnies that tore through the house all day. She was barely thirty, she should be able to keep up with a five-year-old and a three-year-old, but by the end of the day she felt like she'd been training for a triathlon.

Was the triathlon the one with swimming, or was it the one with the shooting? She couldn't remember. Whichever one had the swimming.

Careful to be as quiet as possible, she clicked the door closed and padded down the stairs. Mateo was hiding out in his office, surrounded by paperwork and poking fiercely at the touchpad on his laptop. She crossed to the armchair next to his desk and plopped down, running her eyes greedily over his screen and the papers in front of him.

"They didn't like any of the properties you showed them?" she asked.

"No, and they're driving me nuts. Every house I show them, their criteria change. First they don't want to spend too much, so I figure I'll take them to some fixer-uppers. They're young, whatever they buy now is going to be a starter home regardless. But then, no, she'll have to entertain for her job and she'll need to hit the ground running, so the house has to be move-in ready yesterday. Then I take them to some top-notch stuff, and it's too far out of their price range. I don't know what they think they're going to get."

Anabelle scrunched up her face. "So late in the year, they must be betting someone's desperate to sell 'cause they couldn't move their house during summer."

"Normally I'd say you're right, but she has to start the job first of December. So I think it's circumstance rather than calculation."

"Mmm." As he scoured the listings for the elusive black pearl they wanted him to pluck from thin air, her fingers itched to do her own search. She pointed at the screen. "What about that one? It's been on the market since April. I bet they'd consider even a low-ball."

He clicked it and scrolled, and the details flew past. "You're right. Good catch."

The compliment gave her courage. "You know, I took a look at our budget today. If we want both boys to go to Catholic schools through high school then to even a state university, we need to save more. I really don't want the boys to have to take out student loans."

He frowned, finished what he was writing, and finally looked up at her. "Once you start working, we'll be able to double up and plug that hole. Even part-time, I'll be able to take on a lot more clients with your help. And clients love you. Especially the men." He winked at her.

"Well, that's kinda what I was thinking. Now that Michael's in kindergarten, maybe I could put Marcus in preschool a couple of days a week and start helping out. If we did even just three days a week, I could do a lot. And when we get the rhythm of Casillas & Casillas Realty back in full swing again, we can turn things around."

The frown returned. "That's not what we planned. And we don't have your girl yet." He set the pen down, then reached to stroke his hand up her inner thigh. "Speaking of…"

She shifted out of his reach so he'd stay focused. "I want another baby more than anything. But we're falling way more behind than I thought we were. And, on top of that, I'm going nuts without any adult conversation day after day. Even just a couple of mornings a week would make a huge difference, and we could kill two birds with one stone."

He drew his hand back. "You were the one who wanted kids, not me. I've made sacrifices, too."

She winced. He'd wanted to enjoy each other's company, working just enough to pay for travel and adventures and enjoy being in love, like an extended honeymoon. And they had, for two years, and she'd loved every minute of it. But then she got pregnant and the kids put the romance on hold. He hadn't been happy about that.

He leaned back in his chair. "I'm sorry, but I'm confused. You were the one who wanted to be a stay-at-home mom until they got to school."

She scrambled for a response. She didn't believe in strangers raising her kids at daycare and hated the idea of them being latchkey kids, coming home to a cold, dark house the way she'd had to. But that was before she found out how zombifying it was to be home all day with two little kids. She loved them more than life, but she needed to talk to *adults* now and then, and she *really* needed to get back to work. She'd been just as surprised as Mateo when she fell in love with real estate—she'd never been passionate about anything before, but real estate was fun and she was good at it. And she missed feeling like she could do something other than change diapers and spit out lyrics to children's songs.

Mateo's scowl made it clear she'd ticked him off. She had to fix it.

She shifted over and sat on his lap. "I think I just need some balance."

One of his hands slid under her shirt. "Ah, well, then, no problem. Leo and Bree invited us down to Jamaica for Thanksgiving. That should be a nice break for you."

That's not what she meant, and he knew it. "Is that a good idea? We spent so much on the trip to Italy this summer, we can't really afford—"

It was a mistake—he bristled. "Leo and Bree are getting a villa so they can stay with Rose and Brandon anyway, and they refused to take any money. But it pisses me off that you'd say that, like I'm gonna end us all up on the street. You have to enjoy life, Anabelle, otherwise what's the damned point?"

If she pushed now, he'd just get more upset. So she leaned in and kissed his cheek, and he answered by kissing a path up her neck. Not having to pay for the type of crazy digs the Martins and the Palsers liked to book on vacations would be a help. And it had been a year since she visited her father's family in the Dominican Republic; she could use a little island time, and Jamaica would be almost as good. The sound of the beach, the feel of the air, tropical drinks and romance in the evenings—it would give her time to work on Mateo, really bring home how important it was they got a little more money coming in, and convince him that a morning or two here and there in a daycare wouldn't be a problem for little Marcus.

He ran his fingers over the long box braids that reached down to the middle of her back. "And you just had your hair done. It's like fate, the perfect time for a trip to the Caribbean with your low-maintenance 'do already in place." He slipped her shirt over her head. "Have I mentioned how sexy you look in braids?"

"I need the right hair to be sexy?" She put on a pout and looked up at him through her thick lashes, well aware her Pilates sessions had kicked her lean, curvy figure back up quickly after both births.

He pulled her legs around his waist as he stood. "Baby, even if you shaved your head, you'd still be the finest thing in any room."

She leaned in as he lowered her to the floor. Funny how the very thing you loved best about someone could turn into the thing that drove you the craziest. He acted first and thought later, once it was too late. But maybe she could use that to help her cause, tell him how it was even more important that she help him bring in more business after two expensive trips.

Either way she didn't have much choice. So she tried to put the cost of college educations out of her mind and focused her attention on what Mateo's hands were doing to her hips.

CHAPTER FOUR

One month before

Bree

Brianna Martin Palser curled up into her too-warm bed, sheet pulled up and cradled into her arms, face buried into her pillow. It was Sunday, which meant Future Heroes, the school where she taught children to read, was closed, and thus the only thing that motivated her up and out of bed was missing. Suspended in a miserable catch-22, she couldn't bear to drag herself out of bed without their sweet faces, but if she stayed in bed, all she'd be able to do was obsess about the miscarriage until her brain buried her completely in a deluge of futility and pain.

The miscarriage. Her miscarriage. Her *last* miscarriage, because she wasn't likely to get pregnant again at forty-two. Not when she'd struggled for the last fifteen years, first on her own when her body was younger and it should have been easy, then with the help of invasive, painful fertility treatments and attempted in vitro that only resulted in far more expensive, and devastating, disappointments.

The door to the bedroom opened and Leo crept in. He sat on the edge of the bed and put his hand on her arm. She turned her head and opened her eyes, then closed them again.

"Hey, guess what? I have a surprise. Last night I talked Brandon and Rose into coming for two weeks over Thanksgiving. Anabelle and Mateo are coming, too."

Images cascaded through her head. Of going two straight weeks without seeing the bright eyes of the children at the school, instead forced to plaster a smile on her face and convince the four people who knew her best in the world that she was fine. Of chit-chat and tourist traps and days lounging on the beach with nothing but time to be overwhelmed by their perfect lives and pretend she wasn't dying inside.

"Hon, did you hear me?"

She nodded.

"I thought it would give you something to look forward to. And I thought it would do you good to see the kids."

Of course he thought that. He was well meaning, he really was, and she reached out from the covers and squeezed his hand to let him know she realized that. And of course she wanted to see everyone, including the children. So how could she possibly explain to him that what he was asking was like setting a chocolate cake in front of a starving person who'd have a fatal allergic reaction if they ate it?

"You love being around the kids at Future Heroes. I thought for sure…" He sounded bewildered.

And he had a right to be. He didn't understand that those children were different from Lily and Jackson and Marcus and Michael. The children at the school *needed* her. Some of them had nobody in their lives and—

"I don't know what else to do, Bree." His tone shifted from confused to defensive. "I just don't know what else to do. We've tried everything, and, I know you want to keep trying, but—"

"I just need time," she said into the pillow.

"It's been six months."

She choked back a wry laugh. *Six months?* Was that how long it took to mourn your fifth miscarriage? According to what, some learned website for panicked husbands of infertile wives? Six weeks, six months, six years—she had no idea how long it would take, she just knew the gaping wound in her soul wasn't a skinned knee that would go away after a couple of weeks and some Neosporin. It was more like the piercings in her ears—eventually the edges would cover over and they wouldn't be raw and bleeding any longer, but the hole in the middle would always remain.

"Can you cancel? Reschedule it for the new year, maybe?" she asked.

He tensed and pulled his hand away. She shifted and opened her eyes again.

His jaw clenched and his mouth set in a tight line. "No, I can't. If I can't get them out here soon, very soon, there won't *be* any new year."

"Surely that's a touch dramatic." But she didn't move and couldn't bring herself to put on a Pollyanna smile. Because he'd given himself away—that was the real reason for the visit, not an attempt to help her heal.

"No, I'm not being dramatic. I know it's been hard to pay attention for the last few months, but I'm really not." He stared out of the window into the trees that surrounded the house.

A deeper shadow must have crossed her face, because when he looked back, he made an effort to soften his. "But don't worry. It's nothing we can't fix."

She was silent for a moment, then asked quietly, "Are you sure?"

"Of course I am. I just need a little time with Brandon. So you just do your best to feel better and let me take care of this, okay? It's all good."

She nodded.

He patted her thigh. "Take as long as you need to get up. I'm going to go talk to Sousie about getting a turkey."

She stared after him as he strode out of the room.

He was lying. She could always tell.

CHAPTER FIVE

Four days before

Rose

A blast of hot, humid air hit Rose as the group stepped outside the door of Sangster International Airport.

"Ugh," Anabelle groaned and gathered her braids into a knot on the top of her head. "I always forget how muggy the islands are this time of year."

Rose drank the feeling in. She'd always been the oddball who loved humid weather; dry heat made her feel parched, like she had a bad head cold and couldn't drink enough water. She ran her hand over her ponytail and sure enough, her normally straight hair was already curling up. She smiled—she'd always wished her brown hair was naturally curly, and tropical climates were as close as she ever got. One good thing, at least.

"Over there." Brandon pointed past the looping traffic to the parking lot where Leo hurried toward them, blond hair sparkling in the sun, waving one arm over his head.

Rose gripped Lily's hand and tucked Jackson closer to her body before stepping into the striped crossing. Did pedestrians have the right of way in Jamaica? She hadn't thought to check.

They crossed as quickly as possible while wheeling suitcases and tugging children. Leo embraced everyone in turn, taking special care to fuss over each of the little ones and proclaim how much each had grown. Especially little Jackson, who'd only been a large bump in Rose's abdomen the last time Leo saw him.

"Where's Bree?" Rose asked once the kisses and hugs died down.

"She's at the villa. She went ahead to get everything set up and so we'll have two cars." He grabbed one of the suitcases from Anabelle and headed toward the parking lot. "I rented that white minivan over there to fit all of us, but if any of us have to run off quickly for something, a smaller car is better."

"Translation: you have some business you'll have to tend to," Mateo said.

Leo laughed. "Just some investments I need to keep an eye on."

Mateo threw Brandon a look, but still addressed Leo. "I didn't realize you were looking to invest, I thought you were just here to help."

"That's the main thing. But there's so much to be done, the need for cash infusions are everywhere, and we might as well kill two birds with one stone," Leo said.

The group's energy shifted subtly in a way Rose didn't understand, leaving her uncomfortable. She glanced around nonchalantly for clues. Brandon seemed a bit stiff, and Mateo's expression was bemused. Anabelle chased after her boys who, enthralled by the new surroundings, were pulling her in all directions with an energy only children could muster after a long day of security gates, flights, and customs checks.

Leo hit the remote as they reached the car and the doors unlocked with a thunking click. They navigated the monumental task of loading everyone in—seven suitcases, three diaper bags, four car seats removed from two double strollers, several bottles of water, and a partridge in a pear tree. Once everyone was secured and hydrated, Leo took off down the road.

Rose handed Jackson his caterpillar stacking cups and smiled when he immediately began pulling them apart. Lily reached over and grabbed her hand, and the two of them leaned back into their seats and stared out of the window. Rose made a game of counting the palm trees as they meandered by, knowing Lily would fall asleep almost before she began. Sure enough, within minutes she was gently snoring, and Rose turned to take in the scenery while the husbands talked and Anabelle bargained with her boys, trying to get them to settle.

The streets had tiny sidewalks, nonetheless dotted with pedestrians. Blocky bright-colored buildings squashed together: houses, stores, and gas stations all flowed continuously into one another, divided only by their pinks and greens and blues and yellows. Some were beautiful, lined with flowers and exuding a joyful vibe in their own right, but most had a slapped-together feel, probably because practicality had been their guiding principal rather than architectural aesthetics. Practical choices had a different sort of architectural beauty, one that reminded her of the East Oakland neighborhood she grew up in, a place where people had more pride than money.

But those memories, particularly the ones evoked by razor-wire-topped walls, weren't ones she wanted to revisit—she'd spent far too much time and energy putting them all squarely behind her.

As they continued out of Montego Bay and into the mountains, the sidewalks disappeared completely and the streets narrowed. Trees and shrubs edged right up to the road, like they were driving through a jungle—which, she supposed, they were. More and more of the buildings were old and dilapidated, some not more than shacks made with planks and corrugated metal. Goats and pigs and cows wandered along and several trotted out in front of the car, forcing Leo to slow dramatically. As they cut into the mountain, road conditions became progressively worse, with potholes that turned into pits and stretches of missing asphalt, piles of detritus along the edges, and sunken patches that doubled as people's yards.

Rose shifted in her seat.

Brandon gazed back at her, eyeing her tense posture.

She shifted again. "It's just—I didn't realize the extent of the poverty. It takes me back to my childhood."

Brandon reached back and patted her knee. "She's been a little worried about crime here. I told her it's no worse than anywhere else, and you two know your way around."

Leo smiled at her through the rearview mirror. "Don't worry, Rose, Jamaicans are welcoming and generous. Poverty's only a problem here because the International Monetary Fund has their knee on Jamaica's neck, taking an obscene percentage of the island's GDP each year to pay off international debt. Jamaica supposedly became independent in 1962, but how can they be free with that going on? What you're looking at is neocolonialism at its best, and racism given the predominantly black population, and the country is struggling to gain a foothold. That's why AmericAid is here, trying as best we can to help them on the path to true independence."

Anabelle nodded. "That's why tourism is so important."

"Yes, but not as much as you'd think. Those fancy resorts so many tourists go to? They're owned by corporations in other countries. So yes, the maids and the chefs and the clerks get wages and make tips, but the vast majority of those tourist dollars go back to other countries. And sure, you get to see a beautiful beach, and you can take in the 'ya mons' and drink your daiquiris all day long, but you don't get to see the *real* Jamaica. That's why I rented the villa out in John's Hall."

Rose peered out the window again and tried to beat the childhood memories back. She smiled, trying to be grateful for everything her brother- and sister-in-law were doing to give them all a nice getaway. "I can't wait to see all the things you love about Jamaica."

CHAPTER SIX

Four days before

Bree

Brianna stood in the courtyard of the villa, deciding what to do.

The villa was smaller than she expected—much smaller. The three tiny mustard-yellow cottages were connected by mustard-yellow halls to form a V-shape that faced out over the mountain toward the sea, with a common lounge area and pool enclosed by a twelve-foot mustard-yellow wall. Not that she cared how big any of it was, *she* couldn't care less if they were all staying in a military barracks. But Brandon wouldn't like it. He'd be expecting more, and it would lead to questions. Their father, Reginald Martin, had been the sort of uber-successful stockbroker people tried to eavesdrop on when he was out at lunch, and Brandon had come to expect a certain lifestyle.

She sighed. After thirteen years married to her, Leo still didn't understand that. Because Leo had been raised poorer—both *too* poor, and not quite poor *enough*. Firmly middle class with a white-collar insurance-adjuster father and a stay-at-home mother, he never went without a meal or a roof over his head. But he also didn't get a car on his sixteenth birthday or a tour of Europe for his graduation, and he'd had to pay most of his own way through college. That had put many schools out of reach for him financially, and he resented it. He'd gone to a very fine state university, but that wasn't enough to crumble the chip on his shoulder when he was around the Martin family's wealth and ivy-league degrees.

And even though he'd never quite fit into the upper-scale life, he wanted it, and felt he deserved it. Which would be fine, if he were willing to work for it. But he always looked for the easier way, the shortcut. That was a monumental part of what underlay their current problems, even if he'd never admit it.

An errant chair in the courtyard caught her eye; she shoved it under the table a little too firmly and winced as it screeched. It was all so frustrating, because Leo was *brilliant*. So brilliant he'd been able to pass his classes without trying, and so spent far too many evenings at parties, fueled by his social-butterfly nature. The end result was a solid C average well below his intellectual capabilities. And while he interviewed well enough to snap up an internship with an environmental consulting firm, he again allowed himself to be lulled by his natural talent and lapsed back into a party life rather than taking full advantage of the opportunity. He left with lukewarm recommendations unable to get his dream job at the EPA, and with years of student loans to pay off.

She brought in her and Leo's luggage from the car, and dropped everything in the courtyard. Then she pulled a bouquet of flowers and two bags out of the trunk, hefted them to the outside table, and started emptying them.

She hadn't known any of that about Leo when she first met him, but even if she had, it wouldn't have mattered. She'd always been the awkward sort of introvert who made wallflowers look like glittering belles and faded far into the shadows of her father's and brother's huge personalities. But Leo's easy charm coaxed her out of herself, made her feel relaxed and confident, talkative and fun. Between that and his tall, blond, blue-eyed good looks, she was head over heels in love with him before she learned his last name.

And once she did discover his sagging work ethic, she convinced herself it didn't matter because she complemented him perfectly.

Her brain didn't work with the lightning speed of his, but she was smart and persistent and thoughtful and worked tirelessly at whatever task was in front of her until she completed it. She was the tortoise to his hare. And she'd inherit money of her own anyway, so they'd always be fine.

The southernmost wing's house was the largest—she'd put Brandon and Rose in there. The one in the north wing was almost as big, Anabelle and Mateo could have that one. She and Leo only needed one bedroom, so the center house would be fine with them. She carried their suitcases in and put them in the bedroom.

Back in the courtyard, she arranged the bundle of flowers into separate vases. As she brought them into the houses, she also distributed bottles of water, Red Stripe beer, and Ting soda in each of the small fridges, stocked shampoo, soap, and toilet paper in each bathroom, then did a last walk-through to make sure everything was in order.

Once she finished, she sank down into a courtyard chair and checked the time on her phone. The flight had landed an hour before, so by now everyone should be finished with customs and well on their way. But she had at least a blessed half hour to herself before she'd have to switch into social mode.

Just the thought of it made her want to crawl into bed. Anabelle would be pretty and peppy and fun as always, and Rose would be elegant in her gorgeous clothes with interesting things to say about everything, and there Bree would be, a lump of human flesh just trying to hold it together. Even just appearing normal took more energy than she had.

Hoping an infusion of caffeine would help, she reached for a Diet Coke and noticed a copy of the *Jamaica Observer* stacked with Leo's work folders. She grabbed it and scanned it slowly, trying to savor the last few minutes of her freedom. The headline on the second page grabbed her attention:

MISSING GIRL FOUND DEAD

She went rigid. This was the last thing they needed—when Brandon called the night before to confirm their itinerary, he'd mentioned how worried Rose had been by the Jamaican travel advisories.

She blew a dismissive puff of air out of her nose. Last Christmas, Rose and her mother had taken Lily to New York for a long weekend to do their shopping and see all the Christmas decorations, and she hadn't been worried about the crime *there*. Had the three of them gone for a midnight stroll through Central Park? Of course not, because they'd never have come out alive. Even in small-town Nebraska bad things happened if you didn't make smart choices.

And Rose had nerve acting like her kids were her end-all-be-all when Bree knew better.

Bree pulled the paper closer to read the article.

One of three girls who have gone missing in St. James Parish, Amancia Higgins, 5, has been found dead. Amancia was discovered yesterday in a cove near the shore of the Barnett River. Enclosed in the blanket that wrapped her was a black-beaded Obeah bracelet her mother didn't recognize, and insisted did not belong to Amancia.

Several sources have claimed the Obeah artifact points to a ritual sacrifice. However, an expert on Obeah religious traditions advised the Observer *that "The presence of the bracelet more likely indicates someone was trying to bless the young girl," and that it "suggests someone may have regretted her death." Given previous speculation that the missing girls were kidnapped for purposes of forced labor or human trafficking, it's possible something went wrong with Amancia's kidnapping and the perpetrators had to rid themselves of her body. Neighbors have also suggested that her mother, Rayala Higgins, was involved in the child's disappearance and death.*

Revulsion pulsed through her as she stared down at the paper, no longer seeing it. The mother might have been involved? The very thought of someone sick enough to harm their own child made her stomach roil. Didn't these women realize how lucky they were to have children, that there were countless people in the world who'd do anything—*anything*—to have a child of their own? People whose prayers went unanswered while these ungrateful mothers casually tossed their treasure away?

She read through the article again, and then a third time, obsessing about the implications. She stared off into the distance at the ocean, trying to rein her galloping dark thoughts back in.

After a long moment, she looked back up. Then, with slow deliberation, she folded up the newspaper, took it into her bedroom in the central house, and hid it in her nightstand.

CHAPTER SEVEN

Four days before

Anabelle

Anabelle woke as the minivan came to an abrupt halt outside of the villa, refreshed and excited—the villa was crazy cute. Totally Jamaican, cozy and colorful, not the sort of too-sleek Americanized crap Brandon insisted on when the group traveled together. Like when they'd gone to Mexico the year before—that resort had been set so far from the real Mexico they might as well've eaten Taco Bell the whole time.

This reminded her of visiting her father's family, where she shared a room with whatever cousin had space, in houses packed to the rafters with family who'd traveled from all over to spend time with her. How were you supposed to bond with people when you had to cross endless marble-lined halls listening to your own footsteps echo while you tried to locate anybody? This was more intimate. More fun.

And they could cook some meals here, which would save a little bit of money at least.

From the corner of her eye she saw Michael and Marcus shoot across the grass toward the road, and flew after them. The road curved out of sight in both directions just yards from the house, and they'd never see a speeding car coming until it was too late. "Hey, get back here!"

Once she grabbed their hands and redirected them, she kissed each of their heads, then gave them a gentle, smiling shove toward the gate. "You two are gonna be the death of me."

But when Bree appeared through the gate, Anabelle stopped short. Bree was all smiles and squeals as she scooped up each child and twirled them around, but she looked horrible. Always the thinnest and shortest of them, she was even smaller now, in an unhealthy way that made her look like she'd wash down the shower drain if she wasn't careful. Her puffy, dark eyes popped out from even paler-than-usual white skin, and her auburn hair strained into a tight bun, something Anabelle had never seen her wear before—Bree's thick waves were her best feature.

"Anabelle, that dress is stunning on you." Bree hugged her. "The yellow just lights up your skin."

Anabelle waved the skirt out around her. "Thank you! It's a one-of-a-kind Rose Martin Designs design."

Bree turned her smile on Rose. "Of course it is. Just beautiful."

Rose responded too eagerly. "I brought two dresses I designed just for you. One's a beautiful emerald, and the other's a coral that will bring out the highlights in your hair."

"I can't wait to try them on." Bree barely made eye contact. "Come in, everyone! Let's get inside."

Anabelle winced as Rose hurried to cover her disappointment. It wasn't the kind of thing you could tell someone, that the more they fell all over themselves trying to please someone, the more it was gonna backfire. She'd tried to grease the wheels of their dynamic more than once, but it never worked. In fact, it did the opposite—since Anabelle was Rose's friend first, because Rose and Brandon had referred them as realtors to Bree and Leo, anytime she got caught between the two of them it was just weird, like she was trying to be some sort of family counselor.

Once in the courtyard, Bree pointed to the different houses. "Anabelle and Mateo, you and your boys are over there, Brandon and Rose, you all are in that one. We're in the middle. What do you want to do first, unpack, or eat? I bought a big batch of dongo-dongo and fufu from our favorite stand on my way over here, since they never seem to feed people on planes anymore."

"Dongo-dongo?" Mateo asked, eyebrows springing up suggestively.

Rose waved him off. "It's food. Salt fish and okra. Get your mind out of the gutter."

Anabelle rolled her eyes. "My grandmother makes that every time I visit. But I have to admit, I can't stand okra."

Bree's face fell, and she opened her mouth to speak, but seemed at a loss for words.

Anabelle hurried to fix it, and grabbed Bree in a side hug. "But of course I want some—I mean, come on! It reminds me of family."

Bree smiled again, but it wasn't as full and proud as it had been.

Crap, Anabelle thought. "Is the fufu cassava or yams?"

"Yam, I'm pretty sure," Bree said.

"Yam, yum! That's my favorite." Anabelle beamed at Bree.

"Yam, yum? Mom, why are you always so silly?" Michael said, and smacked her playfully on the leg.

"Ouch! No way did you just hit me!" Anabelle bent toward him with her hands extended in claws. "You know what that means—tickle zombie is gonna come get you!"

"No!" Michael let out an earsplitting squeal and ran to the other side of the courtyard. Anabelle shambled after him.

"Be careful around the pool," Rose called after her. "Does it have a cover? We should probably keep it covered when we're not using it with the kids running around."

Anabelle turned back around in time to see Bree's annoyed expression; Rose must have seen, too, because a flush crept up her face. "That's a really good idea, Rose." Anabelle narrowed her eyes playfully at Michael, who giggled like crazy. "These two can't stay still for more than a minute and better safe than sorry."

Rose shot her a grateful smile.

Leo laughed behind her. "Guys, focus. We need to eat fast because we have to get up to Sousie's before it gets dark."

"Who's Sousie?" Anabelle asked.

"You'll see."

CHAPTER EIGHT

Now

Everyone rushes to Rose's side, and seem to appear all at once in the too-small space. Leo and Bree are in their robes, wiping sleep from their eyes.

"What happened?" they chorus as they peer around the room.

"Lily's gone." Rose still sits on the floor, her voice is shrill and choked. She points to the bed and the curtains fluttering out around it.

"What do you mean she's gone? Lily?" Brandon calls, and begins a search that shadows the one Rose just finished.

"I looked everywhere, she's not here." Rose searches for her phone, unable to remember where she put it. "We need to call the police."

"I'll do it." Bree rushes back toward the courtyard.

"Did you look outside?" Mateo hurries toward the bed, his tan face deathly pale.

"Matty, stop." Leo reaches out and grabs him. "Brandon can do it. If this turns out to be a crime scene, we don't need everyone trampling it."

Rose shoots a horrified look at Leo, and her breath comes in short gasps. "Oh, God. I've already been all over it, twice."

Anabelle hurries to reassure her. "I'm sure Mateo's right, though. She probably just went outside to play. I'm sure she's not far."

Rose bolts past her, into the courtyard and out of the gate to the front yard, screaming into the night air. "Lily!"

But dark has completely fallen, and the area has no streetlights. The only illumination comes from the house windows, and casts anemic bubbles that barely reach the street.

"Lily!"

Rose, Anabelle and Leo radiate out around the small yard, quickly covering the perimeter of the villa's wall, but find nothing.

"We need flashlights, or lanterns, something to search in the forest," Rose calls.

"I don't remember seeing anything like that around." Leo crosses toward her. "Maybe—"

"Have you found her?" Brandon rushes out to them with Mateo at his side. "We checked all three houses, I can't find her anywhere."

"The boys are still in their beds," Mateo calls to Anabelle, and relief flashes across her face. "They were waking up, but I told them to go back to sleep."

"No, we haven't found her," Rose gasps and turns in place, trying to scan anywhere and everywhere all at once. This is all her fault, she should have known better. "If she's lost in the dark—"

"The cars have headlights, we can use those to search. I'll grab the keys." Brandon races back into the villa and reappears a minute later. He throws Leo the keys to the Accord and hurries over to the minivan. "Leo, you head north, I'll head south."

"You're not on the insurance, Brandon," Leo says.

"And you've never driven on the left," Mateo says. "I'll go."

"She's my daughter, Mateo. I'm damned well gonna go look for her."

Mateo starts to say something, but his mouth snaps back shut. "Then I'll drive and you can ride shotgun." Mateo reaches his hand out for the keys.

"And leave three terrified women here alone in the dark?" Brandon sweeps an arm toward their wives, still patrolling the perimeter of the villa.

Mateo nods. "Right. I'll stay here."

Leo glances at the minivan and the Accord. "At least take my car, it's far easier to manage on these roads than that behemoth. I'll take the minivan."

"Fine. Let's just *go*." Brandon catches the keys that Leo tosses back to him, and throws over the minivan's keys in exchange.

Rose watches them drive off in opposite directions, scouring the foliage lit up by their headlights as they slowly disappear around the bend. Something pulls at her elbow.

"Come inside, Rosie. You need to sit down." Mateo's earlier boorishness has transformed into clinging protectiveness. He glances back over his shoulder, tensed like he's ready to race after the cars. "They've got this. They'll be back with her before you know it."

"No, the police will be here any minute—" She ignores the pleading on Mateo's face and wraps her arms around herself against a sudden chill.

Anabelle lays a hand on her arm. "You're shivering. You're in shock. We need to get you a blanket."

Bree steps out through the gate—Rose hadn't even noticed she'd disappeared—cradling Jackson close to her. He is still, miraculously, asleep.

"Jackson!" Rose cries, and pushes past Anabelle to her son. She slips her hands around him and lifts him out of Bree's hands, then pulls him into her chest.

Someone tugs at her elbow again, this time Bree. She allows herself to be led back through the house and sinks into her chair at the courtyard table as Anabelle drapes a throw over her shoulders. Jackson fusses gently as she shifts his weight onto her lap and hunches over him, but he stills again as she tucks him against her abdomen.

"Where are the police?" she gasps, breath short and the world spinning as her nightmare comes true. It was only a matter of time, everything she feared crashing fast and furious, and it's all her fault. Lily's gone, and it's her fault. She knew it wouldn't be safe here—that it wouldn't end well.

Mateo shoots a look at Bree, who glances in the direction of the street. "They're on their way. I'm not sure where the closest police station is. Granville, I think."

Which means nothing to Rose. "Even so, they should have been here by now," she says.

"We're far out from the city," Bree says. "But they're coming. They said so."

Anabelle reaches over to console her. "You've seen how twisty those roads are during the day, honey. It's gonna take a little while. But Brandon and Leo are out there looking, and they'll find her. I'm sure she just wandered off, and they'll be back with her before you know it."

Rose stares off into the distance, berating herself. *All my fault. Inevitable. I never should have—*

She squeezes her eyes shut against the thought and pulls Jackson closer.

Leo and Brandon return empty-handed. The police take another half hour to arrive, but when they do, they come with a mobile crime-scene processing lab and two detectives from the Organized Crime Investigative Unit. Detective Williams is a tall, solid black man with a commanding presence that Rose finds reassuring, while Detective Shaw, a lighter-skinned, muscular woman, asks them for details with a kind, comforting manner. Rose explains how she found Lily missing, then the team work together to secure and document the scene, dressed in white paper scrubs that look like hazmat suits bred with fast-food uniforms.

Rose rocks Jackson in her lap. Why aren't they sending out a search party now?

They wait. Rose's legs go numb under Jackson's weight, and when Bree offers to take him, she gratefully agrees. Leo and Brandon pace the courtyard, ricocheting off each other like ants scurrying along a narrow trail. Bree sits, staring down at Jackson, a blank expression on her face. Anabelle sits tapping one acrylic nail on her teeth as she bites another, not quite chewing it, and silently accompanies the detectives when they need to search the boys' room. She returns a good ten minutes after they finish, reports the boys are back to sleep, and resumes worrying her nail.

Detective Williams calls to them through the gate. "Dr. Martin, Mr. Palser. Would you come here a moment?"

The pacing and tapping stop. Leo and Brandon stride toward the detective, and Rose follows them. Detective Williams looks as though he might object, which angers Rose—she's Lily's mother, dammit, and she's not going to just sit by and wait.

But he apparently changes his mind, and waves them all through. "Please be careful to walk only where I show you, on the areas we've already cleared, to avoid destroying any evidence."

Rose looks down at the path Detective Williams indicates, and follows directly in Brandon and Leo's footsteps.

Williams comes to a careful halt in front of Lily's window, where a tech is carefully lighting and photographing the wall beneath. "Were those marks present before this evening?"

Rose gasps—slashes of red scrawl across the wall. Directly below the window is a symbol that looks like a cross, but with arrows and frills decorating all four prongs. On either side, oddly shaped triangles, half-moons and rune-like scribbles radiate out.

"Oh, God, is that blood?" she cries.

"It's too light to be blood," Leo says, looking at the detective for confirmation.

Williams nods. "We don't know exactly what it is yet, but it isn't blood. Do you remember seeing these markings before?"

"Absolutely not," Rose says. "I would have noticed for sure against the yellow paint." She takes a step back to examine the rest of the house and wall, but Leo grabs her arm.

"Stay put, be careful where you step," Leo says, his voice thick. "I don't remember seeing them, either. Brandon?"

Brandon shakes his head. "What are they? Some sort of code?"

"Obeah," Rose chokes out. "I read about that before we came. Like Voodoo."

Leo's forehead creases, and he looks to the detective.

"They could be any number of things," Detective Williams says, his face blank. "Possibly some sort of graffiti."

Rose gapes up at him. "Graffiti that just happens to show up within hours of my little girl disappearing?"

"We don't want to get ahead of ourselves." He steps carefully to an evidence table on the perimeter of the crime-scene tape, then picks up a plastic evidence bag. "You mentioned your daughter was wearing a pink nightgown when you put her down to bed. Could this be from that nightgown?"

"Yes." A sob closes Rose's throat. "Where did you find this?"

"Near the window," he answers.

Rose turns and scans the area under the window, and starts to take a step forward. Brandon's hand on her arm stops her, and she turns back. "You think it caught on something?"

Williams doesn't answer, but leads the way back to the gate, his face still a practiced blank. He motions toward the courtyard. "Thank you. Please wait back inside."

Rose stands unmoving for a moment, then slips out the phone from the pocket of her sundress.

"Mrs. Martin. I can't allow you to take pictures of the crime scene," Williams says.

"Why?" she demands.

"We must be in control of what information leaves here, at least for the time being."

Rose stares up at him defiantly and considers snapping the picture anyway. But a vision of him taking her phone into evidence, leaving her with no connection to the world, stops her. She slides it back into her pocket and shoots a last glance at the wall.

"Please." He gestures back through the gate, and escorts them into the courtyard. Once they're settled, he leaves.

Rose grabs her phone and pulls up the drawing app she uses to amuse Lily. She creates a new page and transcribes the marks as best she can from memory.

CHAPTER NINE

Four days before

Rose

"Where we going?" Lily asked as Rose belted her into the car seat.

"I don't know, bunny. Uncle Leo has a surprise for us. All we know is we're going to see someone named Sousie." Rose turned to secure Jackson, then handed him his stack of nesting cups to play with.

Lily's face broke into a wide smile. "Surprise!"

Rose laughed, kissed her cheek, then peered past her out the window. The winding roads and intermittent livestock slowed their speed to a relative crawl, and the tempo gave her too much time to think about Bree's frosty welcome.

Their relationship had always been a bit arm's length, but Rose wrote that off to normal sisterly protectiveness. After Lily was born, the relationship had become even more strained, but they both took pains to be civil and supportive of one another—they may not have been best friends, but they'd at least been friend*ly*. Bree wasn't a clothes horse, that was true. But like everyone else, she did in fact *wear* clothes, and she'd made comments in the past about several of Bree's designs that she really liked. So why had she been so cold?

Lily pulled her from her thoughts by demanding a game of patty-cake, and by the time they finished several rounds, the van swung around a wide turn. An open mountain slope appeared before them, lined with a cluster of wooden homes built into the ridge on stilts, peeking out from between coconut trees, pineapple palms, and a thousand other shrubs Rose couldn't identify.

"Look, bunny." Rose pointed out the window.

"Wooow." Lily's eyes widened.

"They look like tree houses, don't they?" Rose said.

Lily nodded, and Jackson, who imitated everything his big sister did, nodded along, still playing with his cups.

"Why they have clothes?" Lily asked, and pointed.

Rose laughed. "You know how Deena puts our clothes in the dryer after she washes them? Some people dry their clothes by hanging them outside."

"To save energy," Michael said, knowingly.

"Not to save it," Bree hurried to jump in. "Because it's hard to get out here. That's part of what Uncle Leo does here in Jamaica. He helps build solar power and wind power for the people who need it."

Michael considered that for a moment. "That's good for the planet."

"It is. We want everybody to have good energy." Leo turned onto a steep road only wide enough for one-way traffic. "In fact, I'm talking to Sousie about getting some solar panels out here for her."

"Ooo, a clue." Rose caught Anabelle's eye, then raised her eyebrows. Anabelle rubbed her hands and giggled. Rose smiled, warmed by Anabelle's enthusiasm.

The van climbed further, then made another turn at the end of a low wall. Two men sat on the wall, one with short locks and the other with a buzz-cut fade, some sort of alcohol perched between them. They watched closely as the van passed. A few hundred yards later, the van swung wide and parked under a corrugated metal overhang.

As everyone climbed out of the vehicle, a thirty-something woman emerged from a shack and strolled toward them, her red dress flapping gently in the breeze as she fiddled with the matching headband in her short Afro.

"Sousie! I brought you my family, just like I promised." Leo turned and introduced everyone.

Sousie squatted to greet the little ones, then stood up and greeted each of the adults warmly. "Thank you so much for coming to visit my farm."

Mateo swiveled his head. "This is a farm? On the side of a mountain?"

Rose took in the two wooden buildings to their right. A paved patio connected them, with a hammock at the far back. A tall web of mesh ran on one side, covered in climbing vines. "Are those peas?"

Sousie's smile broadened still farther. "They are, well spotted." She turned to Mateo. "You've never seen a mountain-side farm before? I'm honored to be the first to show you. Follow me."

She strode toward the courtyard. As Rose turned to follow, two men wandered up the path toward them, watching the group. The two men they'd passed on the wall, she realized with a shiver.

Stop it, she chastised herself. *Of course they're watching us. They must work here, and* you're *the strangers.*

Sousie opened a gate on the far side of the hammock, revealing a steep stone staircase that wound down and disappeared out of sight.

Rose peered down, unsure she'd be able to keep both children safe on the steps. "Brandon, can you carry Jackson?"

Brandon turned to take him, but before he could, Bree scooped him up into her arms. "I'll take him. Come here, my darling."

Brandon fussed slightly, and Rose balked. "Are you sure? He's a little antsy, he might be better off with his father—"

Bree glared for a fast moment, then smiled down at Jackson and hugged him closer. "Oh, don't be silly. I deal with kids all day. And this one's my sweet little boy, isn't he?"

Brandon shrugged, and winked at Rose. He was right, she decided—unless Jackson started kicking up a huge fuss, it probably didn't matter, so whatever made everyone happy was easiest.

She grabbed Lily's hand. "Hold on tight, but don't pull. We're going to go slowly, okay?"

Lily nodded and glanced over to Michael and Marcus, each holding one of Anabelle's hands.

A few steps down the view opened up, and Rose gasped. A series of terraced gardens ran up and down the hillside, staggered into its nooks and crannies. Rocks and planks reinforced each bed, and many had mesh guiding plants upward. Pipes from an irrigation system wove in and out around them.

"That for a giant?" Lily said, voice filled with awe.

"It looks like a staircase for a giant, doesn't it?" Rose laughed and widened her eyes. "But it's a garden. See all the plants growing?"

"Isn't this brilliant?" Leo asked. "You have to get creative when this is the landscape available to you. And the weather here is so lush the growing season is nearly year-round, so farming is very lucrative if you do it correctly. Over there they have cabbage. Okra and peppers, of course. Over there zucchini, and eggplant there."

Sousie laughed, a pretty sound that made Rose picture pealing bells. "Leo, I don't need to give them a tour, you can do it yourself!"

"The view is breathtaking," Rose said. "Imagine spending your days looking out over these beautiful ridges while you work. So good for your soul."

"I know everybody will want to try out restaurants," Leo said. "But we'll pick up some essentials here today, and next week we'll get everything for our Thanksgiving meal here—including pumpkin, and even our turkey."

"You raise animals here, too?" Mateo asked.

"We have pens on the other side. Goats, pigs, chickens, turkeys." Sousie beamed. "We call this our-farm-to-your-table. We grow the food here, then deliver it to our customers."

Leo ran his hand over a nearby plant. "They deliver to people who don't have their own gardens and who live far away from places where they can easily buy food. Or people who don't have transportation. The waiting list is huge, because Sousie can only deliver so much. But the land next to theirs is up for sale, so if they can find the money to buy it, they can serve more of the surrounding communities."

Rose sensed another shift in the group, and glanced around trying to decipher it. Brandon was pointedly looking out over the mountain clefts. Mateo looked like he was solving an exam question in his head. Sousie glanced at Leo, then glanced away again.

"Are these farms associated with AmericAid?" Rose asked.

Leo cleared his throat. "No, that isn't really what they do. But I'm working on getting some solar panels out here to help them with their energy needs."

"It's amazing how quickly we've grown," Sousie said, beaming with pride. "There are a few other farms like this in the area, but we've built a reputation for having excellent quality, and the best variety."

Brandon finally turned back from the wooden railing, his face tight. "Sounds like an excellent investment for you, Leo. Like you said, help your fellow man and make some money at the same time, what could be better than that?"

Leo smiled. "Absolutely. We could all stand to diversify our investment portfolios, right?"

Brandon smiled back, and clapped Leo on the shoulder. "My dad would be so proud to see you and Bree putting his money to good use, and building it up. Ensuring the success of future generations was always so important to him."

Leo's smile faded, and Bree turned sharply away, her back to the group. Rose caught a subtle movement from the corner of her eye—Anabelle giving Bree's hand a quick squeeze, then dropping to pick up Marcus and give him a big hug.

Rose waited, concerned, for Bree to turn back around. But when she did, she was smiling and engaged.

"Shall we go back up?" she asked. "Sousie, you said you were going to show us the right way to fry plantains, right?"

Sousie locked arms with her and led the way back up the stairs. Confused, Rose used Lily's short legs as an excuse to follow last, so she could check everyone's expressions again: Anabelle entranced by the surroundings. Mateo still deep in thought. Leo's jaw firmly set.

And Brandon spitting mad.

CHAPTER TEN

Four days before

Bree

"Would you like to help me make some frozen hot cocoa?" Bree asked Lily as she climbed out of the minivan back at the villa.

Lily's face lit up like she'd been offered the Hope Diamond. "Yes!"

"Yes, *please*," Rose corrected, with a hesitant expression. Bree flushed—she couldn't seriously be annoyed about a little treat?

"Yes, please," Lily repeated, and shook her hands in a little happy dance.

Bree chose to rise above it. Yes, the children *had* already eaten dessert after their earlier meal, and *of course* sugar at the end of the day wasn't the smartest thing for them. But there was a time and a place for everything, and it had been forever since Bree had seen Lily. Didn't she deserve to spoil the children just a little? Was it really so hard for Rose to let everyone alone, not worry about every slip of manners? Lily was only three and a half, for heaven's sake. And given Rose's attitude toward children, you'd think she'd be happy to just let someone else take care of them.

"Frozen cocoa sounds good," Mateo said. "But you know what sounds better? Pina coladas. I've been waiting for them since we first booked the flight. I know I saw pineapple and coconut in there earlier. Who else wants one?"

The adults chimed a round of enthusiastic yeses, except for Rose.

Brandon grabbed her waist and pulled her into him. "C'mon. You deserve a little relaxation."

Rose shot a quick glance down at Jackson, and over to Lily. "A small one should be okay. Any more and I'm going to fall asleep."

"The kids will be fine, we're all here to watch them," Bree said. "It's okay to loosen up a bit."

Rose's smile was watery. "You're right. And it's been such a stressful day." She turned and stepped aside to let Bree and Lily walk through the gate before her.

Bree fought to keep the annoyance off her face. *Such a stressful day.* Right. Such a nightmare spending time with your babies on the way to a tropical paradise!

Bree reminded herself she shouldn't be so judgmental. Traveling with children wasn't easy, or so she'd always heard, and she was being unfair.

But it was so hard to let go of what she knew.

Rose had never even tried to hide it. The first time Brandon brought her home had coincidentally been the ninety-first day of Brianna's fourth pregnancy, and the first time she'd made it out of her first trimester. She'd been terrified but joyful beyond measure to have conquered the initial danger zone and be able to tell Brandon about the pregnancy. Rose had been gracious; truly happy for her, face lit with generous joy for the good fortune of someone who was, in essence, a stranger. And she'd made all the right comments, asked if they wanted a boy or a girl, asked if Bree had any special names set aside, asked how many children they were hoping to have.

Then she'd commented how smart Bree was to wait to start a family until she was *older.* How it was important to *build an identity for yourself* before diving into being a mother. How she herself didn't want to have kids.

Of course Brandon had stiffened when he heard those words. Bree knew beyond any conceivable shadow of a doubt that Brandon needed children more than he needed breath. Their father had imprinted the importance of legacy on both of them: bringing children into the world to continue the family line wasn't an option, it was a *responsibility* to all the ancestors who'd worked so hard to create a life for *you*. According to Reginald Martin, leaving behind DNA and a flourishing business were the two paths to familial success.

All the more important to have children, then, since Brandon had no interest in stock analysis; it bored him so completely his eyes would glaze over whenever Father talked about it. When Brandon refused to take over the business, Father had been so angry he cut Brandon almost completely out of the will. Not completely; he needed to ensure his grandchildren were taken care of, so he left instructions that Brandon would get fifteen percent of Father's estate for each child he'd produced. An additional ten percent of the estate would be put in trust directly for Brandon's children. The rest would go to Bree.

So Bree had been absolutely stunned when Brandon brought Rose to dinner again the following week. And she'd been downright gobsmacked when Rose announced her pregnancy just a few months after her and Brandon's wedding. And she'd been insulted by the mixed feelings Rose exuded about it all. Most mothers couldn't wait to go shopping for the cute outfits and accessories, spent hours researching cribs and strollers and birthing methods. Even at the baby shower, Rose was far more interested in talking about the new dresses she was integrating into her collection.

None of it made sense until the day when, while dealing with stacks of papers from the lawyer as she executed Reginald Martin's estate, she stumbled across Rose and Brandon's prenuptial agreement.

Should the couple divorce at a time when Rose had not produced children, the document stipulated, she would receive nothing in the divorce settlement—including no alimony. If she had borne children, she'd be entitled to alimony, a house of her own, and an additional settlement based on the exact number of children she'd produced. And, in the meantime, for each child she bore, a lump sum of one hundred and fifty thousand dollars would be deposited directly into an account for her, and would not count toward the couple's mutual assets in the case of divorce.

That explained everything: Lily and Jackson were nothing more than a business transaction to her. Rose had grossed three hundred thousand dollars for bearing Brandon two children; they bankrolled her fashion-design company. No wonder Rose was always happy to shove the children off on Brandon or whoever would take them off her hands.

"Auntie!" Lily tugged her hand toward the center house. "Pay attention!"

Bree laughed, embarrassed, and wondered how long she'd zoned out. "So what do you think we need to make frozen cocoa?"

Lily's brown eyes widened. "Cocoa!"

Bree led her into the kitchen. "What else?"

"A freezer!"

Bree laughed, hard. "You're pretty smart."

"You're smart, too."

"Thank you, darling." Bree grabbed her in a hug, kissed her cheek, and deposited her in one of the kitchen chairs. Then she and Mateo wove around each other as if dancing a maypole, gathering ingredients for their respective drinks, while Brandon readied the blender.

"You go first, sis. Let's get the little ones set up before we make the adult drinks," Brandon said.

His devilish grin and the endearment lifted part of the load from her shoulders. His anger was torture for her, all the more so when it was about something like *this*, and she was worried he was blaming her for the display at Sousie's. He'd barely spoken on the drive back, and when she or Leo had spoken to him, his answers were curt. Thank goodness he seemed to be over it.

Beaming up at him, she dumped ice into the blender, added milk, then topped it all off with a generous sprinkling of Roma cocoa powder and a dash of sugar. She pressed the button and sent the blender spinning.

Leo should have gone about it a different way. At the very least he shouldn't have broached it all on their first night, before Brandon even had a chance to wash the airplane smell off his skin. Brandon wasn't stupid—well, except with respect to his choice of wives—and he had the same savage instincts their father had had.

He knew when someone was softening him up and he detested being played for a fool. If he figured out the invitation had ulterior motives, well, that sort of manipulation would get them knocked completely out of Brandon's inner circle. But Leo had insisted time was of the essence, that too much was in motion, and he had to lay the foundation tonight. Everything always had to be his idea, and his way.

Maybe it was good he learned tonight's lesson the hard way. Maybe he'd listen to her now.

She stopped the blender and poured out four frappes, one for each child. "Lily, can you carry yours, or would you like me to bring it for you?"

Lily reached out her left hand—was she going to be left-handed like Bree?—and grabbed for the cup. "I can!"

Bree extended the cup partially toward her. "Okay, but you have to use two hands."

Lily extended the second hand, and Bree gave her the cup. She grabbed the other three, and let Lily lead the way back to the courtyard.

The sight of Lily's perfect little figure stepping carefully to keep the cup safe tugged at her heart. Lily should have been *her* daughter. Rose didn't deserve her.

Why did people get blessings they didn't deserve?

CHAPTER ELEVEN

Four days before

Anabelle

Anabelle hated secrets. She wasn't good at keeping them, and she hated being left out of them. Secrets were bobbing and weaving all around her, and she wasn't sure which way was up.

"What was all that craziness between Leo and Brandon?" she asked Mateo when they were alone in their house.

He shrugged. "You know how they are."

That meant he didn't know either, but wasn't going to admit it.

"Can you get the kids' toothbrushes and stuff out for me?" she asked him. "This'll just take a few minutes and then we can head back out there."

"Sure." He strode off, a look of concentration on his face.

Michael struggled to pull his pajama top over his head, and his voice came out muffled. "But Mama, I don't want to go to bed yet. Why can't I stay up and play with Lily and Jackson?"

"They're going to bed, too," she answered absently, tugging on Marcus' pajama bottoms.

"But Uncle Leo and Aunt Bree aren't." Michael's head popped out, little brow crumpled hopefully.

"I said no. It's been a long day and we have tons of fun stuff to do tomorrow. I don't want you to be grouchy all day."

He puffed up his chest. "*I* won't be. Marcus will, but I'm big."

"So you have to set a good example." Anabelle gave his tush a pat. "Come on, let's brush your teeth."

Michael ran off with Marcus toddling behind, and her mind slipped back to the massive mountain of awkward between Leo and Brandon. So Leo wanted to invest in a farm, so what? Why would Brandon even care? There was something going on under the surface that she didn't understand.

What had Brandon said to Leo? *My dad would be so proud to see you and Bree putting his money to good use, and building it up. Ensuring the success of future generations was always so important to him.* On the surface it seemed like a really supportive thing to say, but that was the moment everything went haywire. Like it was some kind of dig.

She shook her head, frustrated. "It doesn't make sense."

"Are you okay, Mommy?" Michael asked, toothbrush waving in midair.

"I'm fine, baby. And I think you've brushed long enough. Rinse and get into bed while we finish, I'll clear up your toothbrush."

Okay, so assume it had been a dig. When Leo clammed up and Bree's face fell, Anabelle had assumed the part about 'future generations' had made Bree think about the miscarriage—but Brandon didn't know about that.

Which was another thing. Why didn't Bree want Rose and Brandon to know about the miscarriage, or the in vitro trials? Shouldn't her own brother be a part of it all? They could be a big support for her.

She put a pea of toothpaste on Marcus' brush and guided it into his mouth.

Whatever. It put Anabelle in an awkward situation, and she didn't appreciate it. It was only a matter of time before Rose and Brandon found out, and when Rose figured out Anabelle had known the whole time, she'd be ticked off. Especially since Anabelle and Rose had been friends first, and Anabelle had only met Bree through Rose. Rose had every right to feel Anabelle was her friend first and foremost.

She needed to take some preemptive action, smooth the situation over beforehand. Find some way to let Rose know Anabelle was on her side so when the crap hit the fan, it would blow the other way. Definitely doable, so that was good at least.

But that didn't tell her what was up with the farm situation. If the dig wasn't about the miscarriage, what was it about? Was it his way of saying the farm was a bad investment? But if so, why not just come out and say so? And what did it matter where Leo and Bree invested their money? It wasn't like—

The pieces fell into place. Leo had taken them there first thing. He wasn't showing off *his* investment, he was trying to convince Brandon to invest *with* him. And the comment must have been Brandon's way of telling Leo he was on his own. Strange that it had such a big effect on Leo and Bree—having an investment partner must be really important to them for some reason.

Well, if Brandon wasn't interested, maybe she and Mateo should talk to him about it. This would be a great way of getting their money to work for them instead of always working so hard for their money. She had no idea if she'd be able to convince Mateo to let her go back to work anytime soon, and this would at least start bringing in a little more money for the boys' future.

But she had to be careful about it. She'd already hurt his pride about the cost of the vacation, and she didn't need him rejecting the idea because his ego was hurt. And he really wouldn't want to look like he was picking up Brandon's rejects.

She nodded slowly. She had to make Mateo think it was his idea.

CHAPTER TWELVE

Now

An hour later, Detective Shaw returns, her protective gear removed.

Detective Shaw reaches for an empty chair. "May I sit while we talk?"

"Of course," Rose says.

Detective Shaw gestures to another empty chair, and glances at Brandon. "Please."

Brandon hesitates a moment, then slides the other chair next to Rose and sits.

"We've done a thorough search, and we can't find Lily anywhere on the grounds or in the houses," Shaw says.

"What about the surrounding area?" Brandon asks.

"We have another unit on the way to help search while we continue processing the scene. We'll need to cordon off your section of the villa for the time being, at least overnight. Is there a place for you two and your son to sleep in one of the other two sections?"

"Bree and I can go back to our actual house," Leo says, eyes flicking between Rose and Brandon. "You can stay in the center house here."

Detective Shaw turns her steady gaze to him. "That's the address you gave us earlier?"

"Yes." Leo's tone is clipped.

"Shouldn't we stay here?" Bree looks alarmed. "It takes twenty minutes to get here from our house. What if they need us?"

Detective Shaw watches the group's reaction.

"The police are here now. What can we do that they can't?" Leo asks.

"We'll have a second car, at least," Bree answers.

"Please, guys," Brandon says. "Don't feel like you have to stay here. We'll be fine."

"We should be here." Bree clenches her jaw. "Lily is my niece. They may need our help."

Leo's mouth opens and closes, and he wilts slightly. "If that's what you want."

Brandon glances over at Rose. "You can sleep on one of the couches with Jackson and I'll sleep on the other."

"It doesn't matter. I won't be sleeping." Rose waves her hand, but it looks like an accidental spasm. "But I don't understand. You aren't searching the area for Lily?"

"We have two men out and more coming." Detective Shaw nods, and continues before Rose can say more. "Have you found a note of any sort that you didn't mention?"

Mateo's brows knit. "Lily isn't old enough to write notes."

"She means a ransom note," Leo says.

Rose grips the arms of her chair to steady herself. "No. No ransom note."

Detective Shaw looks at each person in turn. "And you've received no call?"

They check their phones and shake their heads.

"The houses here don't have landlines, is that correct?" Shaw asks.

"Yes," Leo says.

"Then we need each of you to make sure you keep your phones charged and nearby. Someone will likely be calling with a demand for money."

"You really think someone *kidnapped* her?" Brandon searches her face. "You don't think she just ran off?"

"Both are possible." Shaw slips a notebook out of her pocket, then looks at Leo. "You're the one who works here in Jamaica. What's the name of your company?"

She asks a series of questions about his job, his colleagues, his friends, and takes down the information. "And where has the group gone since you arrived in Jamaica?"

They recite a jumbled litany of sightseeing.

"But I can't see how that matters?" Anabelle asks.

"Someone may have noticed you and targeted you for attack," Shaw explains.

Rose's mind searches her memory frantically. From their very first day here, she'd noticed people staring at them. But Leo told her she was being paranoid, and the looks were just because Bree is a redhead, something relatively rare in Jamaica. But now—

Brandon shakes his head as though ridding himself of a gnat, then jumps up. "Okay, but if so, they'll call us, right? But if Lily just wandered off, or it's some random pedophile, she's out there, now, and we need to find her. We shouldn't just be sitting here doing nothing—"

Brandon's words chill Rose, and she makes a strangling sound. "She could be huddled somewhere, terrified—or—" She stops.

"We will continue to search the area as best we can in the dark. But your husband and Mr. Palser already searched the main road. If she just wandered away, you'd have run into her. We won't be able to do a full search until the light of day tomorrow."

"But by then, God only knows what—" Brandon starts.

"We *will* search, Dr. Martin." Detective Shaw's voice is still kind, but holds a firm undertone. "If she wandered off, she'll hear us searching for her, or we'll find her when the light of day comes. If she's been kidnapped, you'll get a call tonight asking for money. Our unit has a very high success rate when dealing with kidnappings, one hundred percent success in the last five years. Kidnappers want money, they don't want your child. We'll have this figured out in time for you to have your Thanksgiving dinner on Thursday." She stands up, slides her notebook back away, and returns inside.

They wait again, fidgeting and pacing and staring into corners and out at the ocean as the police continue to process the house. Another car with a pair of police officers arrives and leaves again almost immediately to widen the search as much as possible with mobile floodlights along the road.

They don't find Lily.

Nobody calls.

Both detectives return to the courtyard.

"Mrs. Martin, we need to speak with you alone, please," Detective Shaw says.

When they lead her into the Palsers' house, Brandon follows. Rose expects them to object, but they don't.

The four of them sit at the wooden table tucked into the corner of the yellow-and-orange kitchen. Rose looks up, trying to read their faces, her heart beating an irregular rhythm as she waits for them to speak.

"Please describe the events leading up to when you noticed Lily was missing," Detective Shaw asks.

She thinks back to the morning—can that really have just been half a day ago? "We spent the day at Doctor's Cave Beach. The kids built sandcastles and dipped their toes in the ocean. We left early because the kids overdid it yesterday and weren't feeling well today, so we picked up a couple of pizzas on the way home and ate here. We put the kids to sleep early, then relaxed here in the courtyard."

"Did everyone eat the same thing, even the baby?"

Rose nods. "Yes, he loves pizza. Why?"

"Who put the children to bed?" Detective Williams asks.

"I did," Rose answers. "After we finished eating, around five-thirty, I tried to give them a fast bath. But they were both fussy because they weren't feeling well so I didn't do the most complete job."

"What was wrong with them?" Detective Williams interrupts.

"They were just run-down, I think, and picked up a cold because of it. They've had a lot of excitement since we got here. They were coughing a bit, and had runny noses. So I gave them some NyQuil to help them sleep, then brought them into the bedroom and read them a story while it kicked in. Two stories, in fact."

Detective Williams throws a significant glance toward Detective Shaw before continuing. "You gave them the medicine in the bathroom or the bedroom?"

Rose glances back and forth between their faces. "In the bathroom. Why?"

"You're sure?" he asks.

She stares at him. "Positive. I do it over the sink, in case one of them spills or spits some out. They both hate it."

"Did they have any nausea, or vomiting?" Detective Shaw asks.

Rose shakes her head—what was this, a doctor's visit? "Nothing like that. They didn't eat much, but no, neither of them threw up."

"And nobody else was sick? Maybe had too much to drink, something like that?"

Rose's brows knit as she shakes her head again. "No. At least not that I know of. Brandon?"

Brandon looks mystified, and shakes his head.

"Dr. Martin, did you do any sort of test to see what was wrong with Lily, anything that involved a swab?"

Brandon's mouth drops open. "No—why would I do that? Rose?"

Rose is bewildered. "I clean out their ears whenever they take a bath, with Q-tips. Is that what you mean?"

"Nothing else that involved a swab since you arrived here?"

Rose glances at Brandon, who looks as confused as she does as he shakes his head.

Detective Williams jots a note onto his pad. "And what did you do after that?"

"Then I came back out to the courtyard, and we played cards."

"You said the window was closed when you put them to bed. Did you check it yourself?" Detective Shaw asks.

Rose straightens. "I did. I checked it and the latch on it, because I don't like leaving the kids inside alone when we're out here."

"So they were asleep by six? And you said you found your daughter missing at nine-thirty? What made you go check on the children then?" Detective Williams asks.

"Yes, six is about right. And I didn't like leaving them alone for long when they weren't feeling well, so we checked on them about every hour. It was my turn."

Another significant glance between the detectives. "Who checked the time before you found her missing?"

"I did," Brandon says.

"And Lily was in her bed at that time, around eight-thirty?"

"Yes, that sounds about right."

"Are you sure? Could you have glanced over and seen something in her bed without being sure it was her?"

Brandon's head bobs backward as he nods. "No way. I kissed her cheek and pulled the sheet up over her because she'd kicked it off."

"And you didn't notice anything unusual?"

"No."

"Was the window closed at that time?"

A flush of color rises up his cheeks, and he shifts in his chair. "No, it wasn't. It was open, but Lily was there. I figured Rose opened it at some point."

Rose whips around. "I made it absolutely clear I didn't want that window open!"

Brandon straightens slightly, and his jaw flexes. "I figured you must have changed your mind, and rightfully so. She was hot, that's why she kicked off the blanket."

Tears instantly flood Rose's eyes, and she jumps up. "How could you think I would do that? You know I've been worried sick about the crime out here—" She cuts herself off as she remembers the detectives.

"Because I figured you'd calmed down and realized there was no reason to be worried. I reassured you, Leo reassured you. We're out in the middle of nowhere, a car goes by maybe every twenty minutes—"

"No reason?" Rose points back toward the southern house. "What do you call this?"

Brandon blanches. "It was open when I got there, Rose. So if you didn't do it, who did? Maybe you did it without thinking, or you just don't remember, you know how you—I mean, you did have a few rum punches."

Her cheeks go cold and she feels lightheaded. Her voice comes out low, but steely. "So you're saying I don't remember opening my daughter's window."

He shoots her a look, but then holds up both hands in a surrender gesture. "Look, I'm sorry. I'm just—it's just—*someone* must have opened it."

"Is it possible Lily opened the window herself?" Detective Shaw asks.

"No. It's old and you have to give it a big shove. She's not strong enough." Rose crosses the room and stares out the window to hide her face from everyone as she tries to regain control of her fear and her mind. There's no way she could have opened the window and forgotten about it—except—

No. Just no.

What was far more likely was Brandon had opened the window and didn't want to admit it. He just admitted he thought she was being overprotective and that Lily was hot, and when he thought he knew better than she did, he ignored her and did what he wanted regardless. That was the downside of the confidence she loved so much, and, for the most part, she let him get away with it. Partly because she had to take the bad with the good, but mostly because even though it drove her crazy, it was usually over stupid things that didn't really matter.

But this *did* matter. This was their daughter, their Lily, so tiny and sweet and perfect.

But did it really matter who opened it? The police weren't going to find Lily any faster either way. Someone had, and this was the result. Calling Brandon out would just anger him further.

She took a deep breath. "This isn't time to lay blame. We need to focus on finding Lily."

Detective Shaw gestures toward Rose's empty chair. "Mrs. Martin, we have several more questions we need to ask you both."

Detective Shaw pulls a tissue from a nearby box and hands it to her as she sits back down, and she realizes tears are streaming down her face. She wipes her face clean, and blows into the tissue.

Detective Williams waits for her to finish. "Did you hear or see anything unusual at all, even if it didn't seem like much at the time? A car door slamming, an engine revving, anything?"

Rose and Brandon both shake their heads. "But we might not have heard it if it weren't right near the wall," Rose says. "We had music playing, and we were laughing. Having a good time."

"And were all of the adults together after Dr. Martin checked on the children?"

Rose's mind races to try to remember. "That depends what you mean. All of us at least went to the bathroom at one point or another, like when Anabelle went to check her boys and Mateo made drinks. And Leo and Bree went to bed early, right around the time I checked on the kids the first time."

"Do you remember the exact time they went to bed?" Detective Shaw asks.

Rose squeezes her eyes shut, willing any guess to come up. "I don't. We were relaxing, and, not really paying too much attention."

"And neither of them came back out for any reason?"

"No." Rose looks to Brandon for confirmation, and he nods.

"We noticed the halls that connect the houses have locks on the doors, but they weren't locked. Were they locked earlier?"

"No, of course not, we all know each other." Brandon waves a hand. "Wait. Were any of the windows in the other houses open? Do you think someone got in somewhere else and crept through the houses?"

Detective Williams' expression remains blank. "None of the other windows are open and the only evidence of any disturbance is outside your daughter's window."

"That couldn't be possible, anyway," Rose says. "If they'd come in through one of the other sections, they'd have had to get past Leo and Bree in their house. Bree's a very light sleeper."

Detective Williams clears his throat. "We noticed a nearly empty bottle of rum in the kitchen, and a pitcher out on the table. The adults were drinking?"

"We were, but the kids were asleep, and…" Rose flushes, thinking back to what Brandon said.

"None of us had much," Brandon says.

Another significant glance passes between the detectives. What are they implying? The kids had been asleep. There was nothing wrong with having a drink, even two.

"You said Mateo Casillas made the drinks?" Detective Williams asks.

"Yes." Rose leans forward, eyes flashing. "I'm sorry, but I don't understand how any of this has anything to do with finding Lily. You're wasting time." She points toward the road. "Instead of implying that we're all a group of alcoholics, you should be out there searching, with flashlights or floodlights or whatever it takes. And if you're not going to, I am." She stands up and pushes away from the table.

"Please sit back down." Detective Williams' voice is steel. "We'll need to speak to everyone in turn, and in the meantime, we can't allow any of you to leave the villa."

She opens her mouth to respond, but Brandon's arm snakes out and pulls her down. There's a message in the glare he turns on her: *This isn't home. You don't know how things work here. You can't afford to piss off the police.*

She sits.

CHAPTER THIRTEEN

Three days before

Bree

Bree slept fitfully, tossing and turning over Brandon's reaction at the farm; even though he'd calmed down by the time they got home, that didn't change the underlying problem. His reaction wasn't just a bump in the road, it was a brick wall, and her mind couldn't let go of the major question at hand: *what were they going to do now?*

Then, shortly after dawn, a chorus of joyful voices filtered through the window along with the sun's rays, singing a familiar song.

She threw on her robe and jumped over to the window. Out on the lawn, twenty small figures in dark pants and white shirts swayed as they sang. Wide smiles erupted on several faces as they spotted her, and the smiles spread as children tugged and elbowed each other to pull one another's attention.

Her heart swelled.

"Is that someone singing?" Leo asked from the bed, propped up on one elbow, rubbing his eyes with vague confusion.

"It's the children from the school." She backed away from the window and threw on jeans and a shirt, then hurried out through the courtyard and gate. The children's faces lit up still further but they stayed in their choir formation; Bree hung back, bobbing back and forth to the rhythm, tears streaming down her face. Rose and Brandon appeared within seconds, with Anabelle and Mateo close behind. As everyone listened, the children, led by two teachers, finished the song and sang another.

When they finished, Bree hurried toward them. "What an amazing surprise! I can't believe all of you did this!"

The children ran to her and enveloped her in hugs. Bree turned back toward her friends and family, beaming. "These are my students, well, most of them, from Future Heroes Day School, the ones I teach to read. I was planning on bringing you to visit the school today, but I guess now I don't have to."

The two teachers shook hands with everyone and introduced the children one by one. After each name, the target child chimed, "Welcome to Jamaica!"

Bree couldn't stop staring and smiling—a supernova had gone off in her chest, lighting her up from the inside. These children were so important to her, and to be fussed over like this, to see the joy in their eyes when the littlest one handed her a bouquet of pink flowers? Well. She'd have thought they were paying court to Santa Claus. It shouldn't matter, just knowing she was helping them should be enough, but feeling the love and appreciation made her heart swell in a way it never had before.

Except for one thing.

Bree leaned over and whispered to Miss Rebecca. "Where are Miss Pamela and Miss Denise, and the rest of the kids?"

Rebecca shifted and looked away, and mumbled a response Bree could barely hear about preparations for the day's lessons.

Bree's joy sputtered out like a candle dropped into a well. Why had she asked? Why couldn't she let well enough alone, and just enjoy the lovely moment life handed her? But no, she had to focus on the festering wounds.

She pasted her smile back on and continued conversing politely until the teachers announced it was time to return to the school.

Once the children and teachers waved goodbye, everyone returned back inside the villa to get the children up and have breakfast.

Anabelle grabbed her arm and leaned in as they headed back toward the houses. "What did that teacher say to you? Your face just—" Her jaw went slack.

Bree looked away, trying to hide her expression; it was all too humiliating. "It's nothing."

Anabelle gently held her back as the others disappeared into the houses. "BS. What's wrong?"

Bree winced mentally—she should have known Anabelle wouldn't drop it. "There are just a couple of teachers at the school that have an issue with me, that's all."

"How come?"

Bree raised one hand in a *got-me* gesture, and tried to smile like it didn't bother her. "Something about how I shouldn't have access to children without having to go through the same protocols they did."

"But you're a volunteer." Anabelle's tone was biting.

"I think they just resent me because I'm an outsider. Tale as old as time. Come on." Bree strode quickly off, trying not to give Anabelle a chance to dig any further, and headed into the central kitchen.

Rose grabbed a bag of coffee from the cabinet and turned as Bree entered. "What a charming way to wake up."

Bree smiled, and tried to recapture the warm glow.

"Even better than coffee." Anabelle rubbed Bree's back surreptitiously as she passed. "So what's the plan for today?"

Leo pulled several containers of yogurt from the refrigerator. "I thought we'd go into MoBay and do the tourist drill. Start at Sam Sharpe Square, drive the Hip Strip, wander a little. And I've arranged for a tour of Croydon Plantation after lunch."

Bree tried to distract herself by helping the kids with their breakfast, and then helping pile them all into the car. But once the drive was underway, Miss Pamela and Miss Denise returned to her mind. They'd been kind to her at first, but as time passed, no matter how hard she tried, they became more and more standoffish. She winced; she'd managed to convince herself that she hadn't let anyone at the school see how much she was struggling, but she'd obviously been wrong. Not wrong; delusional. Because the truth was she'd caught both of them giving her strange looks, and Miss Pamela had flat-out warned her about being too affectionate with the children.

She squeezed her eyes shut and tried to pull herself together. They were harpies, jealous of her relationships with the children, and she wasn't going to let their bitterness take away the one joy she currently had.

But the fact was, they'd taken a stand today by not coming with the group, and Bree was sure that was only the beginning. And she couldn't shake the cloud now hanging over her.

CHAPTER FOURTEEN

Three days before

Rose

Rose gripped Jackson's stroller and checked to be sure Brandon had a firm hold of Lily as they approached historic Sam Sharpe Square; cars whizzed past the fountain that dominated the far side of the square and acted as a makeshift roundabout.

But once they were past the danger, Rose was charmed and intrigued. The square felt like an 1800s New England village had dropped through time and space and blended with island flavor and vitality. A blend of Georgian buildings bordered the cobblestone-paved square, draped in Jamaica's vibrant array of colors.

As she headed toward a tiny half-brick, half-stone cottage perched in the middle of the square, her gaze landed on a multi-figure bronze statue next to it. In it, a man with a book—a Bible?—spoke to several other men. A large sign declared him to be the titular Sam Sharpe. She stared at his upraised fist, and that of the front man listening to him; they expressed so many emotions—hope, determination, dignity, power, connection—all frozen in a single moment of time. Something about it pulled at her.

"He was hanged here, in this very square." Leo appeared next to her, following her gaze. "He started a rebellion that led to the abolition of slavery in Jamaica, but it cost him his life."

"So much courage. And look at how inspired everyone around him is." Her voice had a wistful tone she hadn't intended.

He turned to stare at her. "You're brave, and inspiring."

Brave? She puffed a skeptical burst of air through her nose. *If he only knew.* "I'm scared of my shadow."

"You worry about crime, and your kids. We all have fears, and those are reasonable. But you're one of the bravest people I know. You started your own fashion line, and look how it's taking off. And you have a staff of people working with you that are dedicated to your vision. It takes hutzpah to put your life savings on the line for something you believe in, and make a success of it." A strange look came over Leo's face.

They stared at the statue together for a long moment, until a strange voice broke their concentration. "Leo! Great to see you!"

A tall, brown-haired white man in khaki cargo shorts and a beige polo shirt waved from the fountain. "Is that a work friend?" she asked Leo.

"Yep. I guess he has the day off, too. Be right back." He took off, jogging over to the man. They greeted each other and dove instantly into what appeared to be a deep conversation. Leo turned so they both had their backs to the group.

"Rose, how weird is this?" Anabelle called from the stone-and-brick cottage. "It used to be a jail for slaves, and now they sell souvenirs."

Rose pushed the stroller over to Anabelle, then skimmed the signs on the jail with one hand on her hip. "Weird isn't quite the word."

"Right? I can't decide if it's horrible or liberating that a place used to repress humans now sells trinkets."

Rose shook her head and cast a last glance back at Leo's odd posture before entering the building.

*

"Where to next?" Rose asked as they tramped back to the minivan.

"And please can it involve lunch?" Mateo said. "And maybe one of those Bob Marley drinks I've heard of, with the red and yellow and green liquors all separate and set on fire?"

"That's my kinda drink." Anabelle laughed. "One that puts on a show."

"Well, you're both in luck then," Leo said. "I figured we'd take a little stroll down the Hip Strip. Plenty of restaurants, and plenty of drinks. And you mentioned wanting to pick up gifts to take back home, so my suggestion is we walk a little, hit the shops so you can buy whatever you need, then pick one of the ocean-side restaurants for lunch."

Once they'd parked and disembarked again, they strolled their way down the strip, ignoring the vendors cajoling them to enter the boutiques. Anabelle sidled up to Rose and linked arms with her, pointing to different items and making silly observations.

"You're awfully quiet," Anabelle whispered to her when she'd steered them slightly away from the group.

Rose shook her head. "You're right, I'm sorry. I'm still a little tired from yesterday, I think."

Anabelle eyed her skeptically. "I saw your face yesterday, and I've seen you sneaking glances at Bree. Don't let her get to you, the problem isn't you."

Rose started to deny the accusation, but curiosity got the better of her. "What *is* the problem, then?"

Anabelle looked away, uncomfortable. "Oh, I mean, you know. She's just not happy here. Hopefully they'll get to come home soon. I just don't want you to let it ruin your good time. You and I will have a blast, if nothing else."

Rose narrowed her eyes—there was something Anabelle wasn't saying. But she couldn't really push her with Bree only feet away, and what it boiled down to anyway was if Bree didn't want to confide in her, forcing the situation wasn't going to help. She looked away, and nodded.

"Okay, here's what I think has to happen." Anabelle raised her voice and pointed to a row of T-shirts. "I think we need to find the cheesiest, touristy-est shirts they have and buy a matching set for all of us, then wear 'em for the rest of the day."

Rose shook her head and laughed. "You're nuts."

"Of course I am, but in the best possible way." Anabelle hugged Rose's arm.

"The guys will never wear them." Rose gestured toward Brandon and Mateo, who were pointedly pretending they hadn't heard the suggestion.

Anabelle leaned in again. "Uh-huh. After a couple of those Bob Marley drinks, they'll wear anything."

"Probably true." Rose laughed again. "Okay fine, but not this shop." She scanned the row, looking past the more aggressive shop owners to a store fronted by a tall woman with a slicked-back bun and a tranquil smile. "That one."

Anabelle pulled her to the back of the shop where rows of shirts in bold Rasta colors were tacked to the wall, and pointed to one with a large tie-dye peace sign. "What about this one?"

"If we're gonna do it, we need to do it right. I say we go for the tri-color flag shirt."

"Nah, they don't have the word *Jamaica*, they aren't touristy enough. How about that one with the huge blunt?"

"Mmm…" Rose pretended to consider. "I'm thinking making us all look like stoners might be one step too far."

"Fair enough—we'll have to beat off people trying to sell us da ganja as it is."

They continued debating and laughing, finally settling on a set of Jamaican polo-style jerseys.

Marcus started to cry and Anabelle ran out to see what was wrong; Rose waved as she ran off, and turned her attention to the trinkets around her, surprised to find some treasures. Wooden masks, most very touristy, but some so skillfully made they fascinated her. She picked up two that would look bold in their patio area back home, then returned to the T-shirt section and picked out a couple of Jamaican flag shirts for Lily and Jackson.

Then, when she turned the corner, she stumbled onto a section that made her heart pitter-patter: rows of beaded jewelry. As with the masks, most looked mass-produced and touristy, but several sections featured hand-made designs that called to her. She picked up several and considered them, envisioning designs she'd pair with them, outfits dancing in her head like sugar plums. As she picked up an ornate anklet that threaded around the arch of the foot, several resort-wear pieces flashed through her mind fully formed, and she gasped—could she do an extra, resort mini collection for summer?

Brandon was right. The trip was already pushing her creativity in new directions.

After selecting far too many pieces she told herself she'd give away as gifts, she grabbed a few of the cheap toys to make Jackson and Lily smile; a doll, a truck, and set of sidewalk chalk they could use to draw on the villa courtyard. She passed up the emoji key chains, and spent several minutes browsing the shell art before landing at the rows of rum.

Brandon appeared at her side. "You've been gone a while—Wow. That's quite a stash you have there."

She looked down at the items she had carefully balanced in her arms. "I may have gotten a little carried away."

He rubbed his hands together. "Let me at it."

She laughed, and handed it all over. She hated haggling—but he loved it.

He turned to the store owner. "My wife would like to know how much these are. We don't want to buy all of them, we just need to know which we can afford."

The woman rifled through the items, did a count, and gave a lump sum despite his initial question.

Brandon's brow crinkled. "Oh, that's more than we can spend. How much are the T-shirts, do they all cost the same?"

Rose stared on from the side, fascinated as he threw out string after string of sub-offers—*if I buy two of these, will you throw this one in for free? How much if I take four of these instead of two of those?*—until Rose was completely lost, like she was watching a mental shell game where he shifted the amounts and combinations so quickly the shopkeeper herself struggled to remember what prices she'd already offered and what her next move was. By the time he was finished, he had everything she wanted, along with several additional gifts for people in his office, for fifty dollars less than she'd been willing to pay. And if Rose had any doubt he'd worked a miraculous deal, the deep scowl on the woman's face would have erased it.

They joined the others outside, Brandon with a huge smile on his face.

"You look like the cat that ate the canary." Mateo laughed.

Brandon gave a rundown of the transaction.

"Not bad for a *jipato*," Anabelle said. "Even I couldn't have done better."

Brandon's chest puffed out just the tiniest bit. "Why thank you. When you're a surgeon, you have to be able to think on your feet."

"Enough stroking Brandon's ego," Mateo said, laughing. "I'm now officially starving. We have time for a sit-down lunch before we go to Croydon Plantation if we do it now. And Margaritaville is right over there."

"Ugh." Anabelle rolled her eyes. "Why not just go to the Hard Rock Cafe?"

"Hey, don't dis Hard Rock Cafe," Mateo said. "Great music, solid food. Nothing wrong with that."

Anabelle shook her head at him. "Okay, fine. I guess it's only right we have *one day* where we knock out all the touristy stuff. But tonight I want to find the tiniest, most authentic hole-in-the-wall place in Montego Bay and dive into a plate of callaloo. And something made with goat."

Leo threw a hand up, then down, like he was signaling the start of a race. "Let's go!"

Anabelle grabbed Rose's arm, and leaned over to whisper to her. "You feeling better now?"

Rose nodded, and hugged her arm back.

"Good. Retail therapy is *always* the answer." Anabelle spotted Marcus reaching for a stack of bright keychains, and ran forward to intercept him.

Rose smiled as she watched her go. She was so lucky to have Anabelle for a friend.

Especially, she thought, *after what I did to her.*

CHAPTER FIFTEEN

Now

Neither Rose nor Brandon sleep, despite spending the night curled around Jackson on the fold-out futon in Leo and Bree's living room. Rose lies still and numb, feeling the way she imagines a ghost must feel: caught somewhere between the worlds of the living and the dead, her mind going over every detail, chastising herself for every mistake, unable to take any action. Brandon tells her to take a Xanax but she refuses; if the detectives need something, she has to be clear-headed. It's bad enough the police have already implied the entire group is a pack of irresponsible alcoholics, she can't have them thinking she pops pills, too.

"They're positive someone kidnapped her," she whispers to Brandon in the darkness.

"Don't worry. They'll get her back."

"But what if they're wrong? What if she wandered off like that girl, Amancia, the one they found dead near the river? And what if she's out there right now, terrified and alone? Or what if someone did snatch her, but not for—"

He reaches over to stroke her hair. "They're searching, honey. They know what they're doing."

She stares toward him through the darkness. "Two people? That's not a real search, they need a large, organized search party—"

He reaches down and squeezes her hand. "There's nothing we can do. We have to trust them."

"I can't bear to think of her out there alone in the dark. Anything could happen—she could get attacked by some sort of animal. Who knows if we'd ever even find her?" She chokes back a sob, trying not to wake Jackson. "You agreed with me earlier, you said—"

"Honey. There aren't bears or tigers prowling around out there. If she's alone, she's scared, but she'll be okay." He reaches over Jackson and puts his hand on her waist. "And I've been thinking a lot about what they said. They *do* seem sure someone kidnapped her for ransom, and I think they're right. And that's a good thing, because kidnappers just want money. The detectives said they have a good success rate getting people back, so we'll give them whatever they want and this nightmare will be over."

He's trying to sound soothing, but his voice is strained. She studies his face as best she can in the limited light, feeling the tension in his hand and his posture, watching the white of his eyes bounce around the darkness—he's just as desperate and terrified as she is. He's trying to calm her, putting on a brave face for her, taking on the responsibility of getting her through it.

And she knows what she should do—pretend to believe it, pretend to be reassured, join him in the charade so they can both get through the night. That will pull them together, and they'll find the strength together to be brave. So she squeezes her eyes shut and tries to pull herself out of her spiraling thoughts, but she can't, and they keep spinning, because she can't close the distance between the two of them if she can't be honest about everything, all the things she knows and regrets and fears.

So she latches on to the fear she *can* speak aloud. "The only thing is... If she was kidnapped for ransom, why hasn't somebody called?"

Brandon pulls her into him, her head under his chin, pressing Jackson between them. "They'll call. They just want to make sure we know they're serious, that's all. They'll call."

Rose nods and slips one hand under her pillow to grip her phone, reassuring herself it's there, hoping with every cell in her body that he's right.

He *has* to be right.

But nobody calls.

Rose lies awake, following the cracks that cross the ceiling as the morning sun overtakes the police's artificial lights. Jackson stirs and wakes, his nose still running, fussy and confused, and she rises to change his diaper. When she's done, she sets him safely into his portable playpen and goes with Brandon to speak with the detectives. The detectives are gone, the lab technicians report as they pack up. As soon as the sun came up they began a second search of the area, and the techs aren't sure when exactly they'll return.

Rose peers out of the gate on the off chance the detectives may be there. A team of journalists wait outside the crime-scene tape that restricts the yard; they turn toward the gate to see who just appeared. Rose shrinks back, anticipating flashing cameras and yelled questions, but the journalists only watch quietly, curiosity and sympathy mixing on their faces.

Rose hurries back inside and tries to distract herself. Brandon makes coffee while she feeds Jackson fruit and yogurt, stumbling through the feeding by rote, then sits silently, unsure what to do as Jackson plays with a toy cell phone in the playpen.

She reaches for the mug she set on the table, but it's gone. She glances around the room. "What did I do with my coffee?"

Brandon points to the kitchen, confused. "You finished it and put the cup in the sink."

Her brow creases. "I could have sworn I put it right there. I didn't drink much of it—"

"Maybe I'm wrong. But I thought I saw…" He stands and goes into the kitchen, brow creased. "Yeah, both our mugs are right there."

She rubs a hand across her brow, and tears fill her eyes. "I'm just—scattered, I guess."

"You and me both." Brandon sits next to her and pulls her into his chest.

They stay there a long time, Rose trying to keep her thoughts and emotions under control, focusing on the thumping of his heart and the regular pattern of his breath.

The lab techs, now finished loading their van, come tell everyone that most of the Martins' house can be used now, but they shouldn't breach the crime-scene tape marking off the children's room. They supervise as Rose gathers what she needs from the room, and document everything she touches and everything she takes. As they finish up, the detectives return and ask everyone to come out to the courtyard. They all do, except Anabelle, who stays inside with all three boys.

Detective Williams gives them a summary. "We've searched the area carefully, down the road in each direction for about a mile. We didn't find anything, but we're still canvasing to check with everyone in the neighboring properties. This morning we found a family who remembers seeing a strange car lingering in the area, and someone else may have seen something that can help."

"A car? What car?" Leo asks.

"We're still gathering details."

Brandon nods. "What can we do to help expand the search? I can lead a team if you need me to, and I'm sure Leo and Mateo will, too—"

Detective Williams takes a step forward. "Dr. Martin, I understand you want to help. But our team is out dealing with the situation as we speak. You'll only get in the way."

Rose's eyes flick between the two detectives—why are they refusing the help? "But you need to do a *full* search. A professional one that radiates out and covers every inch. You need as many people as possible—"

Detective Williams raises a hand. "Mrs. Martin, please. We need you here where we can react quickly if the kidnapper calls."

"And if she was taken by some sort of pervert who—" Mateo glances at Rose's face and stops short.

Detective Williams' face shows the briefest flicker of a shadow. "Then the only chance we have to track down the culprit is to find someone who saw something suspicious and can point us in the right direction."

The shock that's been numbing Rose most of the night thaws—shatters—and anger bursts through. "So what you're telling me is, you're not going to do a *real* search."

"Mrs. Martin," Detective Williams starts. "Please calm down—"

"Calm down?" She jumps up, voice rising. "We've already lost, what, ten hours trusting you? You should have been searching last night, should have brought in floodlights and twenty, fifty people, whatever it took to search everywhere inch by inch. She could have a broken leg, or be trapped in one of the broken-down sheds everywhere, or God only knows what. We're losing time, we need to act *now*." A sob tightens her chest as she finishes, but she pushes it down. She can't afford to look unstable.

"Mrs. Martin," Detective Williams says when she finally pauses. "I will be blunt with you. It's extremely unlikely your daughter—"

"Her name is Lily," Rose spits.

He nods. "It's extremely unlikely that Lily left under her own power, or was taken by someone who happened to be passing by. You told us yourself that she's a timid girl, afraid of strangers and unwilling to go off on her own. And, it's impossible to see into the room from the outside. But more importantly, the crime-scene evidence just doesn't support the possibility that this was a crime of random opportunity. So yes, we will continue to canvas, but we will do so in a focused, efficient way so we can find the people who kidnapped Lily."

"What evidence?" Brandon demands.

"We're not able to discuss that at this time," Detective Williams says.

"You can't discuss it? I'm her mother, not a stranger off the street. I have a right to know!" Rose cries.

"We must follow standard procedure. As we told you last night, we have an extremely high rate of recovery with kidnappings," Detective Williams says, face still blank.

"You said that, but it's not really true, is it?" Rose's anger twists her face into a desperate snarl, and she taps her phone screen, then holds it up to him. "What about this little girl you just found dead last week? Amancia Higgins? How does *her* mother feel about your nearly perfect record?"

Detective Williams looks at the screen and anguish flashes across his face so briefly Rose wonders if she imagined it.

Detective Shaw steps over to view the phone, and takes a breath. "Amancia's case was an entirely different situation. She is a local girl, and her family has nothing worth ransoming."

Rose wiggles the phone. "Right, of course, it says right here that she most likely was taken for human trafficking. And she was found with an Obeah bracelet, a funny coincidence given those strange markings you found on the wall."

Brandon steps over and takes the phone from her hand so he can read it.

Rose puts up her hand in a *stop* gesture. "And don't tell me that *The Global Daily Gazette* is a trash rag, because I saw it in the local newspapers here, too."

Detective Williams' blank face is pasted back on. "Mrs. Martin, I understand that the police may do things differently where you're from, but crime in Jamaica is different. It's committed for different reasons, by people with different motives and methods, and we fight it in different ways."

Rose's laugh is loud, and nearly hysterical. "Maybe that's just what you say when you fail, so you can preserve your precious record? What about the other two missing girls the article mentions? You haven't found *them*. Are they the same age as my daughter? Because that sure seems relevant to me. I'll tell you what I think—"

Someone tugs at her arm, and she whirls around.

Leo withdraws his hand. "Rose, please. This isn't helping. You need to calm down."

"No, Leo, what I *need* is to find Lily." Rose turns to Brandon. "What *we* need to do is go to the embassy, now. They'll get someone out here to help us. The FBI do that, don't they? Come help when an American is in trouble overseas? And if they won't, we'll hire a private investigator of our own. Something." She whirls back toward Detective Williams, leaning forward with her finger thrust toward his face. "Because you didn't do what you should have done last night and now it's too late and you know it, and you're trying to cover up for it."

Detective Williams doesn't flinch. "You're welcome to contact your consular agency. We can contact them for you if you like. If the FBI believes this warrants their attention, we welcome their help."

Rose balks—she wasn't expecting capitulation. She glances at Brandon.

Brandon, face flushed and confused, gapes for a moment, then reaches for his phone. "I think that would be best."

Rose drops into a chair, and her anger dissolves into vicious sobs.

Leo holds up his hand and pulls out his own phone. "AmericAid works directly with a guy at the consular agency. I'll call them."

CHAPTER SIXTEEN

Now

Rose is surprised—no, disconcerted—when the consular agency in Montego Bay turns out to be tucked into a small shopping complex surrounded by a round, white fountain and watched over by a quaint cream-colored clock tower. Her soul needs something large and commanding, something that oozes government power and endless reach, not this little-more-than-a-kiosk afterthought. As Leo leads the way into a coral-and-peach-building, Rose registers the cool, beachy feel robotically, her designer's brain evaluating the color scheme's intended emotional impact: refreshing, cheerful. Instead, it makes her feel unsafe, alienated, desperate, lost.

Jordan Keppler, the consular officer Leo spoke with, spots them as they enter and crosses toward them. He's a tall, middle-aged white man with the government-employee bearing Rose needs, even if it feels out of place in the setting. He's reassuring, like a tiny island of home in the eye of stormy chaos.

With a grave expression and low voice, he introduces himself and then escorts them to a conference room filled with vapid, mismatched furniture. He pulls a box of tissues from a cabinet in the corner and pushes them gently across the table, careful not to target Rose directly. She doesn't take one, because she's determined not to lose her composure again—the clock is ticking and Lily needs her, and she may only have one shot to convince this man to take her seriously rather than write her off as some hysterical woman who needs a pat on the head.

Keppler expresses his condolences and asks a series of questions about the events of the previous evening. He listens carefully and takes copious notes, both of which further reassure Rose and give her hope. When they finish, he leans back ever so slightly and takes a long, deep breath.

"So, to be sure I understand, what exactly are you hoping I can do?"

Brandon shifts uncomfortably. "We need to find our little girl."

Rose leans forward. "We want to make sure everything possible is being done, including a complete search. I understand they may do things differently here, so if we need to bring in the FBI to make that happen, so be it."

Mr. Keppler nods gently and weighs his response. "I understand your concerns, and I also want to make sure every possible measure is taken to recover Lily."

Rose tenses at his underlying tone.

"But our hands are somewhat tied. I'll call the FBI and ask them to keep tabs on the case, however, they have no jurisdiction here and can only help if the Jamaica Constabulary Force wants them to do so. Even then, they'd need to evaluate the situation to decide if it warrants a team."

"If?" Rose's voice is steel.

He raises a hand. "No matter what, they'll monitor the situation. And if the JCF asks them in, they'll likely send *someone*. But I can't predict what exactly they'd be allowed to do, or when." He leans forward and taps the tablet in front of him with his pencil. "But I'm not going to lie to you, there are a lot of factors working against that happening. After we spoke earlier, I had a conversation with the FBI. The issue they're facing is they need to be certain this is a kidnapping, and as you've pointed out yourself, it's possible Lily just wandered off. There was no ransom letter left at the scene, and nobody's called you asking for money. Normally that happens within the first few hours." He pauses and watches her reaction.

"So you don't think it's a kidnapping," Leo says.

"I don't have the expertise to make that determination. But what I'm hearing from you all is *you're* concerned it isn't. In that case the FBI may not get you what you want."

"It may be a kidnapping, in fact, I think most likely it is," Brandon says. "But is it so wrong to want to make sure no possibilities are overlooked?"

"The detectives won't invest in a real search, either because they can't or they won't, I'm not sure which." Rose pulls out her phone and shows Keppler the news article. "And since several other little girls have gone missing in the area, doesn't it make sense Lily's disappearance might be related? Especially with the possible Obeah link? Shouldn't that possibility be taken seriously?"

Mr. Keppler nods sympathetically. "I completely understand your concern, and it's very possible the FBI may want to follow up that possibility. But it sounds like you'd also like me to see if I can get a larger search of the area done?"

"Doesn't that make sense?" Leo chimes in. "To get as many people searching as possible?"

Brandon raises his hands helplessly in the air. "It's killing me not to go out and organize a search ourselves. If you can get us permission just to do that…"

"The problem is, you don't know the laws or what land is open to the public and what isn't. Without the JCF overseeing it, you won't have the necessary permissions to go on anyone's property anyway." Keppler drops his pencil and flips several pages forward in the tablet. "But we may be able to help there. Along with AmericAid, we have enough grassroots reach in that area to rally the community, if the JCF agrees. I've already made a few calls to get things rolling."

The rush of relief that floods Rose brings the wave of tears she's been holding back, and she grabs a tissue. "Thank you. So much."

"I have a private investigator friend back in Massachusetts," Leo says. "I called him this morning, and he suggested we get in tracking dogs. Is that possible? If she just walked away and is hurt, they may be able to find her, and he said the police down here have been using dogs more and more."

Rose's head whips up. "Oh, yes, that's a really good idea—can we do that?"

Keppler's expression brightens slightly. "I can certainly ask. Most of the dogs they use are trained for drug and firearm detection, but I believe they've been expanding into search and rescue."

"Why haven't they brought dogs out already, then?" Brandon scowls.

Keppler makes several new notes on the tablet. "My guess is they don't think it makes sense. You're saying they believe she was kidnapped, and if she was, the perpetrator would have driven her off in a car and the trail will go dead within feet of your house. And resources like that are very limited, so all their teams may be deployed for other purposes. But we can try."

"What could be more important than a missing little girl?" Rose says, but realizes before she finishes the sentence how it sounds.

Keppler's expression is sympathetic, but careful. "I understand Lily is the most important thing in the world to you. But there are many other dead or missing people who deserve attention, too." He glances quickly at Leo, then back to Rose. "So I should stress that our best strategy is to be as respectful as possible in our dealings with the detectives looking for Lily. Otherwise you may get push-back."

Rose's eyes flick between Brandon and Leo, both pointedly avoiding eye contact with her, then back to Keppler. "What do you mean, push-back? Aren't they professionals?"

Leo jumps in before Keppler can respond. "For heaven's sake, Rose. I'm all about getting whatever resources we can to find Lily as soon as possible. But is it really so hard to understand that you're walking a very fine line between desperate parent and ugly American?"

His words hit her like a brick to the stomach, and her breath seizes. "Ugly American?" she says when she can speak again. "I'm not insisting on non-fat milk in my latte or trying to jump the line in a store. *My child is missing.*"

"Right. But from the day you arrived you've been judging Jamaica through an entitled, white lens. You said it yourself—three other girls have gone missing in the last couple of years. And they're *local,* and *black.* You're an outsider, a rich *white* tourist from another country, coming in and telling the authorities how to do things and already accusing them of malfeasance. People aren't big on being treated that way."

Rose jumps up and pushes back her chair. "I don't give a damn right now about hurting people's feelings. I want my daughter back, can't you understand that? If I see something that needs to be done, I'm gonna say so, and if some detective's ego is too fragile to hear it, too damned bad!"

Brandon stands and puts his arm around her shoulders, trying to guide her back into the chair, but she stands firm.

Leo's finger stabs the air in front of him. "I'm trying to get you to understand. Being openly hostile and offending the police isn't going to help Lily. Mr. Keppler's going to help us, and hopefully the FBI will help us. But maybe in the meantime *not* pissing off everyone in the Caribbean will go the farthest toward getting Lily back safely."

Rose turns to Brandon to back her up, but his expression makes clear he agrees. She looks down at Mr. Keppler, who is discreetly scraping at a spot on his cuff.

She turns and pushes out of the conference room, hand lifted in the air to signal they shouldn't follow. Because they're right, and she knows it. But she also knows that no matter what they say, she can't turn off the lioness waiting to shred anyone who stands in the way of her saving her cub.

She has a secret weapon she's been holding back, and it's time to unleash her claws.

CHAPTER SEVENTEEN

Three days before

Rose

"So what exactly is Croydon Plantation?" Mateo asked as they piled into the car after their Hip Strip lunch.

Leo's face split into a grin. "It's an actual working plantation. They grow pineapples mostly, but other things like sugar cane and the *best* coffee in the world. I thought it would be a good way to get a deeper understanding of the island's history," Leo said.

"You make it sound so boring!" Bree turned to the kids. "It's lots of fun. You get to taste stuff."

Michael looked at Bree like she was an alien. "What kind of stuff?" he asked.

Bree raised her eyebrows. "Have you ever had sugar cane?"

"No," he considered. "Is it like candy?"

"It sure is." Bree wiggled her eyebrows.

Rose watched Bree surreptitiously, considering what Anabelle had said, that Bree just wasn't happy in Jamaica. It made sense—Brandon said *Leo* invited everyone for Thanksgiving, not Leo *and* Bree—maybe Bree was as hesitant about this visit as Rose had been. Coming to Jamaica had been Leo's idea, but Bree adored Leo in a way that would make Romeo and Juliet jealous, and she'd follow him to the dust fields of Mars if that's where he wanted to go. It must have been incredibly hard for her to adjust, and maybe seeing everyone was just making her miss home all that much more.

Rose grimaced at the greenery sliding past the car and chastised herself—she'd been so wrapped up in her own worries she never stopped to consider how Bree might be feeling. Why did she always assume *she* was the one who'd done something wrong? She'd been working for ages on her tendency to blame herself for everything with her therapist, trying to diffuse the childhood events that caused her to behave that way. She shook her head—she needed to get over herself.

When the car finally parked, she and Anabelle eased the kids out of their seats and into the humid embrace of the heat while Leo set off to find their guide. Buzzing insects and chirping birds pulled her attention across the wide stretches of lawn lined with banana and pine trees, through to the ocean view in the distance.

"Mom, it's too hot," Michael complained.

Anabelle pulled out a bottle of water and made the boys each take a long sip. "Don't worry, baby, you'll get used to it in a day or two. You're half Caribbean."

Bree waved a hand. "I wish I were, because I'm still not used to it."

Their guide, Lawrence, led them to a stretch of benches facing a map of Jamaica, and gestured for them to sit.

"I've heard the spiel before," Bree said. "I'll watch the kids."

The familiar knee-jerk hesitation tugged at Rose as Bree grabbed Lily by the hand, but she fought it back. Bree needed compassion right now. And Bree was their aunt—why did her instincts make her feel uncomfortable when she was with them? She was letting her own biases about her relationship with Bree interfere with her judgment, and it wasn't fair or right.

As Lawrence rattled off facts in his warm, rolling patois, Rose fanned herself and Jackson with a brochure and watched Lily run on the lawn in little circles, her arms held out like an airplane.

Children were amazing creatures with endless fonts of energy. Where did that disappear to along the way? When she was a little girl she'd loved swings and she'd pump her legs as hard as she could to go higher and higher and higher, until she felt the tension in the chains disappear because her arc was too high, and in that brief uncontrolled instant a flash of delicious, exhilarating fear stabbed through her, until the chains caught her weight and glided her back onto their course again. Now even just the thought of doing that nauseated her, and the stabs of fear were disabling rather than exciting.

Something about the memory amplified her unease, and she fought down another urge to go stand by Lily. She squeezed her eyes shut for a moment and tried to focus her attention on the information Lawrence was spouting. But a bird flew by, shrieking *braaah-braaaah-braaah-braaaah-braaah,* startling her eyes back open—at the same moment Lily cowered and screamed, then ran toward Rose.

Bree, who'd pulled out sunscreen and was in the middle of applying it to her face, lunged for Lily and carried her back to the center of the lawn. Rose caught Bree's eye and held out her arms, mouthing *it's okay.* Bree scowled, and looked away.

Rose surreptitiously examined Bree. Her face had changed again, but it wasn't a straightforward change. When she was with the kids, especially Lily, she was happy but—there was something else in her expression. Like a shadow that passed over a beautiful garden, changing nothing and everything at the same time. More than just longing for her own children—something far more intense.

Jackson twisted in his stroller and cried out. Rose picked up the plastic toy cell phone he'd been playing with and handed it back to him; as she looked back up, she caught Leo staring at Brandon with his own strange intensity. Her mind flashed back to Brandon's anger with Leo at the farm.

Leo leaned over and said something to him, and Brandon laughed.

She smiled, relieved. That was the thing about Brandon, his moods shifted faster than waves rolling out to sea. He was like her father that way, at least the way her father was after her sister died; his anger would flash sharp and bright like lightning in a night sky, then disappear. But *his* lightning left more than one scorched burn.

Suddenly everyone around her was getting up; Lawrence had finished his presentation. As she followed everyone down the pair of rippled cement paths that cut through the lawn, Lily ran over to walk with her and Jackson. Rose ignored the annoyed look Bree sent after her.

Lawrence paused by a tree and pointed up to a bundle of green bananas. He grabbed what looked like a huge purple teardrop hanging amid the leaves. "The easiest way to find the bananas is to find these, then follow them up." He paused as everyone tested the strategy, then peeled back the outside of the purple pod, exposing little yellow shoots. "And here you can see some baby bananas just starting to grow."

"They look like French fries!" Michael called out, and everyone in the crowd laughed.

"That they do, my little friend." Lawrence smiled, then started them walking again.

Rose peered back at the bananas, considering the little yellow stalks hidden inside their pod.

Funny how dramatically the strangest, smallest seeds grew and transformed over time.

CHAPTER EIGHTEEN

Three days before

Anabelle

"Mama, can I have French fries for dinner?" Michael called.

"French fries!" Marcus squealed.

"I'm not sure what Uncle Leo has planned for dinner, baby," Anabelle said, eyes scanning the neat patches of plants that bounded the pair of cement paths.

Michael stared up at her, head tilted as he thought. "But if they have French fries I can get them?"

She laughed, and pointed a finger at him. "Only if you don't try to get him to take us somewhere that has them."

His face fell for a moment, until he spotted a lizard. He ran toward it and Marcus followed, slow and awkward by comparison, trying to see what his brother was excited about.

Anabelle hung back and waited for Mateo to catch up to her, but he slowed to walk with Leo and Brandon. She was about to give up when Bree grabbed Leo's arm and pulled him to the side. She sidled up to take his place.

"I have to admit, when I pictured a vacation in Jamaica, I pictured lying on deck chairs on the beach, sipping drinks under a tiki thatch umbrella, not taking classes on coffee processing and tropical gardening," Mateo said to Brandon.

"Hey, the kids are having fun." Brandon pointed toward the ocean. "And the view is nice."

"Look at you, putting such an optimistic spin on it. Let me try: Such a beautiful day to be strolling among—" Mateo pointed at the nearby patch of plants "—whatever the hell those are."

"I have a secret weapon." Brandon slipped his hand into his hip pocket and pulled a flask halfway out. "Give me your water bottle."

"I knew I loved you, man." Mateo chuckled like a frat boy and handed over his bottle. "Very resourceful."

"Hey, I was an eagle scout. Always prepared." He winked as he poured out a healthy dose of what Anabelle assumed was rum. "You want any, Anabelle?"

"Nah, there won't be anything left for you." Anabelle laughed. "Besides, I'm still riding the wave of my drink from lunch."

"Psh, that was ages ago. And I have plenty." He swished the bottle of water he was holding in his other hand and bounced his eyebrows.

Anabelle glanced over at the children. Leo, Bree and Rose weren't drinking, and one shot wouldn't hurt her. She held out her bottle, still a third full of water. "Okay, thanks. And they're pineapples."

"Pineapples?" Brandon asked, confused.

"The plants." She motioned toward the fronds springing up out of neat rows.

Mateo stared. "How are those pineapples? They look like spider plants on steroids."

Anabelle tilted her head. "They kinda do. But the pineapples grow right up in the middle. See? There."

"Well I'll be damned," Mateo said, peering at the mini purple pineapples sitting in the center of the plants. Then he shook his head. "And yet, I still don't care."

Lawrence herded them toward a large, wooden table in the middle of one of the lawns, covered with pitchers and plates. He poured a light golden liquid into individual cups and explained the drink was made by steeping pineapple skins and ginger in hot water. After everyone sipped and made the appropriate oohs and aahs, he produced a variety of plates with fruits to sample, including an assortment of different types of pineapple.

Anabelle made sure the boys took only their fair share, then, sensing her moment, turned back to Mateo. "I think there's a theme to this trip. First the farm last night, and now the plantation."

"Yeah, I noticed that, too. Not exactly my idea of tropical paradise." Mateo popped a piece of fresh coconut into his mouth. "But I'll say this—it's amazing how much better everything tastes here."

"It's the island air," Anabelle said in her father's Dominican accent, then selected small pieces of sugar cane for each of the boys. "I guess that's why Leo wants to invest in a farm."

"I guess." Mateo reached for samples of two different pineapple varieties. "I think I'll do a side-by-side."

She glanced around to be sure everyone else was busy with their own conversations. "And the solar panels. That's super smart. I mean, in ten, twenty years, fossil fuels are gonna run out, right? But people will still need energy."

Mateo chewed, and swallowed. "Yeah, but he's going about it in a stupid way. What you'd want to do is invest in a company that produces solar panels, right? Then when the demand goes up, that's when you make your money."

"Isn't that what his organization is doing?" Anabelle asked.

"They're just putting up solar panels, like the one they're providing to the farm." He popped a third type of pineapple in his mouth. "Oh, that's too sweet."

"Huh. Well. Too bad someone doesn't start a company like that, then." Anabelle grabbed a piece of coconut for herself, and tried not to be too obvious. How many more hints did he need? "It's smart of Leo to invest when Sousie's farm is getting the panels now, anyway. It'll give her an advantage, and that has to mean they'll make a good return on their investment. Which is smart, because I have a gut feeling their next in vitro attempt will work, and they'll be in the same boat we are trying to save up money for school."

Mateo nodded as he grabbed a piece of jackfruit. He stared at the boys as he popped it into his mouth.

Anabelle hid her smile.

CHAPTER NINETEEN

Now

"What did you do?" Leo says, face turning red as he stares out the window at the press now setting up on the edge of the road.

Rose stares straight at him, shoulders thrust back. "I contacted Ray Madden. He couldn't get here so quickly, obviously, but he set up a press conference. They're waiting for us to go give a statement."

Brandon groans and drops his head into his hands.

"Who's Ray Madden?" Anabelle asks.

Brandon's head stays down. "He's a PR guy out of Manhattan. He works with a few of my clients, and I did some work on his wife."

"I don't understand," Bree says, looking concerned. "I thought we were trying to get help from the FBI."

Rose keeps her stiff posture. "Mr. Keppler's looking into that. But he's not optimistic, and we need all the help we can get. The first few days are crucial, and the police aren't doing enough. The more attention we get on this, the more likely we'll get Lily back."

Leo storms back from the window, running his hands through his hair. "Rose, are you really that naive?"

The words hit Rose like a slap across the mouth—Leo has never been unkind to her before. "I don't appreciate the name-calling."

Leo's hands drop from his head, leaving his hair sticking out at random angles. "And I don't appreciate you taking unilateral action that impacts everyone. You've just invited the press into *all* our lives. It's like releasing locusts on a field thinking you can make sure they only eat the weeds and not the wheat."

Rose's eyes narrow. "What does it matter? We need to get to the *truth*. Journalists investigate."

The flush in Leo's face drops to his neck, and he barks a short, sarcastic laugh. "Apparently you *are* that naive if you think the journalists that work for rags like *The Global Daily Gazette* give a rat's ass about the truth. When they don't find anything that'll bring in readers, they'll turn to whatever hints or lies sell the advertising space on their website. You just opened Pandora's box."

Anabelle and Mateo pointedly keep their focus on Michael and Marcus, who are playing on the floor with Jackson. Rose's jaw clenches, and she turns to Brandon. She shouldn't be fighting this alone.

He holds up a hand. "Leo, stop with the name-calling. That's my wife you're talking to, and it's not helping."

"I'm not helping?" Leo reaches up into the cabinet for the bottle of Ibuprofen stashed there. "Me. I'm the one not helping? I'm the one who pulled strings to get you an almost instant appointment with Keppler, the guy who's putting pressure on the police and trying to bring in the FBI."

"Right, and the detectives won't even call us back about a dog team," Rose says.

"It's only been two hours!" Leo shouts.

Bree slips past Leo and peers out of the window.

"Three hours, actually," Rose says. "And how long does it take to pick up a phone and say 'We'll look into it?' In three hours my baby girl could have been smuggled onto a boat and be halfway to South America!"

"That's just it, Rose, that's what I keep *trying to tell you*. The more you piss people off, the more they don't bother to go out of their way to return your phone calls." Leo pulls a Red Stripe out of the refrigerator, grabs the opener to pop off the cap, and uses it to wash down the pills.

"Can you pass me some of those, and a beer? I can't kick this headache," Brandon asks.

Rose rounds on him. "You're going to go out to the conference smelling like beer?"

Anger flashes across his face. "It's one beer, Rose. You're not the only one suffering here. You wanted to have this press conference, fine, I'm on your side. Whatever we need to do to put the pressure on, fine. I'll do it. But the thought of going out there and answering questions about my missing daughter is like a nightmare come to life. Cut me the smallest bit of slack."

"I'm just saying, you don't want to—"

Brandon's voice slices through hers. "Enough."

Leo reaches into the refrigerator, then hands him the Ibuprofen, the beer, and an opener.

Bree winces. Rose looks away.

Mateo breaks the awkward silence. "I'm thinking it would be a good idea for someone to go out there with you. Anabelle can stand beside you, Rose, and I can stand behind Brandon."

"If Bree and Leo don't mind watching the kids," Anabelle says, not looking up.

Leo's head jerks back and forth. "This is a mistake, I'm telling you."

"Okay, you've told us," Brandon says. "And I understand your feelings. But the press is here and it's too late now, so we may as well use them to our advantage."

Buoyed by the shift in Brandon's support, Rose nods. "I wrote up a statement on my phone. I'll start by reading it."

"Great," Brandon says, then drains the rest of the beer. "Let's go."

They walk out to the courtyard and through the gate, Brandon with his hand on the small of Rose's back, Anabelle and Mateo behind them. They stop in front of a row of three microphones set up for them, and survey the small crowd of reporters waiting a respectful distance away.

Rose clears her throat, then leans toward the microphone and addresses the crowd.

CHAPTER TWENTY

Now

Less than half an hour after the press conference ends, and *The Global Daily Gazette* alert chimes on Rose's phone. She clicks on the notification, hopeful, but now also frightened by Leo's concerns.

The Global Daily Gazette
TOURIST NIGHTMARE!
PRESCHOOLER KIDNAPPED IN PARADISE

Saturday, November 21st, St. James Parish, Jamaica

Lily Martin, 3, has disappeared from the vacation villa where she was staying with her family in John's Hall, Jamaica. In a scene from every parent's nightmares, the little girl was discovered missing a little past 9:30 Friday evening. Her parents, Dr. Brandon Martin, 43, and Rose Martin, 35, residents of Marblehead, Massachusetts, USA, had gathered with family and friends in the villa's courtyard to play cards over drinks. When they took a break to check on the children, they discovered Lily missing. She appears to have been taken from her bedroom as she slept, because her window was found open.

The couple have another child, aged 18 months, and one of the other couples sharing the villa have two children, 5 and 3. All three were unharmed.

The Martins told GDG *that the police consider the case a kidnapping, and believe the girl is being held for ransom. The police claim ransom kidnappings are common in the region. In most such instances, the motive is generally monetary and the individual is returned or recovered unharmed.*

However, at a press conference, the parents stated they aren't convinced the child was kidnapped, at least not for ransom, because they found no ransom note and received no ransom call. They worry that Lily wandered off, or was taken by an opportunistic malcontent passing by, and are worried that the police are not investigating adequately. "We just want to make sure all options are being covered," *Brandon Martin said at the press conference.* "We're appealing to the police and the public to help search the area, and we've requested that the police bring in search-and-rescue dogs. Whatever it takes to find our little girl."

"I don't understand it, not at all," *a source close to the Martins said.* "Why aren't they investigating all possibilities? The only possible reason is they're covering something up. I read several other girls have gone missing in the area that they haven't found, and one even turned up dead. They couldn't solve those cases, and I think they're worried that international attention will expose their incompetence."

The Global Daily Gazette *has previously reported on this spate of missing girls in the area over the past two years. The three previous victims were all local Jamaican girls, and were several years older than Lily. But one was recently found dead, only a week ago, and the coincidence seems strange. Is Lily Martin a victim of the same perpetrators?*

And, it does appear that the police are not being fully forthcoming. When questioned about possibilities other than ransom kidnappings, they would only say that the family seems determined to do whatever they like, even if it hampers the police investigation. In their official statement to GDG, the Jamaica Constabulary Force justified their focus on a ransom kidnapping by stating that two suspicious-looking men were reported loitering in a car around the area, and gave descriptions now confirmed by a second witness. The man driving the car, a dark-blue Nissan Note, had shoulder-length African locks, was large, and had a wide mouth, while the other man was slighter, with short hair under a cap, and a narrow nose.

As of now, the search is ongoing. The parents made an emotional appeal during their meeting with the press, asking that "If you have Lily, please return her to us. Bring her back, or leave her somewhere safe, because we just want our baby back."

Lily is white, has brown hair and brown eyes, is about three feet tall, and was last seen in a pink nightgown; a recent photograph of her is included below. If you've seen her, or either of the two men reported near the area that night, please contact the Jamaica Constabulary Force immediately.

"What the actual hell?" The words slip out before Rose can stop them.

Everyone turns to stare—she doesn't swear often—and she glances down at Jackson. He doesn't seem to have noticed.

She hands the phone to Brandon, and recaps the article for everyone else. "They told the press we aren't cooperating. That we're actively causing problems."

Leo tosses down the paper he's reading and shakes his head with an unbelieving smirk. "What did you expect? You accused them of not doing their job, of course they're going to turn it back on us. Do you think this is their first time dealing with angry parents?"

"But it's just not true that we aren't cooperating! We've done everything they've asked."

"Rose, I told you they wouldn't like you going to the press," Leo continues. "This may be a vacation for you, but it's my *reputation*. I have to look my coworkers in the eye. I can't have all of this going on around me."

Rose tries to slog through the implications. Is Leo right, has she made a mistake? Maybe she has been naive, maybe she should have known she was throwing down a gauntlet. But Ray Madden is a pro at this, he'll make sure that—

"I'm sorry the disappearance of my child has inconvenienced you, Leo," Brandon snaps.

Leo stops pacing to stare at him. "You know that's not what I mean."

"Then what do you mean, Leo?" Brandon asks, voice icy. "Because I just heard you say your reputation is more important than recovering our missing child. *Your* missing niece."

Leo's eyes widen—he realizes he's gone too far. "Of course finding Lily is the most important thing. But we could have done it without all this. I'm entitled to an opinion when my livelihood is involved, aren't I?"

"Your livelihood." Brandon's posture tenses, and his eyes narrow to slits. He leans toward Leo. "No, Leo. Your *livelihood* doesn't matter one damned bit. Don't forget for a single second what we're facing here."

Rose slips her hand into Brandon's, still glaring at Leo. Thank God for Brandon—there's no way she'd be able to deal with all of this without him. She'd be a quivering bowl of jelly rocking comatose in a chair the way she'd been back when Lillian Marie died. Maybe if her father had done this rather than—

Mateo cleared his throat. "The question is, what do we do now?"

"I don't see that we can do much except wait," Brandon answers.

Anabelle makes the sign of the cross over her head and chest. "And pray."

Pray.

Rose stares at Anabelle as the word tugs at her psyche, insistent and indelible, and a desperate hope clutches at her heart. How long has it been since she's even been inside a church? Not since—she presses her hand against her eyes to short-circuit the thought—and maybe *that's* the whole problem. She needs to pray. Not just for help and for strength, she realizes with blinding surety, but for forgiveness.

She's been trying to push down all her guilt for years, to pretend like none of it ever happened, like if she ignored it she'd never have to face a reckoning. But she can't hide from herself, or from God, and she should have asked for forgiveness long ago. How can she be surprised that God has forsaken her if she's forsaken Him?

"Is there a church nearby?" she asks. "I'd like to go, now."

"There's one about half a mile from here," Bree answers.

Brandon's head snaps around, and Rose shares his surprise—neither Bree nor Brandon have ever been big on church, they weren't raised that way. Leo also looks confused.

Bree clears her throat, and grabs her purse. "I've been going lately."

"To church?" Brandon asks.

"Yes." She finally makes eye contact. "Every week. What's wrong with that?"

As they drive, Rose listens absently as Bree makes a series of phone calls, her obsessive thoughts spiraling. Bree manages to get in touch with the priest who oversees St. Anne's Catholic Church; he's heard about the kidnapping, and will be there to welcome them.

Maybe she should ask him to hear her confession?

She scrutinizes the church carefully when they arrive, hoping for solace. St. Anne's is small, set slightly up a hill, with a flight of stone steps that feel like a pilgrim's path. A square tower rises in the center, flanked by two wing-like structures that form an almost-triangular facade of white stone masonry covered with meandering tendrils of ivy. Like a stylized angel—strange, but welcoming.

Rose and Brandon climb the steps hand in hand, heads bowed, with Leo and Bree following behind them. A man in priest's robes emerges from the church and strides out to greet them.

"I'm Father Delroy." His voice is deep, strong, and soothing. "I'm so sorry for what you're going through. Please, come in."

Rose dips her finger in the holy water by the side of the door and crosses herself; old habits die hard, even those untapped for so long. They follow him inside, past a confessional at the back, between red wooden pews that line the room, up to an oval altar framed by a stained-glass triptych.

Father Delroy turns to them. "If you like, I can lead a small service? Or would you prefer to be alone with your prayers?"

Brandon looks at Rose.

The confessional is too close by, and it can't be soundproof. She searches her memory—are confessions confidential if they relate to crimes? She knows there are exceptions, but she's not sure what they are. She can't take the risk.

"Alone, if you don't mind. May we light a candle, Father?" she asks.

"Of course. Just there." He points to the left side of the room. "I'll be waiting in the back when you're finished."

She genuflects before turning from the altar, then approaches the spread of pillar candles and tea lights burning near the wall. She selects a pillar and lights it; when she finishes, Brandon already has a bill pulled from his wallet. She inserts it into the box, then returns to the pews where Bree and Leo are already praying.

As soon as she lowers herself onto the kneeler and dips her head, tears stream down her face. *Please, God. Please let Lily be safe. Please bring her back to us. Please forgive me—please don't make her pay the cost for my demons.*

She repeats the prayers in a mantra designed to atone, and to break a cycle of obsessive thinking. How many times has her therapist told her to chase away anxiety with reason and facts? *God doesn't work that way*, she tells herself. *This isn't because of you.*

But how can it not be? It's too much. It's too coincidental.

Stop.

She short-circuits the cycle of thoughts and returns to the prayer.

But Brandon was right—

Stop.

This isn't her fault. It can't be, it just can't.

Unless it is.

Lily's face pops into her head, the wide, dark brown eyes and the soft brown hair—

Stop.

She refocuses on the prayer, desperate to chase away the demons circling her mind.

Divine punishment.

She blanches as the thought rips through her mind, and her eyes fly open. She searches the stained-glass Jesus facing her, begging for answers, but he only stares back, silent, turning the questions on her.

No, she tells herself, trying to seize control. *You're losing it, and you can't afford to lose it. Divine punishment doesn't work that way.*

She glances back at the confessional. *Please bring my baby girl back. Bring her back to me and I'll do whatever you need me to do to make it right. Bring her back and I'll make sure it never, ever happens again.*

CHAPTER TWENTY-ONE

Two days before

Rose

Rose woke Wednesday feeling groggy, wishing for an extra few hours sleep, but could already hear Jackson calling out from the other bedroom. She turned over and kissed Brandon softly on the cheek.

He groaned, and pulled the pillow over his head. "Too early."

Rose laughed. "I'll go take care of the kids if you make some coffee."

"Deal," he said, but didn't move. She shook her head and laughed again, then went off to tend to the day.

Leo announced that he'd booked a tour of something called Ahh... Ras Natango Gallery and Garden, a relaxing nature walk through a sanctuary filled with birds and flowers and ferns, and suggested they eat breakfast there. More than happy to avoid making breakfast while stifling a series of yawns, Rose agreed, and enjoyed sipping a portable morning coffee as they strolled the beautiful path. As her brain slowly woke, she snapped dozens of pictures as the colors and shapes around her triggered designs for caftans and bathing suits and rompers in her head.

"So what'd you guys think?" Leo asked as they drove down the bumpy road away from the gardens.

She and Anabelle gushed their approval, and Brandon nodded.

Mateo yawned. "This was great, but I'm beat—I was up 'til four last night with the heat. Any chance we can make it to the beach sometime soon? Or maybe just hang by the pool?"

Leo shot a finger gun at him. "Don't worry, I got you. All next week we're gonna just hang out, on the beach or around the pool at the house. And right now I have the ultimate relaxing afternoon booked for us." He paused to glance back at everyone. "We're heading over to the Languid Lake Country Club. It has a golf course so Brandon and I can relax over nine holes, while you all go get some treatments."

Rose watched something flicker over Brandon's face as Anabelle gave a little squeal. "What kind of treatments?"

Leo beamed. "Whatever you want. They do facials, some sort of weird mud bath thing, another one with kelp, and something with a salt cave? Or you can just get a massage. That's what I signed you up for, Matty, since golf isn't your thing."

"I could curl up on a couch somewhere and save you the cost. I'll fall asleep the minute I lie down." Mateo laughed.

Rose's mind skipped among the blissfully escapist options. She could use a day of pampering, to just relax and— "Oh, but the kids—"

Leo raised a hand to cut her off. "They have a little daycare there. Very highly recommended, lots of people associated with AmericAid go there. That way everybody can have a break."

Rose tensed at the thought of leaving the kids, but caught herself; she'd seen these types of swanky golf-spa resorts before. They catered to rich and famous clientele, the sort of places that had a skilled staff and plenty of activities for the kids, all under copious video surveillance. She'd even heard of some that allowed you to check in on your kids via webcam. And she had to admit… she could really use a massage.

"I suppose if they sleep on the drive, that could work." She smiled up at Leo. "Thank you so much, that's such a lovely thing to do for us."

He smiled back. "Great. That's settled, then."

But despite their best attempts, Rose and Anabelle weren't able to get the kids to sleep. Just as one nodded off, one of the others would do something that woke everyone back up, and by the time they closed in on the resort, not only hadn't they slept, they were fussing and crying for lack of sleep.

Rose's heart sank as she faced the inevitable. "The kids need a real nap, they're still over-tired from traveling. I can't leave them in a spa daycare when they're grumpy like this."

Mateo yawned into his hand. "That's what the staff is paid for, to deal with grumpy kids."

Rose shook her head. "No, I mean I literally can't leave them. When Jackson gets like this, he won't leave my side. He'll throw a screaming fit, and then Lily will burst into tears and she'll be too upset to leave me, too."

"Huh." Mateo gave her a skeptical look. "Our boys were never like that. Can't they just cry it out?"

Anabelle's wry smile and head shake told Rose that *yes, their boys had been like that*, Mateo had just never realized it. Rose smiled back in solidarity. "They'll scream bloody murder and the staff will just call me right back to get them. And there's no way I'd be able to enjoy anything knowing they're miserable anyway. Is there time to drop me off with the kids at the villa? I can take the boys, too, that way Anabelle can still go."

Leo met her eyes through the rearview. "It'll take us an extra forty minutes to get there and back. But don't worry about it, I'll just switch the appointments to another day, and we can head home. Hon, can you call for me?" He slipped his cell phone out of his pocket and handed it to Bree, who shot Rose an annoyed look.

Just what she needed—another reason for Bree to be angry. "I don't want to ruin everyone's good time. How about I drop you all off and take the kids back to the villa myself? The van has GPS, doesn't it?" But as soon as she said it, she realized it was ridiculous. She'd never driven on the left before, and the roads up to the villa were narrow and treacherous. And, alone with four children, she'd be the perfect target for anyone looking for a helpless tourist to rob. "Or, no, you know what? I can just stay in the van with the kids while you all go in. If we leave the air conditioning on, they can sleep in their car seats, and I can read a book on my phone."

Brandon shook his head. "No, you're right, they need real beds. I'll go with you."

Disappointment, and something else Rose didn't recognize, flashed across the strip of Leo's face in the rearview mirror. "I don't want to play golf by myself, and neither of you is on the insurance for the van, anyway."

Mateo rubbed a hand over his eyes. "I'll go with her. My insurance covers me for any car I drive. And I drive on the left all the time when we visit Ana's family. I'm just gonna fall asleep anyway, I might as well do it at the villa."

Rose tried to read his face. "You're sure you don't mind?"

He smiled. "Not at all. A few quality ZZZs will get me back on track for whatever Leo has planned this evening."

The children fell asleep almost as soon as their heads hit their pillows. Despite that, Rose stayed with Lily and Jackson until she finished the story she'd started for them, about a cat whose white shoes get dirty, but who doesn't let that stop him from appreciating his blessings.

As she read the final page, she sat for a moment with the moral of the story. Why was it so easy to focus on the bad, and so hard to remember the good? When you had a toothache it was impossible to forget the pain, but once it was gone, you didn't sit there appreciating how good you felt, you just got on with your day and didn't think twice about it. You had to make a special effort to remember, something her therapist called 'mindfulness.' Brandon claimed that was the problem with her anxiety—that she focused too much on the negative. Which was true, to a degree. It did interfere with her ability to enjoy what she had, but it was really all just fear of losing what she loved so much.

Still, there was truth in the power of appreciating what you had, so she sat mindfully in the quiet with the ceiling fan casting gentle eddies of air around her, watching the face of her babies. Jackson, asleep in the crib, his left arm thrust up and over his head like he wanted to ask a question, mouth hanging ever so slightly open, rosy lips tracing a vague 'O.' And Lily, curled into herself, her breathing heavy, her thumb tucked loosely into her mouth. Rose smiled and shook her head—she'd have to break her of that habit before it interfered with the shape of her jaw. But she secretly loved the preciousness of it, the little-girl innocence it symbolized. Tomorrow they'd be bigger, and different, so she was thankful for the reminder to bask in how small and perfect they were today.

"That's a pretty picture," Mateo whispered, startling her.

Leaning against the doorway, he smiled as he watched her. She stood and crept out of the room, closing the door softly behind them.

"Did the boys go to sleep easily?" she asked, trying to push down the wariness that tugged at her.

"Pretty much. I've been watching you since the cat's shoes turned brown."

She rolled her eyes as she passed him, and put on a laugh. "Because that's not creepy at all."

His hand reached out to her waist, and gently pulled her toward him. "We've got the houses to ourselves. Nobody can come home until we go get them... I say we take a little nap of our own."

She pulled his wrist off her. "Mateo, stop it."

"What? We aren't hurting anybody. We're on vacation, here to relax and have a good time. What people don't know won't hurt them." His hand caught hers, and he raised it to his lips. "And it's not like it hasn't happened before."

Guilt wrenched her stomach. "That was the biggest regret of my life, and it can't *ever* happen again."

He leaned back from her like he'd been slapped. "The biggest regret of your life? That's a little harsh, don't you think? You enjoyed it well enough at the time."

Heat crept up Rose's cheeks. "I remember being very drunk and very angry at Brandon for cheating on me. Not trying to make excuses, because there is no excuse. I'm just saying I'm not proud of it, and I'm not going to do it again."

He leaned forward again with a devilish grin. "If the alcohol will help, I can whip up some margaritas in a hot minute."

She snatched her hand back. "I asked you to stop it."

"He's cheated on you a hundred times since, Rose. Let's not pretend all is well—"

Anger flashed through her—*how dare he attack her marriage*—and her hand flipped up to silence him. "Two wrongs don't make a right. He's accountable for his mistakes, and I'm accountable for mine." She narrowed her eyes at him. "Mistakes have consequences, and I live with mine every day."

His brow creased, and his demeanor shifted, suddenly serious. "What do you mean? Did he find out? Is that why—"

"No, he didn't. But he could figure it out at any minute, and that's my constant fear."

He seemed relieved. "I'm certainly not going to tell him, and neither are you. Is this one of your anxiety phobia deals?"

The condescension of his words scraped against her like broken glass, and anger flushed her face again. "No, it's not one of my *anxiety phobia deals.* I wish it were."

His face broke into another lascivious smile. "Then let it go. Enjoy yourself. Brandon doesn't appreciate you, and you deserve a little fun—"

"Brandon's not the only person who matters here. What about Anabelle?"

His hands snaked back toward her waist. "That's for me to worry about."

She slapped his hands away. "No, it isn't, because she's *my* friend, and I hate myself for betraying her trust." She caught her voice rising, and with a quick glance at the children's door, lowered it to a harsh whisper. "No means *no.* As it is, I'm struggling to hang on to my last shred of self-respect. You might be okay with having possible evidence of your worst moments toddling around, but it creates a fair amount of stress for me."

Realization dawned on his face, and his hands drop to his side. "Wait. You mean—"

"Dawn breaks over Marblehead," she spat. "Didn't you ever do the math? You never wondered about the timing? How lucky men are to be able to be so oblivious."

"You mean—" His head swiveled to the children's door. His jaw dropped, and all the color drained from his face. "She's mine? Are you positive?"

Deep sadness suddenly took her over. "I don't know for sure. But yes, I think so."

He stared at the door as though there were a ghost on the other side, a discordant blend of terror and pride on his face. "She could be *my* daughter?"

"Maybe." Rose took advantage of the shock to push past him. "So let's not do anything that puts us in even deeper water than we're already treading."

CHAPTER TWENTY-TWO

Now

After an hour and a half, Rose feels Brandon tugging at her elbow, his signal he's ready to leave.

She resists—if she had her way she'd stay hidden here, wrapped in the comfort of the church until Lily is found. The iconography of her childhood has reached into the core of her soul and the act of praying, of putting everything into God's hands, has almost allowed her to believe all this can be fixed. Back at the villa they can only sit in oppressive silence and stare at one another, endlessly waiting: waiting for the police, waiting for the consulate, waiting for a ransom call that doesn't seem to be coming. The church gives Rose a sense of agency, and a salve for her flagging hope. Bree continues to kneel, suggesting she feels the same way.

But Leo and Brandon, both men of action, are restless, and it isn't right for her to find refuge at the cost of their peace of mind. So she rises, takes Brandon's hand, and allows him to lead her out of the church.

Before her seat belt's even buckled she pulls out her phone to check the news. She gasps, not able to trust what she's reading.

"What's wrong?" Brandon scours her face.

Rose reads the report out loud.

The Global Daily Gazette
TWO PERSONS OF INTEREST DETAINED IN THE LILY MARTIN KIDNAPPING CASE

Saturday, November 21st, St. James Parish, Jamaica

Earlier today, GDG reported that Lily Martin, 3, went missing from her villa in St. James Parish, and that residents who live nearby reported two suspicious-looking men loitering in a dark blue Nissan Note not far from the villa. The Jamaican Constabulary Force has now confirmed that two men matching these descriptions have been brought in for questioning.

Police confirm they hope the interview will provide information central to the disappearance of Lily Martin. They would not comment on whether they hope to recover Lily soon, but will release another statement as soon as they're able.

Bree reaches back and clasps her hand. "That's wonderful news!"

"I'll never doubt the power of prayer again," Brandon says, eyes wide. "Is there more?"

"That's it, at least for now. Leo, can we call Keppler?" Rose asks.

"Of course." He blasts his horn as a goat runs out into the road. "But it sounds like they're playing things close to their chest. If they didn't call us directly about this, I'm not sure how much more they'll tell us, even through him."

Adrenaline courses through Rose, and she's almost light-headed with hope. "But this is good, so good! Their recovery rate on kidnappings is almost perfect, right? So this must mean they're getting close."

Brandon wraps one arm around her and nods. "Thank God."

"Right," Bree says, eyes scanning the floor of the minivan. "It's just… I don't understand. Why didn't they confirm an actual arrest of the men?"

Brandon's head jerks toward Leo. "Do they have different laws about that here, or…"

Leo's shoulders rise sharply, more stab than shrug. "No clue."

"Maybe they're only releasing part of the information," Rose says.

"They're certainly only releasing part of the information." Leo glances to his left in advance of a turn. "The question is what are they holding back?"

Brandon's brows knit. "And why?"

CHAPTER TWENTY-THREE

Two days before

Anabelle

Anabelle's arm snaked through Bree's as they pushed into the sleek, all-wood interior of the Luminous Lake Spa building and tried to make sense of the sunken lily pond in the center of the room. Because, just, *why?* She snuck a look at Bree's face, and managed not to laugh at the disdain there—she could practically hear Bree's thoughts: *Pretentious nonsense with no function. There's a reason you keep ponds outside, not in.*

The attendant led them into a treatment room also covered in wood—hardwood floors, treatment beds on raised wooden platforms, bamboo wall and ceiling—with *another* sunken lily pond, this one right under a wall-sized window with an up-close view of lush plants. Eucalyptus and rosemary perfumed the air, at once refreshing and woodsy, and two low chaise lounges hugged the floor on either side of the pond, pointed toward the garden enclave.

"Okay, I get it now," Anabelle said once the attendant left. "It's supposed to be like your own private jungle. Like you're outside when you're really inside. *Très bougie.*" She flipped her hand as she stressed the final syllable, then turned to laugh with Bree.

But Bree's face was squashed in pain. Anabelle reached out for her arm. "Oh, girlie! I knew you weren't okay. What's going on?"

Bree turned away and unrolled the robe on her treatment platform. "Nothing you don't know. It's just all hitting me hard. Please, don't mind me, I didn't mean to let it show."

Anabelle slipped into her own robe as she watched Bree's movements. Bree's emotion seemed more raw than it had with her previous miscarriages—something more was going on. "You're losing hope that you'll get pregnant."

Bree dropped onto the platform, hunched over, and stared out the window. "There's no hope left to lose."

Anabelle sat next to her and hugged her shoulders. "There's always hope. Plenty of people still get pregnant after forty. You're only forty-two, and you froze your eggs. The in vitro will buy you time."

Bree's face went blank. "Most places won't do it after forty-two, forty-five at the oldest."

"Well, then, you still have three more years to try!" Anabelle added extra pep into her tone, and squeezed Bree's hand. "And if they won't let you, you can always get a surrogate."

"That's just it. I can't try again. It's—" She stopped and shook her head, and her face changed in a way Anabelle had never seen on her before.

Anabelle waited a long moment before prompting. "It's?"

A tear slid down one of Bree's cheeks. "Do you know how much a surrogate costs? Seventy-thousand dollars minimum." She held up a hand to stop Anabelle from speaking. "And even if I found someone who was willing to do it for free, the IVF alone costs twenty-thousand a cycle."

"I know it's expensive, but it's all you've ever wanted. That's gotta be worth—"

Bree laughed, a dry, bitter sound. "We've done seven cycles, Ana. You're excellent with numbers…"

A hundred and forty thousand dollars. Anabelle's eyebrows rose as she imagined what she could do with that sort of money.

"Okay, I get it, that's a lot. But what's the point of having money if you can't use it to get what you want in life? Both you and Leo want a child so much, you have to keep trying. You're so close!"

Bree puffed air through her nose. "Close? What does that mean, realistically?"

Bree's bitter tone surprised her. "Wait. Is the problem Leo? Does he not want to try again?"

Bree wiped the tear from her cheek. "The problem is the clinics don't run on credit."

"But your father's money—"

Bree stared out the jungle window. "Is gone."

That stopped Anabelle short—how was that even possible? She didn't know exactly how much Bree had inherited, but she did know, since she and Mateo had been their realtors, that Bree and Leo paid just over a million dollars for their Marblehead home. In cash, without breaking a sweat. Which you didn't do if it took you down to your last dollar.

"All of it?" she asked.

Bree nodded, and wiped another tear away.

The implication hit like a slowly amplifying burn. "Are you—are you okay? I mean, not with money for IVF, but with—you know, just living?"

"For now. But not for much longer."

Anabelle's gaze slid around the room—an afternoon in a place like this had to be a cool thousand for the two of them at least, let alone for the golf and Mateo's missed massage. And the villa—Mateo said Leo had insisted on paying for that. She bristled for a moment—was this some kind of charity? Anabelle and Mateo might not be as well off as either the Martins or the Palsers, but well enough off to pay their own way—but almost before she finished the thought, she realized this wasn't about her and Mateo, and it wasn't about charity.

It had to be about pride.

A vision of her mother's stubborn face flashed across her mind. *We have our pride,* she always said. Anabelle never understood that—what good was pride if your kids were hungry and your electricity was off? But her mother wouldn't even take extra money from their *father,* even when he had plenty, after he finished school and got the marine biologist job. *We'll take what the court gave us and not a penny more,* she'd say. *I don't want to owe him anything.* So she worked three jobs and always kept her head held high, and her three daughters grew up never knowing their mother.

But maybe she was wrong, and that had nothing to do with it. "I'm sure Brandon would lend you whatever you need—"

Bree whipped toward her and clutched her arm, eyes wide with panic. "You can't tell him. Or Rose. They can't know. Promise me."

Exactly like Anabelle's mother then, filled with the same stupid, pointless, stubborn pride.

Anabelle took a deep breath before answering. "Of course I won't if you don't want me to. But I really think you should, especially since time is an issue. He understands how important children are."

"You have to trust me on this. Leo has a plan, and if Brandon thinks there's an ulterior motive it'll never work."

The pieces fell into place. "Is that what this stuff with the farm and the solar panels is about?"

Guilt washed over Bree's face. "Leo just needs money to get it all off the ground. The farm alone would be enough—once Sousie can afford to buy the other property, we'd have money coming back to us within months, and the farm's income will double in the next year. And if he can convince Brandon to help fund the solar panels, it will triple, maybe even more. We might even be able to generate enough for a final round of IVF before all the doctors say I'm too old."

"So just tell Brandon—"

"No." Bree gripped her hand and stared at her with scared blue eyes. "He'll never *give* it to us. It has to be something he'd invest in for himself, not for us. That's a win-win, and he never has to know."

Anabelle raked her teeth across her bottom lip. That plan wasn't going to work, Brandon was too smart and suspicious. But Anabelle could see her mother in the set of Bree's jaw—no way was she gonna get her to believe anything different. "Are you going to ask him soon?"

Bree glanced back to the picture window. "It has to be just the right time, in just the right way, because Leo complicated things by diving in too fast."

Anabelle made a split-second decision. "Okay, look. When Leo was talking about the farm expansion, I started wondering if Mateo and I should invest in it. I'm sure we don't have as much as you need, but maybe if Mateo offers to invest, that'll convince Brandon it's a good idea? You know how guys are, total FOMO. Who knows, maybe it'll turn into some bro thing they can do together."

For the first time, a glimmer of hope lit up Bree's eyes. "Do you think he would?"

Anabelle rubbed her hand across her eyes. "I don't know. But we're falling behind in our savings plan for the boys' education and we have to do something. He doesn't want me to go back to work yet, so I've been dropping hints that this might be a good way to go. So maybe if I mentioned to him that Leo was hoping Brandon—"

"No," Bree cut her off. "He might say something to Brandon, and we can't risk that. We can't look desperate, or Brandon will completely pull away."

"Okay." Anabelle tried to push back her frustration. "So what should we do?"

"I'll talk to Leo. Maybe he can figure something out."

CHAPTER TWENTY-FOUR

Two days before

Rose

After inadvertently carpet-bombing Mateo, Rose hid in her section of the villa, afraid of the fallout. She'd known about the possibility for three years; he'd only known about it for a few minutes. He'd have a cascade of emotions to struggle through, each more unpleasant than the rest, and she'd be the easy target.

She tried to distract herself with the cheap paperback she'd purchased at the airport. But the thriller, about a man with two secret wives, inadvertently kept pulling Mateo's words back up, circling them through her mind.

He's cheated on you a hundred times since, Rose.

Most likely something Mateo had said to get her in bed, she kept repeating to herself. But, the possibility it was true nagged at her, because she'd struggled so much to forgive the one indiscretion, she wasn't sure she could forgive another.

Brandon had promised her it meant nothing. He didn't even remember the woman's last name, and he certainly wouldn't ever see her again. Nothing more than the unfortunate consequence of both he and a random pharmaceutical rep having far too much free alcohol at a conference mixer.

She only found out because his grandmother fell and broke her hip while he was at the conference, and Rose needed to let him know. The tramp picked up the phone, and she heard Brandon's drunken laughter turn to anger in the background when he realized the call wasn't about the room service they'd ordered.

Heartbroken wasn't a strong enough word for what she'd felt. *Destroyed? Devastated?* Still not strong enough, because she loved Brandon more than she loved her own life. He was her savior in so many ways, the only thing that had made her feel secure since the day Lillian Marie died. And that had taken her so much by surprise, because she never even thought she'd get married, and she definitely never wanted to have children. She channeled her energy into winning a full scholarship to Boston University, then into keeping her grades, and her portfolio, in shape so she could land a job at a fashion house. She'd dated along the way, but nothing serious, just a string of dead-end relationships with emotionally abusive men that reinforced her commitment to putting her nose to the grindstone and establishing a reputation for herself.

Just like the saying claims, as soon as she stopped looking, she found *the one*. Brandon was fresh off a divorce, and newly moved back to the Boston area. Born and raised in Marblehead, he'd gone off to medical school at Stanford and had started his career out in California. But after an ugly divorce because his wife didn't want children, he returned to Massachusetts for a fresh start.

She noticed him right away at a cocktail party, not because of his sandy-haired-blue-eyed good looks, but because of the way he handled himself. Several of his childhood friends were there, ribbing him mercilessly about his divorce and relocation, and she'd been impressed by the way he'd parried each of their thrusts. Later, when one of them asked her out and refused to take no for an answer, he appeared at her side.

"Give it a rest, Todd," he'd said. "Go learn some manners."

Todd had tried to punch him, but Brandon caught his fist and froze him mid-swing. Todd then broke away and stalked off.

"That's a useful trick," she'd said, trying to cover how much Todd's aggression had upset her.

"Nah, not really. He's so drunk he can barely stand, so I have a club soda advantage." He rattled the ice in his water, then looked into her eyes. "Are you okay?"

She gazed back into his and fell instantly in love. So much so that when he told her how much children meant to him, she'd fought back all her instincts and agreed to have kids. He'd been worried she'd change her mind—she couldn't really blame him—and had insisted on putting a clause about it into their prenuptial agreement. That was fine by her; if it made him feel secure, she'd sign whatever he needed.

Somehow, *that* was the part that hurt most of all. That her love for him was so encompassing she'd faced her deepest fears to give him what he wanted, but he'd been willing to toss their marriage away for a little midnight delight.

After days of reassurances that his indiscretion was a stupid mistake, after oceans of tears that seemed like they'd never stop coming, she forgave him. Everybody made mistakes, she decided, especially when alcohol was involved, and you didn't just give up on people you loved. And if she was going to stay with him, she knew she had to let it go.

But something deep inside wouldn't let her. Her pride whispered to her with annoying regularity: *What kind of pathetic woman stays with a man who cheats on her? How little respect do you have for yourself?*

It left an imbalance between them that festered, a resentment she knew would destroy them eventually. So when Mateo came on to her, that dark patch of wounded pride whispered that *this would make it better, put them back on the same level so they could move forward and rebuild trust from an equal footing.* She convinced herself it was almost an altruistic act to save the marriage, and allowed the alcohol to take her over the way it supposedly had taken over Brandon.

She tossed down the novel and rolled her eyes at herself. Because *that* was complete and utter bullshit. She knew that—now.

The truth was simple: it was an excuse that let her allow Brandon to stay. If *she* could sleep with another man and have it mean nothing, then she could convince herself that the same was possible for Brandon. She could cling to the delusion that her marriage was fine and Brandon truly loved her.

But if he'd cheated again, if it was still happening—then her carefully constructed house of cards came tumbling down. And that meant she was *exactly* the sort of pathetic woman who stayed with a man who cheated on her—except she was also now the sort of treacherous bitch who betrayed her dearest friend along the way.

The front door swung open, startling her out of her thoughts.

"Hey, honey." Brandon crossed to her and leaned over to kiss her head. "I'm sorry you had to miss the spa. How are the kids?"

She fought to keep her thoughts off her face. "Still asleep. They were even more tired than I realized." She searched his face. "Is everything okay? You look annoyed."

He pinched the bridge of his nose. "I suspected it was coming as soon as he mentioned golf, but hoped he legitimately just wanted to play. I mean, come on, the signals I sent were pretty damned clear. But sure enough, as soon as we finished our first drive, he started pushing me about investing."

"I meant to ask you about that last night. That's what the farm thing was about?"

He dropped into the wicker chair facing her. "The farm, the solar panels, and now wind turbines. For someone who came out here on an international mission to help beef up the island's infrastructure, he's sure looking to make money anywhere he can."

"I'm sure he means well. Maybe he just thought you'd want to be involved?"

He barked a bitter laugh and stared pointedly at her. "Right. Just a nice, familial venture. That he couldn't wait for us to unpack before he smashed over my head, then went through Olympic-level gymnastic contortions to corner me about it today."

Well, when he put it *that* way… "Why the urgency, do you think?"

"I don't have to think." He kicked off his shoes. "I know. They also use Mason and Ranstad."

She shifted in her seat. "Our accountants told you about Leo and Bree's money?"

"Not exactly. I noticed a few odd changes even before they moved here to Jamaica, so I did some checking. Asked a few questions here and there. Then paid someone to look into it."

Rose glanced over her shoulder to make sure the door was closed, then lowered her voice. "You dug into their personal finances?"

"Their *personal* finances?" He turned incredulous. "There's nothing *personal* about their finances. That money was my *father's*. He spent his whole life building it up to secure his family legacy, for his grandkids and their grandkids. It's *Lily and Jackson's* money. *Not* Bree and Leo's."

Rose stiffened. This topic was never pleasant—the way Reginald Martin distributed his estate was a massive flashpoint for Brandon. But not because of the money itself. The real issue, the disease-ridden tick burrowed firmly into Brandon's psyche, was that Bree was not Reginald Martin's real daughter.

She was his *step*daughter. Brandon's *step*sister.

Reginald Martin met Bree's mother at a grief-counseling group, a year after Brandon's mother was killed in a car accident and six months after Bree's father died from colon cancer. If you asked any friend of the family, they'd gush about how Reginald had always treated Bree as his own. And it looked that way from the outside—he'd cherished and spoiled her—but in a strange, opposite sort of way, it wasn't actually true.

Rose had never been able to figure out if it was because Brandon was his biological child or because he was a boy, but Reginald's expectations had always been much harsher and more intractable for Brandon than Bree. Brandon had to scrape and fight for every ounce of attention and approval he got; he had to get perfect grades, excel at sports, win class president, go on 'young leader' retreats.

His future had been predetermined: he'd take over the family stock-analysis business, marry the right sort of wife, and have children who would carry on the Martin genes. None of that pressure had ever been there for Bree, and of course that bred resentment. So when Reginald left the bulk of his estate to Bree after all the emphasis he'd put on legacy, it was a knife in Brandon's chest.

"Bree and Leo are struggling?" Rose asked.

"If by 'struggling' you mean they're flat broke, then yes, they're struggling."

Rose's head spun. She'd heard Brandon spit out the figures often enough: Bree had inherited one-point-six million dollars to his five hundred thousand. "It can't all be gone?"

"You'd think that, wouldn't you? But they're living off fumes. Based on how desperate Leo is to get me to invest, it's even worse than I thought."

"But how? They don't live lavishly. How did they blow through all that?"

He rubbed his brow. "Oh, that's the ironic part. They've spent a fair amount on fertility treatments, and nobody can blame them for that. But the majority has been due to *bad investments*. The man who's trying to pull me into speculating is basically a very high stakes gambler with absolutely no instincts for the game."

"Fertility treatments?" Rose's mind flew to what Anabelle had said about Bree's mood. Rose knew Bree had been trying to get pregnant forever, but she'd never mentioned extensive treatments. "And investments? Here in Jamaica?"

He shook his head. "They were in trouble well before. More than likely the main reason they came to Jamaica was to take advantage of the infrastructure issues here. Probably thought it was an opportunity to get in on the ground floor of solar and wind power here. Of course, that's misguided for a slew of reasons."

Not the least of which was the morality of profiting from a country trying to find its economic feet—maybe Leo wasn't quite the righteous champion she believed him to be. "So he asked you outright to invest, and you said no?"

"Damned straight I said no. They pissed my father's money away, and now I'm supposed to let them piss away mine? I have my children to think about." He grimaced. "So as much as Dear Daddy thought he'd get the last laugh by turning his legacy over to Bree, it looks like it's back on *my* shoulders after all. Thank God my practice is doing so well, and I've kept the family name standing tall."

Rose took a deep breath as she tried to process all the information. The thought of Bree and Leo in dire straits broke her heart—they were family, and they needed help. And if they needed money to help them have a baby—well, wasn't helping the right thing for family to do? But she was walking a minefield now, and had to compose her response carefully.

"It's funny. I fell in love with the farm when we were there, and was already wondering if we should invest," she lied. "Sousie seems very savvy, and she's doing good work for the community. Maybe it's worth doing regardless, and if Leo and Bree get a boost because of it, well, that's a nice side-effect?"

Brandon glared at her for a minute, then strode into the master bedroom, his jaw clenched. Rose followed, and said nothing as he selected a clean shirt from the bureau, then pulled the one he was wearing off over his head.

Finally, he responded. "So let's say the person who makes this shirt comes to you, as a fashion designer, and wants you to invest in their company. Says that with your money they can expand their line and make five times as many shirts next year, and with it, five times the profits. What would you say?"

Her fledgling hope dimmed. "Right, I get it. Even if he showed me some sort of business plan that supported those claims, it's not what I do. It would take focus and capital away from my goals, without adding in any real way to my long-term future."

He touched his index finger to his nose, then pulled on the clean shirt.

She knew he was missing the point on purpose, and that she should let the issue drop, but she had to try for Bree's sake. "I guess I was thinking it would be a little push to help them get back on their feet, and—"

Anger twisted his face. "So basically you're saying I should bankroll their mistakes, but do it in an underhanded way that keeps them from having to take responsibility for themselves?"

She winced. *They're family*, she wanted to say, but there was no point.

She pulled out a clean pair of chinos for him. "Well, I hope you turned him down gently."

"No, frankly, I didn't. I really resent being brought here under the guise of a pleasant vacation only to discover they're just trying to get money out of me."

"I'm sure the main reason for the trip was still for us to be together over the holidays—"

He flipped up a hand to interrupt her. "This is why I love you, Rose. You have a big heart and you can't imagine the people you love doing something to hurt you. But, the sad truth of this world is, the people who love you are the very ones who can and will hurt you the most. You have to set clear boundaries." He held her eyes. "So if Bree comes to you trying to get to me, I want you to shut it right down."

She nodded. "I understand."

He smiled, and squeezed her hand. "I know it's unpleasant. It's hard to watch people you love go through something like this, but the fact is, this is a situation *they* created, and they shouldn't put us in this position. And you know I'm not going to let them starve, or end up on the street. Everything will be okay. Alright?"

She smiled. "Alright."

He kissed her gently, then flashed a silly grin. "Then we better get a move on. Leo has a tour booked for some place called Rose Hall, and you don't want to miss out on your namesake."

She smiled and followed him to the children's room to wake them and get them ready, then out to the courtyard. As Anabelle and Bree chatted to Mateo about the crazy sunken ponds in their spa room, Leo stood jangling the keys in his hand, face blank.

As soon as he caught sight of Rose and Brandon, he turned to lead them all out. "Guys, we should get going."

She scanned everyone's faces as they secured the kids and themselves into the minivan once again, trying to make sense of the difference between her perspective and Brandon's. To her mind, these people mattered far more than money ever could, no matter where it came from or who should have gotten what, or who hadn't made the best choices. Maybe it just came down to the difference between being raised rich and being raised poor—family, and the friends you loved like family, was all you had when you didn't have money. And if you managed to get your hands on some, the most important thing you could do with it was take care of the people you loved, and who loved you.

CHAPTER TWENTY-FIVE

Now

The press conference has the desired effect: articles continue to appear over the course of Saturday evening, and a slew of other outlets flood Rose's and Brandon's phones with requests for interviews. But more importantly, despite having detained the two suspects, the detectives show up Sunday morning with a plan to conduct a full, organized grid search, and two trainers show up with sniffer dogs.

While Anabelle keeps the children occupied safely out of sight in her section of the villa, Detectives Williams and Shaw call together police and volunteers, and set up a command center a safe distance away from the still-cordoned section of grass. They distribute photocopied pictures of Lily and give specific directions to the civilian volunteers about what they're looking for—not just Lily herself, but her nightgown, any stray children's toys, or any out-of-place items, especially those that might be used to bind or gag a child. The search shouldn't just be visual, they instruct, so volunteers should call out and listen carefully in case the child is stranded somewhere out of sight.

Rose pales at the blunt descriptions and the horrific images they call up in her head, images she's been trying desperately to keep at bay. Lily weak and in pain at the bottom of a trench or ravine. Lily trapped inside a well. Lily lying dead amid long grass, broken and twisted like an abandoned doll. Rose longs to be out searching with them, but for reasons they don't explain, the detectives insist all three couples remain inside the villa. So she paces, fighting a continual wave of nausea and tries to blot the images back out with her prayer mantra: *Please let her be okay. Please let them bring her back to me alive and well.*

Once the volunteers set off down the road, Detective Williams clicks on his radio and says something Rose can't hear. Almost immediately, two cars arrive on the scene, each containing a sniffer dog and a pair of handlers.

Detective Shaw approaches the group. Her demeanor is still kind, but has a new edge of wariness. "We've brought in a search-and-rescue dog and a cadaver dog to search the premises and the surrounding areas," she says. "Are you familiar with what these dogs do?"

"I didn't realize there were different kinds," Rose answers.

"Search-and-rescue dogs are trained to follow the scent of a live human being. We'll need something of Lily's that has her scent on it, ideally an article of clothing she wore recently that hasn't yet been washed. A cadaver dog is trained to search for human remains, and they alert to scents associated with human decomposition." Detective Shaw's eyes scan each face for understanding.

Rose nods. "Should I get you some of her clothing now?"

"Please."

"Everything she wore recently is in the hamper in the children's bedroom. Do I need to put on one of those suits, or booties?"

"No, it's not a problem," Shaw says. "We've already processed the scene, and your hair and DNA are everywhere in the room anyway. I just need to accompany you and make note of what we remove."

This surprises Rose, but she doesn't say anything more, just follows Shaw to the children's door and waits while she lifts the crime-scene tape. Rose digs into the laundry bag and pulls out the purple bathing suit and shirt Lily wore the day she went missing. The tears return instantly as she stares at them, remembering that day's trip to the beach. Only two days ago, but an entire lifetime, a parallel existence where she was happy in a way she can't ever imagine being again.

She clears her throat so she can speak. "We did a load of laundry just the day before, so there's only one outfit that hasn't been washed. And it's been sitting in here mixed with Jackson's clothes, so I don't know if that will confuse the dogs?"

"That's fine." Shaw's face is soft as she holds her hand out. "It won't be a problem. The dog will know to follow the predominant scent."

Rose releases the clothes reluctantly. "Okay."

They return to the courtyard where the rest of the group is waiting, and Detective Shaw selects the shirt carefully as she speaks. "We'll take these out to the search-and-rescue dog. Because we don't know which way Lily went, we don't know which way the dog will go, so it's important that everyone stay out of her way. Same thing when we release the cadaver dog."

Everyone nods.

"Thank you. Please follow me."

She leads them through the courtyard and positions them near the outside of the gate. She then joins Detective Williams and the waiting dog teams. A policewoman pulls out a camera and begins recording.

The first trainer, a tall, thin man called Tom, crosses the lawn with a German shepherd named Heidi, and the two of them stand in front of the children's window. He places the shirt in front of Heidi's nose, gives her a moment to take in the scent, then says, "Find it, Heidi."

Heidi immediately takes off across the yard, away from them. Rose watches, heart in her throat, expecting the dog to head down the road.

But she veers to the left, toward the minivan, then turns and alerts to the fender of the Palsers' Accord.

That's wrong—that can't be possible. Rose steps forward to object, but Detective Williams' hand shoots up, warning her to stay in place.

"Lily's not in there, we checked to be sure she wasn't hiding in the car several times," Leo says. "The dog must be picking up an old scent."

Tom shakes his head. "She's trained to alert to the strongest scent, so that's the most recent. The last time Lily was in the area, she came, or was brought, from the window to the car."

Rose's hopes plummet. She'd been so sure that the dogs would help—she'd spent half the night reading success stories about missing children and adults recovered by search-and-rescue dogs. Heidi must be new to this, or tired. "That's not possible. Lily wasn't anywhere near that car on Friday. I'm pretty sure she's never been in that car at all. The dog must be making a mistake."

"Heidi's the best at what she does." Tom's expression is guarded. "But we can try from another starting point to be sure."

"Yes. Please," Rose says.

Tom leads Heidi out into the middle of the street, several hundred yards down the road. He again exposes her to the shirt, then gives the 'find it' command.

Heidi takes off again, nose in the air, and veers toward the window. She picks up the trail, then returns first to the side of the minivan, then to the Palsers' Accord, where she alerts at the fender.

Detective Williams steps toward Leo. "May I have the keys to the vehicle, please?"

Leo reaches into his pants pocket and extracts them. Williams hits the remote to unlock the doors.

"Not the doors," Tom says. "She's alerting to the trunk."

The trunk? Rose's blood rushes so hard the sound of it echoes in her ears.

"Let's be certain," Williams says.

Tom walks Heidi to the front of the car, and gives the command again. She runs directly to the fender, and alerts.

Before Rose can object, Detective Williams holds up his hand again. "I'll collect fingerprints from the handles, and then we'll check inside."

He crosses to the vehicle he and Detective Shaw arrived in and digs a small black duffel-type bag out of the trunk. With the camera still running, he gloves up, dusts each handle, transfers the prints he finds, then carefully opens each door and leaves it ajar. He does the same to the rear of the trunk. Once finished, he removes the gloves and uses the remote to pop the trunk, then signals Tom.

Tom walks Heidi to the front of the car, exposes her to the shirt again, then gives the command. She bobs and dips around the doors, alerting again at the fender. This time she sticks her head into the open trunk.

"No," Rose whispers. "She's wrong."

Expression grim, Detective Williams instructs Tom to take Heidi away, then signals the other trainer, a short man he calls Alfie, who's waiting in the middle of the street with a collie called Rex—the cadaver dog. Alfie gives the command, and Rex first runs to the side of the minivan, stands in place, and barks. Alfie gives him a treat and gives a release command; Rex heads immediately to the Accord's trunk. This time he sits before he barks.

"What does that mean?" Rose asks, although she knows full well.

"It means your daughter was in this trunk." Detective Williams speaks somberly. "And Rex is a cadaver dog, which means she was dead."

Rose goes numb. "No. It has to be a mistake. The dogs are confused by something else."

Neither of the detectives nor the trainers will look her in the eye, and Williams turns to talk to the others in a low tone she can't hear.

Rose stares at the car, willing it all to make sense. This has to be wrong, it *has* to be. There must be another explanation.

Detective Williams puts on a new pair of gloves and reaches into the trunk. Leo keeps the car clean, so Rose can see easily inside. There's a small emergency kit, and—a central spare tire compartment.

Rose grabs onto Brandon, trying to keep her knees from buckling; he pulls her close to him. She can't breathe as Williams grabs the compartment's release, then lifts the cover.

The spare tire sits cradled inside.

Rose chokes on a gasp of air and squeezes her eyes shut in relief, clinging onto Brandon's arm. He pulls her head into his chest and strokes her hair.

"Have the keys to either of these vehicles been missing at any time?" Detective Williams asks.

Leo's voice comes out unnaturally high. "No. I keep them in the kitchen inside the middle house. The only time they've been gone is when *you* checked the cars to see if Lily was hiding inside the night she went missing."

"And you always keep the windows up and the doors locked?" Williams continues.

Leo nods. "Always."

"Please wait here with Detective Shaw," Williams says to them, then motions Alfie and the policewoman who's recording the proceedings to follow him.

Everyone watches as they disappear through the gate, toward the Martins' section of the villa.

Rose has a sudden desperate desire to run, to be anywhere but beside this car, and she fights to take in ragged breaths as she roots herself in place.

After an eternity, Williams reappears, face professionally blank. Alfie leads Rex over to the car they arrived in, but doesn't get in. Williams gestures to the policewoman; she fiddles with the camera, then holds up the display so Rose and Brandon can see. The others watch over their shoulders.

The recording shows Williams bringing Alfie and Rex to the door of the children's bedroom. Alfie then gives the signal to Rex, and he begins sniffing the room. He works his way to Lily's bed, where he immediately sits and barks.

The policewoman closes the camera.

Williams clears his throat. "Lily was dead before she was removed from the premises."

CHAPTER TWENTY-SIX

Two days before

Rose

"You're quiet again," Anabelle whispered as they drove toward Rose Hall. "I thought you were feeling better about Bree. Between you and Leo it's like a hospital waiting room in here."

"Oh, sorry, I'm zoning out. I think I should have taken a nap along with the kids." She gave an exasperated headshake and turned back to the window.

She had too much going on in her mind, and needed to process it all before they arrived. Leo was sullen—not surprising considering Brandon had shot him down, and the implications weighed heavily on her. If they were in dire straits, Brandon's decision would only make things worse. They were in pain, and now they'd have to spend the next week and a half pretending they weren't, and it disturbed her that she couldn't think of any way to help.

And she'd been watching Mateo as surreptitiously as possible, not sure what to expect in light of the news he might be Lily's father, but he was acting like absolutely nothing had happened. She glanced briefly at his profile, completely perplexed as he made jokes about a patch of marijuana growing alongside a parking lot. Either he just didn't care that he might be Lily's father, or his ability to hide his true feelings was borderline pathological, and both possibilities made her deeply uncomfortable.

But part of her envied the ability, because Mateo's come-on had brought back her guilt about betraying Anabelle with a lion-like roar, and try as she might, she couldn't push it back down. She tried repeating the same arguments she'd made to herself initially after sleeping with Mateo—that she couldn't undo it after the fact, and that confessing to Anabelle was not an option, because she truly didn't want Anabelle hurt, either. It would be a cruel thing to do just to ease her own conscience, and far too easy a way to let herself off the hook. The weight of her guilt was a penance she needed to bear, to remind her the only amend she could make was to be the loyal friend Anabelle deserved from now on.

But the words rang empty in her head.

All too soon Rose Hall appeared in the distance, the white Georgian architecture looming high over the rolling green hills like a wedding cake abandoned by a runaway bride. She leaned over and pointed. "Lily, Jackson. Look at the beautiful house!"

"A princess live there?" Lily asked.

"It's pretty enough for a princess, isn't it?" Rose asked.

"People say that a witch used to live there," Leo said from the driver's seat, breaking his silence.

"A witch!" Michael yelled. "I want to meet a witch!"

Lily's brow furrowed. "A witch?"

"Leo!" Bree shot him a dirty look.

"What? There's a witch in every Disney story." He shrugged.

"A witch is there now?" Lily asked, apprehensive.

Bree sent a laser death-ray stare to Leo as she answered Lily. "Of course not, my love."

"Oh." But Lily's little brow remained furrowed.

"Do you see those white letters on the lawn?" Rose said to distract her. "Do you know any of those letters?"

Lily studied them. "That's a 'L!' L for Lily!"

"That's right! Two of them."

As Lily guessed letters, Rose tried to remember what she'd read about the 'white witch' of Rose Hall when she'd researched the trip. She hadn't paid it much attention because the too-casual historical use of the word 'witch' bothered her, ever since she heard a talk in Salem about how the women labeled 'witches' during the trials were the ones who inconveniently threatened male egos. The terms 'witch' and 'witchcraft' had been too-often used to stigmatize and repress women who were deemed problematic or didn't fit society's mold; women who were intelligent, landowning, or even those who struggled with mental illness. As an intelligent woman who suffered from panic attacks and owned her own business, the history unsettled her, especially because the talk had gone on to illustrate how its legacy was more present today than women might want to believe.

They parked, then walked up the cobblestone path that led to the huge mansion. A twenty-something woman in colonial-era dress greeted them as they approached.

"I'm Delia." She led them through the main doors into the house. "I'll be leading your tour. If you have any questions, please don't hesitate to ask."

Bree reached for Jackson's stroller. "I've seen the house before. I can wait out here with the baby if you want. And Lily."

Bree's frosty tone annoyed Rose, but her conversations with Anabelle and Brandon tugged at her. Between the money situation and struggling harder than Rose had realized to have a baby—it would be downright uncharitable for her to refuse.

"That would be great, thanks." She pushed the stroller over to Bree. "Lily, do you want to stay here with Aunt Bree?"

"No. I wan stay with you! Don't like witches." Her little brow pursed.

She smiled at Bree and shrugged her shoulders. Bree stared wistfully at Lily.

Rose sighed and hurried after the group—everything was caving in on her today. Thankfully, the interior of the mansion was the answer to her prayers, and her mouth dropped as she gazed around the entryway, creative connections exploding in her mind as her eyes bounced from one element to the other.

"Can I take pictures?" she asked.

"Of course you can," Delia replied.

She released Lily's hand to pull out her phone. "Stay right with me, bunny."

Lily nodded, her hands tugging at her dress as she stared around the room.

Rose raised the phone and snapped. Almost everywhere she looked, something called to her, and Delia's stream of facts about the plantation and its history faded into the background. The lines of the sprawling staircase curving around wood paneling made her imagine a structured, but flowing, skirt silhouette. The monochromatic white-on-beige vine-patterned wallpaper begged to be turned into evening gowns. She'd never seen bottom-quarter-only paneling before, and her mind instantly turned the proportions into a street-wear ensemble she knew she had to add to her next collection. Her brain whirred and clicked and cataloged.

As they climbed the stairs, Anabelle slipped her arm through Rose's. "Ah, much better. Looks like you're enjoying yourself."

Rose tried not to tense up. "This house is amazing."

"Tell me about it. The way the floors creak when you walk on them? The smell of that wood polish? I'm in heaven." She put her other hand over her heart.

"Guys, check this out!" Brandon called from the other room.

Marcus and Anabelle rushed in, and Rose ushered Lily behind them.

"Over here," Delia stage-whispered conspiratorially as she stroked a large wooden urn. She pulled up on the top, separating it from the section below, like the retro cigarette holders that splayed cigarettes out in a circle. But in this case, it revealed a flat surface lined with slots. "Annie, the mistress of the hall, would hide knives in these around the house, so she always had a weapon nearby should anyone try to attack her."

Rose's eyebrows shot up. "A secret stash of knives around her own house?"

Delia laughed. "Well, Annie was cruel to the slaves, and she murdered three husbands, so she had reason to be afraid." Delia closed the urn as she continued. "She killed her first husband in this room, with arsenic. She stabbed the second husband in his sleep, then poured boiling oil in his ears. To keep the doctors away, she told them he'd died of yellow fever—it was so contagious, nobody dared to come in. The third she strangled with the help of her lover, a freed slave. She had slaves retrieve the body and carry it out through a secret tunnel—and of course she killed those slaves once they were done."

Brandon shot a horrified look at Rose. "That's a lot of crazy packed into one woman."

"Mentally ill," Rose said. "So not a 'witch,' then." Mentally ill to a terrifying degree, to be sure—but mentally ill just the same, with demons that drove her to harm the people she loved.

"It's not real." Anabelle must have seen her expression, and leaned in close to her head. "People have researched it and there's no truth to it. It's just flashy nonsense they keep telling because it pulls the tourists in. Michael, I told you not to touch anything!" She hurried after her son.

Brandon tugged at her arm and whispered so only she could hear. "I'm sorry, I shouldn't have said it that way. That was insensitive."

She nodded. He kissed her forehead and followed Delia into the next room.

She lifted her phone to snap a picture of the beautiful smoked-sage wallpaper, trying to recapture her excitement over it. As she dropped it back down she spotted Mateo, who'd hung back in the far corner of the room.

He was staring at Lily, jaw clenched and eyes hard.

Rose slipped her phone back into her pocket and hurried Lily out, close to her, with both hands.

The tour ended in the dungeon where Annie had punished her slaves, now converted to a gift shop.

"The boys have had enough," Anabelle said. "They're getting all fidgety, and it's only a matter of time before they destroy something in here. Or everything. I'm gonna take them out as soon as Mateo gets back from the restroom."

"I'll go with you," Leo said. "I should check on Bree."

"Speaking of the restroom, I should go now while I can," Rose said.

"I'll take Lily. Meet you outside." Brandon squeezed her hand, then headed toward the stairs.

Once inside, Rose sagged against the side of the stall, glad for the moment to herself. She should have known Mateo wasn't as sanguine as he'd seemed about it all. But the way he'd looked at her, and Lily—she didn't know what she'd expected, fear maybe, or avoidance, or even a bit of fatherly pride—but certainly not that degree of anger.

She took her time washing her hands, delaying the moment when she had to go back out. As she finished, she caught a glimpse of herself in the mirror, looking frightened and unsure, and forced herself to stand straighter. He'd get over it, she told herself. He didn't have a choice, any more than she did.

As she made her way out of the dungeon, she glanced around for the others. But before she spotted them, someone pulled at her arm from behind, and she jumped—Mateo.

Her hand flew to her chest. "You scared me. Don't do that."

"I need to talk to you. We're in deep shit. I didn't believe you at first, but I took a close look at her, and you're right, she may be mine. Why didn't you tell me about this before?"

Rose took a step away from him. "I didn't see the point of worrying you when I don't know for sure."

He jutted his head toward her. "But I *am* worried. I've been checking her out, and her hair is darker than yours, and so are her eyes. And not just the color, but the shape. It's only a matter of time before someone else notices."

She shrank further back. She never should have told him, for his sake and her own. But she'd been angry and desperate to get away from him, and it was too late now. "Look, I was upset when we talked, and melodramatic. Lily looks more like me than anyone, and if Brandon had any suspicions about anything, he'd have said so by now."

He kept his eyes ahead, toward the group. "Oh, Brandon's clueless. I'm worried about *Anabelle*."

"I know." She squeezed her eyes shut. "We just have to hope she doesn't notice."

"I need more than *hope*. I can't lose Anabelle." He leaned closer and hissed at her. "Make some excuse to cut out the play dates. Don't ask her to babysit. Start making the changes now, in case Lily starts to look even more like me. Keep that girl away from my wife. I will *not* lose my marriage over one stupid mistake."

All of the emotions Rose had been struggling to push down bubbled up and out in a bitter laugh. *Now* he was worried about Anabelle? He wasn't worried about Anabelle, he was worried about himself. She hissed back at him, hands on her hips. "Oh, *come on now*. If your marriage is so sacrosanct, how did you *just* try to have sex with me while she was off having a massage?"

His eyes narrowed. "That's the problem with women. You can't separate love from sex. Just because I want to have a little fun on the side now and then doesn't mean I don't love my wife. What's the infidelity rate among married people? Fifty percent, for both men *and* women? Including, by the way, both you and Brandon."

CHAPTER TWENTY-SEVEN

No, it's not possible. How could Lily have been dead before she left the house?

Panic swells in Rose's chest and bursts, because she can't make sense of the implication. How could she have been in the Accord's trunk, when nobody but the six of them could have gotten into the car? None of it's possible. There has to be a mistake.

A forgotten detail comes rushing back. "Lily was bleeding the day she disappeared. She cut her foot as we were leaving the beach, on a shell. That must be it, that must be what they're smelling." Rose stares at each skeptical face in turn, and her voice rises as her words flood faster. "That makes sense because Bree helped clean it up and put the Band-Aid on her, and she must have gotten some of the blood on her. Then she must have transferred it when she put something in the trunk of the Accord?" She turns to Leo and Bree, desperate for confirmation.

Bree looks as panicked as Rose feels, and her eyes dart around as she searches her memory. "I can't think of anything," she says. "But I—I wasn't thinking about that sort of thing, so—"

Detective Williams' tone is tight and controlled. "If that were the explanation, Heidi wouldn't have alerted on the same spot."

"But maybe—" A river of electricity buzzes through Rose as she scrambles frantically for an explanation. "Maybe whoever took her set her down on the car? Maybe they stopped to check if it was open, or if they could force it open, and maybe her foot started bleeding again? Or maybe Heidi just made a mistake and Rex imitated her, these dogs aren't perfect, I've heard about that…"

The detectives' eyes fill with pity, which frightens her more than their previous blank expressions.

"Was there ever a time when Lily was inside the Accord?" Williams asks.

Silence presses down on them as everyone thinks. Rose scours her memory of every day since they arrived, but can't remember anything. When nobody else responds, Bree answers, her face grim and resigned. "The kids have only been in the minivan. That's where the car seats are, and we'd never let them ride anywhere without those."

Brandon and Leo shoot Bree a look. Mateo mumbles something under his breath Rose can't hear. Rose starts to object that it doesn't matter, because the issue is blood transfer—

"Mr. Palser, when was the last time someone went into the trunk?" Detective Williams asks before she can speak.

Leo's expression is desperate. "I don't know."

"When is the last time you're certain you did?" Williams asks.

Leo turns to Bree. "I don't remember going into the trunk since everyone arrived. I think the last time we opened it was when you unloaded everything while I picked everyone up at the airport."

She nods slowly. "I think you're right. We've done everything else in the minivan."

"So none of the Martins' luggage was transported in that trunk?"

"No." Leo's voice is reluctant.

"Anything at all belonging to either the Martin or Casillas families?"

"I can't think of anything. Can any of you?" He casts his gaze around, begging someone to come up with something.

They stare at one another and shake their heads.

"We'll need to take the vehicles into custody so we can analyze them," Detective Williams says. "If there's a mistake, we should be able to clarify quickly."

"Both? We need some way to get around," Leo objects.

"Perhaps your consulate officer will drive you to get a rental car," Detective Williams says.

Leo shoots Rose a glare.

CHAPTER TWENTY-EIGHT

Now

The detectives instruct them all to stay inside the villa while the tow trucks remove the vehicles, and they spread out in the courtyard like ants scattered from their hill. Anabelle comes out with the children, and Rose dives onto her phone to search more information about the reliability of sniffer dogs. Leo says he's calling Jordan Keppler, and disappears into his house with Bree behind him. Mateo grabs a beer for himself and brings one to Brandon, who has an arm around Rose, watching over her shoulder.

When Leo comes back out, Brandon asks him to make arrangements for the rental car, since Leo will need to drive it, and they'll need a friend from AmericAid to pick it up. He surreptitiously hands Leo his credit card.

Rose continues to scour page after page of articles about sniffer dogs, latching on to anything that allows her to believe this is a horrible mistake. She even considers the possibility that the police somehow planted evidence to make the dogs alert, but there's no way they could have managed it—at least one of the six of them has been around the vehicles the entire time since Lily went missing.

The villa's gate opens, interrupting her thoughts. Jordan Keppler waves back toward the police as he steps inside and closes the gate behind him. His expression is far more somber than it had been at the consular agency, and the sight makes Rose's hopes sink still further.

Leo jumps up and gestures to an empty chair. "Thanks for coming. Please, sit. I don't think you've met Anabelle and Mateo Casillas."

Keppler shakes hands with each of them, then sits. He nods to the kids playing with Matchbox cars across the courtyard. "Are those your boys?"

"The two older ones are Michael and Marcus." Anabelle tilts her head toward them. "Jackson is Lily's brother."

He nods, then casts a glance back toward the gate. "Well, we'd better jump right into it. I've talked to the police representatives."

"What did you find out?" Rose says.

"Nothing you didn't already tell me, at least not much. And, given the direction this has turned, I don't see the FBI getting involved. If Lily was dead before she left the premises and placed inside the family's car, this isn't a kidnapping."

"Because the dogs alerted to the car?" Rose asks. "I was just reading about that. There are a hundred reasons why that could happen."

He shakes his head, expression unchanged. "The dogs will just put it over the top. We need to get you a lawyer, because they want to talk to you again once they're done out there. Do you have one at home you can call, possibly have them listen in on speakerphone? Or should we find one for you here?"

"Why would we need an attorney to talk to the police?" Anabelle asks.

Keppler waves a hand reassuringly. "It's always a good idea to have an attorney when you're talking to the police."

Brandon pulls out his phone. "I have an attorney that deals with my practice, I'm not sure how much help that'll be—"

Keppler nodded. "He can likely refer someone to help you, and in the meantime, whatever sort of law he practices will be better than nothing."

"She," Rose says. "Audrey MacMillan."

Keppler acknowledges the correction with a slight bob of his head. "Please call her."

As Brandon explains the emergency situation to Audrey's office manager, Rose squeezes her eyes shut and continues to analyze the dog's behavior. What exactly had they all just seen? The dogs alerted to *something* in the back of the car. But only the search-and-rescue dog was responding to Lily's specific scent. That could just mean whoever kidnapped her set her down on the car for some reason, maybe while opening the door to their own car. Space was limited in front of the villa, and the trail would seem to dead end there, because once a car drove away, her scent trail would disappear.

But the cadaver dog was alerting to cadaver odors, not specifically to Lily's scent. Rex might have been responding to someone else's injury—could someone else have been bleeding around that trunk, or even killed in it?

"Leo, your Accord. You bought it here, didn't you? It's used?" she asked.

Leo's attention shifts from Brandon and it takes him a moment to process her question. "Yes. Too expensive to bring one of our cars from home, and it wouldn't be set up to drive on the left, anyway."

"So you don't know the car's history? Like, if anyone bled in the trunk or anything like that?"

Leo's brows shoot up. "No. You're right, anything could have happened in it before I bought it."

Keppler bounces a palm on the table. "They're checking for blood and DNA, so they'll know if there's something specific to Lily in the car."

The attorney's voice breaks through on Brandon's phone. "Brandon? What exactly is going on right this moment?"

Brandon explains the situation. When he finishes, Audrey responds. "Is there any reason why you shouldn't speak to the police about what you know?"

"Of course not," Brandon responds without hesitation.

"Then my advice is to answer their questions as best you can." She rattles off a phone number. "Call me on my cell as soon as they come back in, and I'll stay with you via speakerphone. In the meantime, I'll send out feelers and see if I can find a criminal defense attorney who can talk to you today."

Brandon calls Audrey back once the detectives reappear in the courtyard.

"We have several issues we'd like to clarify with you all," Detective Williams says.

Keppler responds. "The Martins have their attorney on the line. She's advising them to speak to you, but only if she can be present by speakerphone."

Detective Williams nods. "Of course. In fact, we'd like to record the interview, to help ease everyone's concerns."

"I have no objection, as long as you allow us to record, as well," Audrey said.

"As you prefer," Detective Williams says. "We'd like to talk to everyone at once, please. Detective Shaw will sit at the end of the table, and I'll sit at the head, with everyone along the sides."

They make the adjustments to the seating, and Audrey directs Rose to start the voice recorder on her phone and place it in the center of the table, next to Brandon's.

"Thank you," Detective Williams says. "When we spoke to you last, you weren't certain how the window in Lily's bedroom was opened. Have you figured out how that happened?"

Brandon shakes his head. "The window was open when I checked on Lily."

"And Mrs. Martin, you say the window was closed when you checked on Lily earlier in the evening?"

Rose shifts in her seat. "It was."

"So, then, we need to know why someone would open the window and not admit to it." He glances down the faces lining the table.

"You're making assumptions," Bree says. "Most likely Brandon or Rose opened it without thinking. It's the sort of thing you do automatically."

Williams nods. "Mrs. Martin, can you tell us again where you administered the NyQuil to the children?"

"In the bathroom, before I brushed their teeth."

"And you're positive? You were on vacation, rightfully enjoying yourselves. If it's possible the rum punch made the evening a bit fuzzy, that's understandable."

She bristled. "No. I gave it to them as soon as we got home, before I had even a sip of alcohol. Completely sober, and as I told you before, I always give them liquid medicine over the sink because they spill."

Detective Williams' eyebrows raise. "Very interesting, because that seems to be exactly what happened. We found several spots of NyQuil on the bedroom floor, and a spot directly on Lily's bed sheets."

Rose's mouth drops open, and her gaze darts around the table. Everyone looks as shocked as she feels—except Detective Shaw, who is examining everyone's expressions as carefully as Rose is. "There must be a mistake then. Maybe some of it came back up once she was in bed…"

She winces as she realizes that wasn't possible. She'd brushed their teeth, given them a drink, and read them a story before leaving them. By that time, the medicine would have been long swallowed and gone.

Detective Williams continues. "Did Lily's nightgown have some sort of rip or cut in it before she went missing?"

Rose's mind flies to fabric they found outside the window. "Of course not. It was intact when I put it on her. That scrap you found was pulled off when she went through the window."

Williams turns to Brandon. "And was it also intact when you checked on her last?"

Brandon seems taken aback. "I—I'm not sure. I didn't really look."

Williams takes a deep breath. "The problem is the material we found wasn't ripped off, at least not fully. The fibers are cleanly severed on one side, so they must have been cut by scissors or a knife and then ripped from there. Do you have any idea how that might have happened?"

Rose shakes her head and wraps her arms around her chest as a chill runs through her. He knows the answers before he asks the questions—he's weaving some sort of web.

Williams continues. "The evening Lily disappeared, when precisely did your son wake up?"

"He was asleep when I looked into the room, and then woke briefly when I screamed for help," Rose says.

"He was asleep again when we arrived on scene. He fell back asleep amid all the bustle?"

Rose looks at Brandon, then at Bree, annoyed by the question— it's a trap, but she has no idea how or why. She rubs her forehead as she struggles to remember. "Pretty much immediately, I think. I don't fully remember, I was focused on Lily. But I remember Bree brought him to me when we were searching outside, and he was asleep then. And then Bree held him for a while—did he wake up then?"

Bree fidgets with the cup of water in front of her on the table. "No. He shifted a bit here and there, but never fully woke."

Rose nods. "Then he slept between us on Leo and Bree's living room floor, and didn't wake again until morning."

"Is he normally such a sound sleeper?" Williams asks.

"No, actually he's not. He never has been," she answers, throat tightening.

"But when you give him NyQuil, that allows him to sleep through the night?"

She takes a deep breath before answering, trying her best not to let his Columbo impersonation upset her. "It helps, yes."

"Well enough to remain drowsy through everything that happened?"

A heavy dread hits, and compresses her chest. Between the NyQuil spill in the bedroom and Jackson's unnatural sleep, the implication is clear: someone administered a second dose to the children.

And someone cut into Lily's nightgown. And opened her window.

She looks into Detective Williams' eyes, and the courtyard becomes impossibly bright. Black dots dance in front of her eyes.

The police believe Lily's dead, and they no longer believe she was kidnapped. Probably never did. If what they're telling her is true, if they aren't manufacturing evidence, they believe someone staged the crime scene to *look* like a kidnapping. And now they have the confirmation from the two sniffer dogs Rose insisted they bring in.

Detective Williams came in today with an agenda, and he deployed it very, *very* skillfully.

He's looking to prove someone inside the villa killed her.

CHAPTER TWENTY-NINE

One day before

Rose

Rose woke Thursday morning with a pounding headache, more agitated than she'd been since Brandon first mentioned the trip to Jamaica. Partly because of how badly Mateo was handling the news about Lily, but mostly because of what the day held in store.

She'd known all along she'd have to face this at some point. But now that it was here, she wanted to grab her children and run far, far away.

You're being ridiculous, she chanted to herself. Dunn's River Falls was one of the most beautiful waterfalls in the world. She was lucky to get a chance to see it. Even just the pictures were stunning—the series of smooth stones and graduated pools transported her to a magical fairyland, the sort of place you'd expect the elves from *Lord of the Rings* to congregate. And when she was a little girl, waterfalls had always been so soothing to her—the way they danced and splashed, and she could spend hours staring into them. But ever since her sister's death…

The falls are safe, she kept repeating to herself. *The pools are shallow and there are so many guides around you couldn't drown if you tried.* And since Jackson and Lily were too young to climb up the falls anyway, she could always just suggest she stay with them in the kids' water park while everyone else climbed up.

But even the kids' water park made her feel like someone was standing on her chest.

And, to top it off, Anabelle and Mateo wanted to stop at the Luminous Lagoon on the way back. That meant not only a second body of water in the same day, but water after dark—the lagoon was filled with bioluminescent microorganisms that lit up when anything moved the water, like an underwater light show, only visible at night.

She'd tried to object. "It's too much for the kids to do all in one day. We should pick one or the other."

"It's a two-hour drive to the falls and two hours back." Leo's mood had still been dark after Brandon's flat-out refusal to invest. "The lagoon is on the way back, so it doesn't make sense to do the drive twice when we could be using that time for other things."

"I'm sure the kids will fall asleep in the car," Anabelle said with a bright smile. "They'll be fine."

She'd tried to enlist Brandon's help. "They had so much trouble falling asleep after Croydon Plantation, and they'll be even more overstimulated after the water park at the falls. They always end up getting sick when they get overtired, especially several days in a row like we've been going. And if they're sick, they'll be moody and ruin everyone's time."

Brandon had patted her shoulder. "It's okay, hon. Lily's getting older now, and Jackson can always sleep in his stroller. I'll help you with them."

"And we have a relaxing day at the beach tomorrow," Leo said. "They can recuperate then." He turned and walked away, putting the kibosh on the conversation.

More water. Rose covered her fear by mouthing *'relaxing?'* at Brandon with a wide-eyed expression. Brandon covered his laugh, because, really, what in the world did a relaxing day at the beach with a toddler and a baby look like in Leo's head? Did he think Lily and Jackson would kick back in lounge chairs sipping pineapple juice while reading the latest James Patterson? Or maybe nap while they worked on their tans? It would have been hilarious, if the idea of them veering into the water and being pulled away by tides and undertow didn't make her break out in a sweat.

She'd scoured her brain for something else she could say or do. But everyone else clearly wanted to go, so she wouldn't get anywhere pushing the issue. If she admitted her fears about them drowning, she'd look like a complete mental case—she couldn't even get them to take the government travel advisories about crime seriously, how would she get them to listen to her insane phobias?

So she pulled herself out of bed, took four Ibuprofen for her headache, and told herself she'd keep an eagle-eye on the children anytime they were anywhere near the water. It would have to be good enough.

Once they arrived, they made their way toward Central Gardens, the kids' water park. Michael and Marcus gasped when it came into view, and Lily ran excitedly with them toward it.

"Hey, come back here," Rose called.

The kids came running back, jumping up and down like little pogo sticks. Not surprising—the bright colors and constant flow of water were designed to pull kids in. The large, main pool had yellow ovals that looked like lily pads with spouts bubbling water up over them, and in the center, tall faucets splashed water into multi-colored buckets that dumped over onto anyone standing below. A large red-and-blue water slide wound enticingly around the back, but from what Rose could see, the water was extremely shallow most places, and relatively safe.

"How are we going to work this with the kids?" Anabelle asked.

"I figured I'd stay here with them all so you guys can do the climb," Rose said, pulling out sunscreen to put on the children.

"All I really need is to see the view from the bottom once you're done, and snap a few pictures."

Anabelle's hand shot out to Rose's shoulder. "No way, that's not fair. We'll take turns, that way everyone gets the full experience."

"There's no reason for that." Bree stroked Lily's hair. "We've seen the falls before, and we want to spend as much time as possible with the kids. You all go ahead and we'll stay here. Right, love?" She shot a look at Leo, who was staring back toward the car, lost in thought.

Leo turned and caught her expression, then smiled. "Sure. Sounds like a great opportunity for some quality time."

Rose's stomach flipped at the thought of leaving the kids. "All of them? Four are a lot to watch when water's involved."

Hurt flashed across Bree's face. "I watch multiple kids all the time at the school."

A sudden spike of frustration ripped through Rose—why did Bree have to make this difficult? Couldn't Bree just back off for *once* and meet her in the middle? She'd been trying to be understanding about all that Bree was going through, but this was beyond draining, like they were caught inside some strange battle for control. They were *her* kids, not Bree's. They were *her* responsibility and *she* made the decisions, and it was time Bree respected that.

The anger flared out quickly and she felt ashamed of herself. She was the lucky one, and the point of the trip was to spend time together. She was letting her fears leak over into the situation with Bree.

She forced a smile on her face. "Thanks so much, I'd really appreciate that."

Bree looked taken aback, and grudgingly returned the smile. "Great. Take your time and enjoy yourselves."

CHAPTER THIRTY

One day before

Rose

When they turned the corner to the base of the falls, Rose gasped. The series of step-like pools, surrounded by impossibly smooth and random rocks like a cross between frozen floes of lava and clumps of Play-Doh, seemed lit from within by the blue-green water cascading over them. The flowing water's rhythm pulled at her, lulling her like a Disney villain's sleep spell.

Their guide, a medium-sized man wearing a dark jersey labeled SAM on the back, stepped over to greet them. Rose put on her water shoes while he gave the introductory talk.

"If you want to be romantic," he said with a wink, "hold hands as you climb up, and see if you can make it to the top without ever dropping them."

Rose smiled up at Brandon. He smiled back and reached down to kiss her forehead. Sam was right, it was romantic—she'd focus her thoughts on that, on trying to cherish this happy moment with her loving husband.

Rose stepped into the pool, sinking to mid-thigh level, and shrieked when the water turned out to be far colder than she expected. The others laughed—she managed to laugh with them.

"Don't worry, you'll get used to it before you know it," Sam said, heading toward the rocks on the right side of the falls.

Brandon led, holding Rose's hand behind him; Rose held onto Anabelle, and Mateo trailed up the back. She stepped carefully, mesmerized by the water rushing over her feet as though trying to wash them away. The water shoes gripped the stones; after a few tentative steps, her confidence grew enough to look up and enjoy the magical view of water and lush rain forest.

After several minutes of climbing, they stopped in one of the mini lagoons for a rest. Mateo sidled up to Brandon.

"So what do you think about that whole farm-to-table venture?" Mateo said.

Rose's heart dropped as Brandon stiffened. "Did Leo put you up to this?" he asked.

Mateo stammered. "I—no. I just—I heard you guys talking, and thought if it was a good opportunity, I might jump on board. But I know houses, not farms or solar systems."

Brandon searched his face for a moment, then his posture relaxed slightly. He pulled out the water bottle zipped inside the pocket of his shorts. "I didn't know you were looking to diversify."

"I wasn't." Mateo still looked confused. "But the kids are getting older, so I'm considering my options."

Suddenly very much in need of something to do with her hands, Rose stuck them into the stream of water cascading off the rocks in front of them. Anabelle followed her lead.

Brandon drained the bottle. "Then I'd recommend going to a financial consultant. I can give you some numbers."

Mateo nodded, and pulled out his own bottle of water. "I guess I'm thinking less of stocks and bonds, and more, like, entrepreneurial."

Brandon barked a laugh. "Then stay far away from Leo." Brandon shoved the bottle into his pocket, and turned to the rocks along the pool. "You guys ready to keep going?"

This time they didn't hold hands as they climbed, and Rose had to intermittently grab stones and tree branches in the wall of vegetation beside the falls to keep her balance.

"Watch out for spiders," Sam said.

Rose jerked her hand back and wobbled, but caught herself. "Are they poisonous?"

"Mostly not." Sam shrugged, grin wicked.

Rose reached out to grab Brandon.

They stopped again when they were almost to the top, and Rose gasped as she turned to look back down the falls. When looking upward, the sheets of vertical water running over the rocks felt active, busy with peaceful continual motion. But from this vantage point the view was almost ominous, akin to a bubbling pool, frothing around the people dipping and climbing, like a series of mouths opening to suck them in. She stepped back and braced herself against a shelf of rock.

"Now for the best part," Sam said. "If you sit on this spot right over here, the water will pull you over into the pool below, like a water slide." He showed Mateo how to lean back, and the water gently swooshed him over into the pool below.

A pit opened in Rose's chest as she watched him splash below.

Anabelle went next, and Rose's breathing sped. She pressed harder against the rock, mind suddenly filled with visions of Lily and Jackson plummeting into the pools never to resurface. *They're not here*, she repeated to herself. *They're safe*.

"Your turn, honey," Brandon said, tugging at her arm.

"No." Rose pulled her arm away. "I don't want to. You go."

Brandon's brow creased. "Do you feel okay? You look pale."

Rose's hands flew up to her cheek, and her stomach churned. "I'm fine. I'm okay. I don't want to ruin it for you. You go."

Brandon glanced at Anabelle and Mateo below, both now watching with worried expressions. "It's perfectly safe, Rose. Look, there's no way anything can go wrong, it's not high enough or deep enough."

"No, I don't want to." She turned away, searching for the fastest path back to the rocks, then scrambled up onto them.

Then, as fast as she could without slipping, she fled.

CHAPTER THIRTY-ONE

One day before

Bree

Bree pulled her floppy hat down farther on her head as she watched Lily chase Michael and Marcus from one yellow oval to the next, splashing water in front of her as her little feet pounded along.

"Be careful," she called, holding Jackson's hand as they walked toward a giant purple sprinkler-head fountain that sprayed water in a circle like a manic daisy. She lifted Jackson to swing him into the spray and Jackson squealed as the water hit, giggling and waving his arms trying to catch it. She set him down out of the spray and he wiped his face with his hand. "Again!"

She repeated the pattern several more times, trying to keep her sensitive skin out of the sun as best she could while swaying him. Then, suddenly, his giggles turned to a cry of pain.

"What's wrong?" Bree's heart thudded in her chest as she turned him toward her. Her only clue was the hand clamped over his eye. "What's wrong, my love?"

But Jackson only wailed louder—of course he couldn't answer, he'd just barely started to talk. "Is it your eye?" she asked.

"Eye," he repeated.

Lily ran over, followed by Leo, whose head flicked back and forth between them and Anabelle's boys.

"You okay?" Lily asked Jackson.

Jackson threw himself at his sister, wailing. "Eyeeeee."

Frustration bubbled up in Bree. Was something actually wrong with his eye? Or was he just repeating the word *eye* because she'd said it? And why did he go to Lily, but not to her?

"Did something get into his eye?" she asked, which was ridiculous because Lily couldn't know, she was only three. Bree turned to Leo, panic taking her over. "Did you see what happened?"

He shook his head. "No, I was watching those three. Did the water hit his open eye or something? Maybe he's allergic to the chlorine?"

"Let me look." Bree tugged harder on Jackson's arm, but he clung fiercely to his sister. "My love, I need to see where it hurts."

But Jackson's arm stayed firmly in place.

"Kiss it better?" Lily said.

Jackson nodded, still crying, and pulled his head away from Lily's chest. Lily leaned in, kissed his eye on the lid, and said, "All better."

Jackson, calmer now and crying more softly, rubbed his eye again.

"Let me see, darling," Bree said.

He turned his face toward her this time.

"Can you open your eye for me?"

He struggled, but managed to open his eye. It looked red and irritated, but as Bree peered in, she couldn't find anything obviously wrong. "Leo, do you see anything?"

He bent over and studied the eye. "Nope. And he's already opening it more. I think he's okay." He rubbed Jackson's arm. "Hey, buddy, do you want some ice cream?"

Jackson's face brightened, and his eye opened almost all the way. "Keem."

Leo's smile broadened. "Ice cream it is, then! Come on, guys."

Michael and Marcus ran over, and Leo led the four of them off toward the little-brown-cottage kiosk selling pizza and ice cream. Bree plopped down, still half terrified, onto the stone bench they were using as home base and dug into her backpack for a bottle of water, hiding her emotion from the happy families surrounding her.

She felt completely useless. What the hell was wrong with her thinking she had any right to be a mother? She had no idea what to do to help Jackson, had completely panicked when he needed her. Little Lily—only three years old—knew better how to handle the situation than she did. Absolutely pathetic.

She glanced at the families in the play area. Two little boys in matching lime-green swim trunks, their mother young and beautiful in a yellow bikini, laughing and splashing with her boys. An older girl playing with a younger girl and boy, their father watching from another stone bench. Two women who could be sisters watching over a passel of five kids, all standing under the splashing buckets. A mother waiting at the end of the water slide as a father escorted their little boy to its entrance. All of them happy and at ease, all perfectly calm and able to care for their families.

This was a message from above. A comeuppance. She'd spent the last three years judging Rose, feeling she didn't deserve the kids she had and believing she could do a far better job if given the chance. She'd sniffed at Rose earlier, full of righteous indignation that she watched over multiple kids every day at the school. But she didn't, really, did she? She was never alone. The experienced teachers and mothers dealt with any *real* problems that occurred. And several of *them* had now made it clear they didn't think she had any right to be near their children.

Perhaps it was time to accept they were right.

Was that why God hadn't given her any kids? Because she was too judgmental? Too prideful? She'd sensed a hesitation in Rose all week, and had been righteously indignant about that, too. But as it turned out, Rose was right not to trust her with the kids. Rose was the one who should be judging *her*.

"Hey. I think you're making them uncomfortable," Leo whispered in her ear, breaking her out of her trance.

The mother of the lime-green-trunked boys was staring at her, frowning. But once Leo and the kids sat next to Bree, her face cleared and she turned her attention back to her boys.

"I'm useless," Bree whispered back. "All of these parents would have known what was wrong with their child."

Leo wrapped an arm around her shoulder. "Of course they would have. Because they've known their children from birth and they've learned, step by step, how to take care of them. You think they started out that way?"

Lily stuck her cone up into Bree's face. "Share?"

Touched, Bree smiled. "What kind of ice cream did you get?"

"'Trawberry," Lily said. "Jackson gots chocolate."

"Strawberry's my favorite, too," Bree said.

Leo kissed the top of her head. "I'm sorry, hon. I really thought this visit would help."

She forced herself to smile. "What's really important is getting the money from Brandon. Are you sure you don't want me to talk to him? Maybe if it comes from me—"

A shadow settled over his demeanor. "No, he made himself more than clear."

She nodded. Brandon didn't like to be pushed. "So I guess that's that."

"Don't give up yet. I have a few other cards up my sleeve," Leo said, then nodded toward the water park's opening. "Here they come."

She opened her mouth to speak again, but he cut her off. "Shit, something's wrong."

She swung around to see—Brandon's arms were wrapped protectively around Rose, who looked embarrassed and shaky. Bree jumped up and ran over to the group. "What happened?"

"I'm okay, I promise. I just had some weird version of vertigo, that's all. I have my land legs back now." She pointed to the bathroom. "I'll be right back."

Bree waited until Rose was out of earshot. "What happened?"

Anabelle answered. "We were doing these little slides over the falls, where you can let the water push you off the rocks and into the pool below? She totally freaked out."

"Yeah," Leo said. "I wondered about that."

Everyone turned to stare at him.

"What do you mean?" Mateo asked.

Leo shrugged, looking surprised at their surprise. "She's always been strange about water. You guys must have noticed? Remember when we went down to the Cape? She didn't even want to get her toes wet. Can she even swim?"

"She can, but she doesn't like it. I wonder if this has to do with…" Brandon's eyes skimmed the ground as he thought.

"What?" Bree asked.

He looked back up, his expression wary. "It's not something she likes to talk about, even to me. Her sister, Lillian Marie, the one Lily is named for, drowned in a lake when they lived in California. That's why they moved to Massachusetts."

Anabelle's jaw dropped. "Brandon, I swear to God."

He stared at her, confused. "What?"

"How are you that clueless? She's been worried about coming to Jamaica, and we've all been brushing her off like she needs to up her meds. Now you tell us her sister died in a lake when they were kids?" She crossed her arms and tilted her head. "Gee, I wonder why she didn't want to come on a vacation that revolves completely around beaches, swimming pools, lagoons, rivers and waterfalls, especially now that she has *two young kids*?"

Brandon's brow creased. "Oh come on, Anabelle, that's a leap. She's been obsessed with the crime here, she never once mentioned worrying the kids are going to drown."

Bree threw up her hand to stop Brandon. Because Anabelle was right, and Bree's heart broke as the pieces fell into place. Rose's anxiety on this trip wasn't because she didn't trust *Bree*, it was because she was already dealing with terrifying fears of her children dying. *That's* why she'd been hesitant to have children in the first place.

"You said she doesn't like to think or talk about it, even with you. Maybe she doesn't even allow herself to really think about it," Bree said. "She may only realize she's scared to come here, and when she sees the travel alerts, it all blends in her mind."

"That," Anabelle pointed to Bree.

Brandon grimaced skeptically. "You're saying my wife has deep-seated trauma around water and children and she doesn't even know it?"

"People's minds do strange things to protect themselves from trauma. Or, she might also be afraid to be honest with you about it," Bree continued. "You're not always the most understanding person."

Brandon's face flushed red. "Don't project your crap marriage onto me. I'm an excellent husband and father."

Leo took a step forward, placing himself protectively in front of Bree. "Except you don't even know when your wife is fighting a deep-seated trauma just to please you."

"Oh, stop, please, I can't with you. You'd drag your wife into malaria-filled jungles if you thought it'd make you the next easy-money millionaire—"

Anabelle cleared her throat loudly and flashed her eyes toward the restroom, where Rose had just emerged. "I see the kids have had ice cream. So should we just do something light for lunch?"

Bree jumped to follow her lead. "I'm not that hungry today for some reason. So snacks would be fine by me."

Rose pointed toward the empty ice cream cups as she reached the group. "Ice cream sounds really good for some reason, if that's okay."

"I think we deserve it after that climb," Anabelle said.

Brandon put his arm around Rose and started in the direction of the kiosk. "Sounds perfect. What kind do you want?"

As Bree watched Leo snatch up their backpack, she struggled to keep the rage off her face. Her whole life she'd put up with Brandon's angst, let him take it out on her because she knew how much their father had screwed him up. But it was one thing to do it to her, and another to do it to someone she loved. He didn't want to invest with them, that was fine. But he had no right to talk to Leo like that, to humiliate him in front of Anabelle and Mateo. It was cruel, and it was unacceptable.

This time he'd gone too far.

CHAPTER THIRTY-TWO

Now

Anabelle rushes to Rose's side as soon as the detectives leave. "Are you okay? Your hands are shaking again."

Rose looks up at her, mind chugging sluggishly. "They think Lily's dead, and they think one of us did it."

"No, honey, they didn't mean that, they're just trying to tie up loose ends." Anabelle grabs her hands and starts rubbing them. "They couldn't possibly think one of us did it."

"Of course they're going to try to pin it on us," Leo says, pacing again. "They need to preserve their perfect kidnapping recovery record."

A notification chimes on Rose's phone. She forces herself to pick it up and check.

The Global Daily Gazette
A GRIEVING MOTHER?

Sunday, November 22nd, St. James Parish, Jamaica

Rose Martin, the mother of the three-year-old girl who went missing from her family's vacation villa in St. James Parish, turns out to be no stranger to tragedy. When she was nine, her younger sister Lillian Marie, then five, was found drowned in Lake Merritt, Oakland, California—after disappearing while Rose should have been watching her.

According to news reports from the time of the accident, Rose and Lillian Marie were on a family trip to a small amusement park, Children's Fairyland, with their father. A by-the-day construction worker, he received an urgent page regarding a potential job, and needed to return it immediately. In a time before cell phones, he was forced to find a pay phone, and left the girls alone by the park's merry-go-round. When he returned, Rose was talking to a school friend, and Lillian Marie was nowhere to be found. The staff locked down the park and searched thoroughly for Lillian Marie, and when they couldn't find her, the police broadened the search outside of the park. An hour later, Lillian Marie's body was found floating in the water near Bellevue Avenue, a short walk from the Children's Fairyland park.

The medical examiner was not able to conclusively determine whether the child had slipped and fallen into the lake on her own, or if she was intentionally drowned by some person or persons unknown.

Rose's friend told police she'd seen Rose in the bathroom shortly before running into her again near the merry-go-round, and that Lillian Marie wasn't with her at that time. Rose strenuously denied leaving the area, insisting she'd been reading a book on a nearby bench the entire time Lillian Marie rode the merry-go-round. She refused to waver from her story even after the police and her own father assured her it would have made sense for her to go to the bathroom while her sister was safely on the ride. Rose also told police during her interviews that she couldn't remember significant portions of the day.

Subsequent reports claimed several friends and family members told police that Rose didn't get along with Lillian Marie, and resented being tied to her much younger sister.

Now another child in Rose's care has gone missing, one with a similar name and similar in age. Lightning may not strike twice, but apparently horrific coincidence does—if you're Rose Martin.

Rose looks up from the article to find the world is spinning around her, and the light of the sun is impossibly bright. The phone slips from her hands.

CHAPTER THIRTY-THREE

Now

Brandon picks up the phone and reads the article about Rose's sister's drowning out to everyone, and the words sting like a thousand needles shearing into her soul.

You did this to yourself. You insisted on involving the press.

The words ring through Rose's head, and when her vision clears again, she sees them reflected on Leo's face. She looks around, expecting confused expressions, but they're not confused—Brandon must have told them about it all. They're all staring at her with *that* expression, the same way everyone looked at her after Lillian Marie went missing. The mix of suspicion and disbelief, caution and pity, takes her right back, like no time has passed—because they don't want to believe she's responsible, but given the evidence, they can't be sure she isn't. Just like everyone back then.

Her chest constricts and her heart thuds, and she drops her head into her hands to hide their faces and tries to bury it all again, the way she's been trying to bury the implication of it since Lily went missing—that if she were responsible for Lillian Marie's death, if she blocked out parts of *that* day in some self-protective reflex, she very well could have done the same with Lily's disappearance, too.

Because she can't believe it. She *won't* believe it. She loves her daughter more than breath.

So she squeezes her eyes shut harder, but that only clears the way for the series of scenes that flash through her mind, the only jagged bits and pieces she has from the day Lillian Marie went missing. The fragmented parts she *can* remember.

The tantrum she threw before they left the house, when Lillian Marie asked to spend the day at Children's Fairyland. Rose was too old for such a babyish place, she'd objected. Why did they always have to spend Daddy's day off doing *stupid* things? She loved Lillian Marie, but it was hard being her sister. Hard because as the older sister, her parents expected her to be 'mature' about always having to do baby things.

And mostly she was mature about it, but that day it was too much for her, because she'd gotten a new pair of Rollerblades for her birthday and Daddy kept promising to take her someplace with more than the few feet of space so she could play with them, but Lillian Marie was *too young* to rollerblade. So Rose had pouted and stuffed her paperback copy of *A Wrinkle in Time* into the pocket of her jacket, determined to read it in the car rather than talk to them so she could show her dad how angry she was.

Then another flash of Daddy's pager beeping when they were inside Fairyland, then telling them he had to make a call. He put Lillian Marie on the merry-go-round and told Rose he'd be back as fast as he could. But no way was Rose going to stand there just to wave every time Lillian Marie swung past, so she sat on the bench next to the ride and read her book. Then a few minutes later—at least it felt like only few minutes later—clammy hands clamped over her eyes and Tiffany's annoying giggly voice cried out 'guess who?' into her ear. Then Dad came back and asked where Lillian Marie was, and the cold panic took over.

It was like Rose's brain had short-circuited. She couldn't understand what was happening, and people kept asking her questions all at once and Tiffany said she'd seen Rose in the bathroom but Rose *hadn't* gone to the bathroom, at least she didn't *remember* going to the bathroom, and they kept insisting she was lying, and she couldn't take it anymore and she fell down onto her knees and put her hands over her ears and started screaming.

That was the last thing she remembered until her mother had come home from work. Her mother melted down—of course she did—and screamed at both of them for being careless. Then screamed at Rose to remember what had happened—why couldn't she remember?—and cried, and shook her, and accused her of lying, accused her of hating Lillian Marie because Lillian Marie was Mama's favorite, then screamed at her again to remember.

But she couldn't, no matter how hard she tried. And the strange part was, it wasn't like there was a block of time missing. To her, it was seamless—as far as she could tell when she thought back, she wasn't missing any memory at all. And yet, there were whole details of the search she couldn't remember, whole chunks of the day that were missing. So how could she know what she was remembering and what she wasn't? How could she even know what she did wrong?

Everyone else felt the same way. The only question they had was whether she was lying about remembering or not—but either way, they all believed she'd done something to cause Lillian Marie's death. She could see it in their eyes, hear it in their whispers, feel the weight of their silences on her. More than one newspaper article said flat-out that the only reason for her to lie about being in the bathroom was because she'd done something herself to harm Lillian Marie. Her mother gave her the looks almost daily: *Why weren't you paying attention? What did you do?*

She'd become anxious and depressed. She lost weight and her grades dropped and she stopped seeing her friends, preferring to spend hours with her Discman listening to the B-52's' 'Cosmic Thing' over and over again. Nobody talked much about depression and anxiety back then, and tweens and teens were expected to be roiling cauldrons of hormones on the best of days, especially during the grunge era when teenagers dressed like they'd rolled out of bed at Goodwill. Her parents weren't the sort to believe in psychotherapy even if they had been able to afford it, and fifteen years passed before Rose figured out there were people and medications that could help her.

Even so, they'd only helped so much. Her therapist convinced her that a nine-year-old should never have been left in charge of a younger sister in a public place. That Children's Fairyland was an extremely safe place, so the whole incident was a one-in-a-million occurrence. But Rose still couldn't let go of the guilt that her negligence had contributed to her sister's death; at the very least, she shouldn't have been reading the book, she should have been watching her sister.

And she could never bring herself to even tell her therapist about the debilitating, thrumming fear hiding in the deepest shadows of her mind, that she hadn't just contributed to her sister's death, but that she'd lashed out at Lillian Marie that day because she was so jealous and resentful and maybe had gone too far, and her mind had blacked it out because she couldn't deal with the guilt of it.

And because of that fear, she promised herself she'd never, ever have children. Never. She couldn't trust herself to keep them safe. She couldn't trust they'd be safe from *her*.

And the looks on all the faces surrounding the courtyard table tell her everyone there is thinking that exact same thing.

CHAPTER THIRTY-FOUR

One day before

Bree

Bree stared out the window of the minivan on the drive from the falls to the Luminous Lagoon, trying to get some solid ground back under her. Her failure with Jackson, and Rose's secret fear of water, it all turned everything she thought she knew on its head—it was hard to admit, but she'd been diving so far into her own ocean of self-pity she hadn't been able to see the shore. She'd seen herself as *the* victim. But Rose had pain, too. Bree shifted in her seat, uncomfortable with her guilt. But it was too late, and she couldn't change any of it now.

Brandon was another story. He only cared about himself. She'd always known that on some level, but hadn't allowed herself to admit it, but there was no way around it now. He knew about their financial issues, had known for some time, but instead of reaching out to them and trying to help, he'd shut them down—rudely—and was now throwing it all in their face. He was every bit as self-righteous and self-obsessed as Reginald Martin had been, and was resorting to the same manipulations Reginald had used on him to now control her and Leo's behavior: withholding his approval, and love, via money.

They arrived at Magic Lights Lagoon Tours just in time for the dinner of chicken and rice—jerk for the adults, chicken fingers for the kids—served alongside flowing punch, with generous amounts of rum added in for the adults. The adults chatted awkwardly, trying to restore a normal dynamic. Michael and Marcus, ravenous despite the ice cream after the day of water fun, tore into the food with vigor, but Lily and Jackson seemed uninterested. Bree offered to feed Jackson so Rose could focus on Lily, and was relieved when Brandon said he'd take care of it.

"I'd like to make a toast." Mateo lifted his paper cup. "To Leo and Bree for arranging such an awesome vacation, to friends who make everything a good time, and to bioluminescent organisms that turn lagoons into light shows after dark."

Anabelle smacked his cup with hers a little too vigorously. "I'm so excited—the kids are gonna love it."

"It's pretty cool, truth be told." Leo tossed back the rest of his rum punch. "There're only a few places on the planet you can see it, and ours is the brightest and the best."

"I'll go grab one last round of punch to take on the boat." Brandon collected the empty paper cups and tossed them out on his way.

Rose carried Jackson on her hip as they lined up for the boat; he shifted non-stop, and when she tried to steady him, he whined in protest while Lily hugged Rose's leg and pulled at Rose's dress. Michael and Marcus pushed and pulled each other while Anabelle struggled to get them to stop; Michael pushed too hard, and Marcus fell, then started to cry.

They all should have listened to Rose, Bree realized. It was too much for one day.

"Carry me," Lily whined louder, competing with Jackson for attention.

Rose leaned down toward Lily. "I can't hold you both, bunny. You want Daddy to carry you?"

Lily shook her head against Rose's thigh. "No. You."

Rose glanced over to Brandon, who was sharing some private joke with Mateo. "Brandon, can you take Jackson? Lily wants me to carry her."

Brandon held up a single finger. "One sec. Or maybe Bree can take her?"

She gritted her teeth and turned to Rose, reaching out her arms wordlessly for Jackson. He was tense and squirming, and instead of the normal feeling of warm happiness she got from holding the kids, she felt anxious and annoyed.

The boat pulled up, and they boarded. Seats lined each side of the long, open-air rectangle under a plastic awning, with a narrow strip to walk in the middle if needed between the thirty or so passengers. Leo walked toward the bow and selected seats on the port side; once the other passengers boarded, the guide revved up the engine and moved on out.

Bree's phone rang. She pulled it out and peered around Jackson, trying to see the number. Danica Edwards, the director at Future Heroes, calling far later than she should be.

She turned to Rose. "I'm sorry, I have to take this."

Rose shifted Lily off her lap onto the seat next to her, and took Jackson. "Is everything okay?"

She smiled. "I'm sure everything's fine. It's just work."

Bree edged as far away into the aft of the boat as she was able before she answered. "Hello?"

"Bree, hi, how are you?" Danica's voice sounded guarded.

"Good. How are you?"

"I'm good. I'm sorry to call you so late, but I'm afraid this can't wait."

Bree froze against the boat's back railing. Someone near her laughed in a frantic burst; she stuck her finger in her unoccupied ear and strained to hear Danica's voice over the sound of the motor, the music, and everybody's chatter.

"There's no easy way to say this, so I'll just cut right to the chase. I just finished a meeting with Tom and Richard. I'm afraid we can't use you here at Future Heroes anymore."

Bree's heart plummeted, and she stood, silent.

"Are you there?" Danica asked.

"I'm here," she replied. "Why can't you use me?"

Danica took a long moment to reply. "Bree, I like you. I think you mean well, and I truly believe you want the best for all our students. But not everyone agrees with me."

"I know Pamela and Denise don't like having me there. But the other teachers—"

Danica cut her off. "It's not just the teachers. I had several parents express concerns with how attached you are to their children, and several were worried by their visit out to see you this week."

Bree barked a laugh. Of course they had concerns—at Pamela and Denise's urging.

"I'm sorry, Bree, I really am," Danica continued. "I know you've been through a hard time and I wish I could help. If you need any type of reference, anything like that, please let me know."

"Thank you, I appreciate that." Bree barely managed to get out the words. Was Danica sorry? She doubted it. But it didn't matter either way. "And thanks so much for letting me know personally."

"Take care of yourself, Bree," Danica said.

Bree tapped the phone to hang up the call, and stared out over the dark water of the lagoon into the blue light trail left in the boat's wake.

CHAPTER THIRTY-FIVE

One day before

Rose

Rose pressed herself into the bench on the side of the boat, trying to hold herself together as she stared out at the shifting surface, ominous and endless, like a cloud of shimmering sludge waiting to engulf her.

She should have brought her Xanax with her. She should have known a panic attack was a possibility—no, a probability—once she got the children near the water. But she'd deluded herself into believing she was fine, especially since they wouldn't be near the actual falls. Fine *enough*, anyway.

And she had been, mostly. Until the water turned on her, into some amorphous beast trying to reach up and swallow her whole.

She'd texted her therapist from the restroom, but hadn't heard back. Not surprising—her therapist would be done work for the day. So she'd allowed herself several minutes to cry, done her deep-breathing exercises, then cleaned herself up and pinned an optimistic look on her face. She'd laughed over the ice cream, played with the kids on the drive, and chatted with everyone at dinner. But the whole time her chest had been in a vice and she'd barely been able to breathe. All she wanted to do was run far away from here, back home where she was safe.

But now she was surrounded by murky black water, with two fussy children, one next to her and one in her lap, both squirming like they were actively *trying* to fall over the side of the open-air boat.

"Ow, Mommy." Lily pouted up at her.

Rose released her grip on Lily's shoulder slightly, and kissed the top of her head. "I'm sorry, bunny. I just want to be sure you're safe."

She glanced over her shoulder at the water and spotted Bree heading back toward her, picking her way as fast as she could over everyone's feet, looking like she'd just seen a ghost. As she squeezed her way back onto the bench, Jackson started to cry; Bree tried to comfort him, but he only screamed louder.

Rose stroked his hair with her free hand. "Are you tired, sweetie? It's okay if you want to go to sleep."

"No!" Jackson screeched. Rose glanced around the boat apologetically.

Bree took over stroking his head. "Oh, darling, it's okay. You're a good boy."

Jackson pushed her hand away.

"Was everything okay with your call?" Rose asked.

"Of course." Bree flashed her a fake smile. "Where's Leo?"

"Over there, talking to the first mate, or whatever he is."

Bree nodded, pulled out her phone, and made a big show of creasing her brow as she tapped and scrolled.

Rose clasped Jackson tighter and leaned down to sing softly near his head, as much to soothe herself as him. Bree was lying, and shutting her out. On another day, in another place, Rose might have pushed a little more, tried harder to be supportive. But she couldn't, not right then, not with the darkness strangling her and her babies fighting her—she was so emotionally drained she felt like she'd burst into a thousand pieces any moment. If Bree wanted to keep her at arm's length, so be it.

She pulled Lily closer and sang to Jackson and kept trying to hold it together.

CHAPTER THIRTY-SIX

Now

Bree brings Rose tea and she sips it absently, staring out across the water, trying to convince herself she wasn't the one who opened the window in Lily's room. The caffeine and the sugar reach her bloodstream and she feels slightly less lightheaded, but nausea now rushes over her.

"How did they even find out about Lillian Marie?" she whispers. "That was twenty-six years ago, long before everything landed on the internet…"

"It's a matter of public record," Leo says. "Journalists are masters at searching records and newspapers, and everyone is digitizing their archives now. All they had to do was plug in your name and the word *death* and it probably came up on page two of the search results."

"That's horrible." Anabelle shakes her head, but the conflicted expression is still on her face.

"Oh, God," Mateo cries. "There's another one."

"I'm sure it's going to be reprinted on all the sites," Leo says, disgusted.

"No, a different article on the same site." Mateo pauses. "This one about Bree."

Bree flushes red and snatches up her own phone as Rose refreshes *The Global Daily Gazette* page on hers.

The Global Daily Gazette
BARREN AND UNSTABLE?

Sunday, November 22nd, St. James Parish, Jamaica

Rose Martin isn't the only person associated with little Lily Martin, missing from her vacation villa, who has a tragic secret to hide. Brianna Martin Palser, Lily Martin's aunt, has been pouring hundreds of thousands of dollars into in vitro fertilization, with no success. Our reporters have discovered a series of no fewer than five attempts, possibly more, none of which have achieved the desired results.

Further, sources close to her indicate that Brianna Palser, who volunteers at a local elementary school, has shown severe signs of depression in recent months, so much so that she's recently been fired. "She comes to work sad all the time. She tries to hide it, and some days she succeeds. But more often we catch her just sitting and staring at the children, not moving or speaking," one of the teachers at the school said.

"There's something about her that feels strange to me. Off," one of the parents told us. "Like there's a crack that will break wide open at any minute. I don't trust her around my daughter."

GDG was unable to verify whether Brianna Palser is taking medication or undergoing therapy to help her with her difficulties. "Reginald Martin believed in strength, and that only the weak need outside help," an old friend of the family told us. "But if any family ever needed therapy, it's them. If you ask me, being around her brother's beautiful babies was more than she could handle."

Bree emits a low, guttural, animalistic noise.

Rose swallows hard. Bree may not be the warmest sister-in-law, but she doesn't deserve this—

Does she?

Rose's mind spins—her own instincts have rebelled against Bree's contact with the children since the beginning of the trip—even before the trip. She's tried to tell herself she's being unfair—but has some part of her been responding to signals too subtle for her conscious awareness to understand?

Mateo squints down at the article. "They can't just insinuate that she hurt Lily with no evidence, can they?"

Leo stares down at Bree's phone. "Of course they can. They worded it very carefully. They never insinuated it—the anonymous source did."

"Still, it's irresponsible to—"

"No, it's not." Bree throws up her hand, face twisted in pain. "They're right. It's all true."

She stands, turns, and strides into the center house without another word.

CHAPTER THIRTY-SEVEN

Now

They all stare after Bree, unsure what to do, as she disappears into the center house.

"Just because she's been depressed, that doesn't mean she'd ever hurt a child—" Anabelle says.

But nobody else speaks.

Pointedly avoiding Rose's gaze, Leo gets up and follows Bree.

An oppressive cloud descends on the group. Rose drops her head into her hands. Leo was right, she underestimated how viciously the press would tear into them. She certainly never expected they'd splash Bree's private business across the globe, not to put the deepest, darkest corner of her past out on the shutter for everyone to see.

And the strategy backfired, regardless—now the police were turning everything around on them, looking to blame Lily's disappearance on an insider. But what else was she supposed to do when nobody would listen to her, just shut up and do nothing while her baby vanished into thin air?

She honestly doesn't know. Nothing makes sense anymore.

Anabelle reaches over to her arm. "The boys should eat. Do you want me to feed Jackson, too?"

Rose shakes her head. "I'll come. They'll need a nap after, too."

The boys don't want to eat; they can sense something is wrong, and Jackson is still struggling with the sniffles on top of it all. Once he finishes his lunch, she gives him a carefully measured dose of the Dimetapp, then turns to put it away—and hesitates.

She shoves the bottle toward Anabelle. "Can you put this somewhere safe?"

Anabelle opens her mouth to say something, but rethinks whatever it is. "Of course. Let me know when you need it."

Her hesitation is meant as a kindness, Rose knows. She doesn't want to say flat-out that she's also worried what Rose might do to Jackson, accidentally or otherwise. Everyone is thinking it, but nobody will say it, and as much as it rips Rose apart, there's a perverted comfort in the familiarity of their expressions and the sideways glances they try to hide. This, at least, she's used to dealing with.

Jackson fusses as she rocks him, taking far longer to be lulled by her singing than he normally would. But eventually his thumb lands in his mouth and his eyes stare up into hers, the connection of their gazes comforting her as much as him, and his lids begin their dance, closing and opening, closing and opening, more and more slowly, until he's finally asleep.

By the time they finish, Leo's friend has dropped off the rental car, and Mateo has thrown together a stack of sandwiches for lunch in the courtyard. As she and Bree slip into their chairs around the table, Brandon's phone rings.

"Keppler." Brandon answers the call. "Mr. Keppler, is there news?"

Brandon's face screws up as he listens intently. The pause seems to last an eternity, and then the blood drains from his face.

"We're on our way," he says, and hangs up.

He turns to Rose, his voice tight and panicked. "They found a body. They think it might be Lily."

CHAPTER THIRTY-EIGHT

Now

"No," Rose chokes, her entire body numb. "It can't be Lily. Those men kidnapped her—"

Brandon grasps her shoulders. "You're right, it can't be her. But they need us to confirm that for them. I can go check it out, you can stay here—"

"No." She stares toward the gate, eyes wide. "I have to go with you—"

Leo pulls out the key to the rental car. "I'll drive."

Brandon and Bree flank Rose and lead her out to the car. As Leo speeds, Rose stares out at the green blur and prays. *Please let it not be Lily*, she repeats to herself. *Please let it not be Lily*.

Bree breaks the silence. "Where exactly did they find—whatever they found?"

"A shack on the edge of a field about half a mile north of the villa," Brandon says.

Not Lily. Not Lily. Please don't let it be Lily.

"Don't worry, Rose, I'm sure it's not her." Leo turns to meet her eye for a moment, his expression an odd mix of skepticism and confidence. Does he really believe it, or is he just a good liar? Either way, she stares at him long after he turns back to the road, oddly reassured. Of course it's not Lily. She'd know it in the depths of her soul if her daughter were dead.

It can't be Lily. I'd know if it were Lily.

Everybody lapses into silence again, and she clings to this new refrain, chanting it in her mind on an endless loop, drowning out possibilities that are too horrible for her to contemplate.

They round a bend in the road. In the distance, along an open stretch, they see the flashing lights of several police cars. A swath of crime-scene tape cordons off a stretch of grass and greenery around a very small shack set several yards back off the street; it looks to be made of plywood and corrugated metal held together by bubble gum and electrical tape. Several individuals kitted out in personal protective equipment surround it.

Keppler stands near the crime scene tape. Leo pulls up behind him and the four of them pour out of the car.

Rose runs to him. "What happened?"

"The man who sells soup out of this stand came back from visiting his family in Kingston, and when he approached, he was alarmed by the smell. When he opened it up, he found a little girl inside," he says.

"But they'd know if it were Lily." Rose sounds hysterical even to her own ears. "They have her picture. They would have said."

Keppler looks uncomfortable. He clears his throat and speaks hesitantly. "People can look very different after the body begins to—well—to break down."

Rose's stomach lurches. She reaches for Brandon—he's green, like he's about to vomit, and the fear in his eyes terrifies her. He pulls her close.

Detective Williams strides toward the edge of the tape closest to them.

"Is it Lily?" she asks without preamble.

"We're not certain yet. We need one of you to identify her," he answers.

Rose nods, but the black spots dance in front of her eyes again, and she knows if she takes a step she'll collapse. She can't do this, can't go look at whatever tragic little girl is in that shack, can't bear to think of the images that will be burned permanently onto her brain. She clings to Brandon to keep from falling. *It can't be Lily. It can't be.*

"I'll do it," Brandon says, voice barely above a whisper.

Detective Williams nods. "Follow me, but stay outside the tape. We'll need you to put on protective equipment."

Leo and Bree take his place at Rose's side, propping her up, and she watches as Brandon skirts the edge of the road. An officer helps him into one of the ridiculous suits, then into booties and a hair cap and gloves. Detective Williams leads him across the grass, carefully directing him where to step, to a door in the side of the shack.

Rose waits, not breathing, unable to hear, unable to see the expression on his face. A millennium passes, and Brandon turns— but not toward her. He ducks under the tape and the officer helps him take everything off in reverse order—gloves, cap, booties, scrubs—and puts it all into a bag that he then seals and labels.

Finally Brandon turns toward them. But he keeps his head down, and he won't look at her.

Rose's legs buckle. She falls to the ground, accidentally cross-legged, and the world spins around her.

CHAPTER THIRTY-NINE

Now

Rose barely registers the two officers who manage to get her back into the car and escort them back to the villa, following behind in their own vehicle. Once they arrive, Leo whispers to Anabelle and she disappears into the north house with the children. Someone wraps her and Brandon in blankets, and Bree announces she'll make them each a strong cup of tea, sounding like she's speaking through a long tunnel.

As she watches Bree work, Rose's brain stutters, spitting out nonsensical questions. *What is it with the tea? Not just Bree, but everyone in a crisis, always making tea. I hate tea, I never drink it, and neither does she. What makes people think tea has some sort of magical properties?* But when Bree hands her the cup she gulps it down without tasting it. Brandon does the same, his eyes wild over his cup.

"The detectives will be here after they've finished at the crime scene," one of the officers says. "They've asked that you stay here until they come."

Rose nods, but can't manage a verbal response. Keppler pulls up next to the officer's car, then hurries in and expresses his condolences. Bree offers him tea, of course. He accepts it, and she hurries to make it.

"It keeps people busy," Rose blurts out.

Mateo jumps. "What?"

"The tea," she says. "Making it keeps people busy. Gives them something to do."

They look at her like she's insane. Brandon crosses the kitchen and pulls a bottle of whiskey down out of the cabinet, then raises it in a silent question. Leo and Mateo nod; Rose and Keppler shake their heads. Brandon pours two fingers each in three glasses and distributes them. He sits back down next to Rose, downs his in one gulp, and wraps an arm around her.

"I managed to get a little bit of information from the detectives," Keppler begins, and glances around the table, waiting for confirmation that he should continue.

Everyone stares at Rose. She nods.

"Her throat was—uh—cut, so that appears to be the cause of death," he says.

A sob rips through Rose as the image takes her over. "Did she s-suffer?"

Keppler clears his throat. "I don't know. I don't think so."

"Was she… hurt… in any other way?" Mateo asks.

Keppler clears his throat again, and Rose wishes Bree would hurry with his tea. "Not that they can tell right now," he says. "They'll have to do a more complete examination, but they seemed to think that it would be obvious if so."

"Thank God," Mateo says.

"Do they have any idea how she got there? It must have to do with those two men. Isn't that in the direction where they were spotted?" Brandon asks.

"They wouldn't say. They're still investigating."

"Do they know when she…" But Rose can't form the word.

"They said it's impossible to get a precise time of death, but based on insect activity, they believe she's been there since Friday night. Given that the cadaver dog alerted to her bedroom, they believe that's further evidence she was dead before she was removed, or died in the process."

Rose wraps her arms around her abdomen and rocks back and forth, still sobbing. "Those men kidnapped her. They kidnapped her, and it went wrong. That's why the ransom call never came—they messed up and killed my baby—"

Brandon pulls her into his chest, and she turns into the embrace. That shows they're wrong, she tells herself. If Lily was in that shack since Friday night, the police were wrong about one of them being the perpetrator. Nobody left the villa before Lily was found missing. None of them could have done this.

Including—thank God—Rose herself.

"What about the bracelet, did they say anything about that?" Brandon asks.

Rose pulls away to stare up at him. "What bracelet?"

"She had on some bracelet. Williams asked me about it, if it was hers and we just forgot to mention she was wearing it. I told him I'd never seen it before," Brandon answers, then turns back to Keppler.

Rose goes rigid. "She had on a bracelet?"

Brandon peers into her face. "What is it?"

She reaches for her phone and searches for the article, then holds it out to Brandon. "Amancia Higgins, the kidnapped girl they just found a few days ago. She had on an Obeah bracelet, and her mother said she'd never seen it before. Did the bracelet look like this?"

Brandon pulls the phone closer for a better look, and pinches the screen to zoom in. "No. The one Lily had on was different. It was hard to see because—well, I could see it was reddish."

Rose thrusts the phone toward Keppler, and her voice rises. "It has to be the same killers. Those strange symbols we saw on the wall under Lily's window, those looked like Obeah symbols. Oh

God—is this some sort of Obeah ritual? Like some sort of human sacrifice, with children?"

Keppler studies the picture and skims the article, his jaw clenching and releasing. "No, that's not possible. Obeah doesn't involve anything like that."

"That's not true!" Rose jumps up. "After I saw that article I looked up Obeah, and blood sacrifice is definitely a part of it."

"Rose, you're veering dangerously close to racism here," Leo says. "Just because you don't understand the religious traditions here doesn't mean—"

Keppler holds up a hand to stop him, and puts a soothing tone in his voice. "Obeah involves animal sacrifice, not human."

"Not when *sane* people do it, but what about if some sort of psychopath is doing this?" Rose's sobs have stopped, and her voice is shrill. "There are some really sick, disturbed people out in the world, and if you can kidnap and hurt a child in the first place, how much of a stretch is this? I'm not blaming *Obeah* for this, Leo. Insane people who do horrible things have claimed all sorts of religions, like the mass shootings against Muslims. I'm saying *that bracelet is a clue that can help us*. It's not a coincidence that both cases involve something that points to Obeah. It means *something* and we need to figure out what!"

"Rose." Mateo reaches out and puts a hand on her shoulder. "We'll talk to the police, they'll figure this out—"

She shrinks from his touch. "The police have made up their mind one of us did this, and they've already shut us out. They aren't going to investigate other theories. And if my own brother-in-law thinks I'm a racist because that bracelet worries me, the police are going to be even more dismissive—"

Anabelle strides through the doorway, takes Rose's face into her hands, and stares into her eyes. She speaks calmly. "The boys can hear you yelling. I need you to listen to me for a sec, okay?"

The thought of the children stops Rose in her tracks, and Anabelle's calm voice focuses her. She nods.

"You're right that the police think someone here did this," Anabelle says. "So *we're* going to find an expert ourselves and see what they have to say about all this. If this is a perversion of local religions, local experts will be furious, and will want to call it out as much as you do. Okay?"

Rose nods, and picks up her phone. "And since the press can't seem to come up with constructive things to investigate about this case on their own, let's see what they can dig up about this bracelet."

CHAPTER FORTY

Now

The Global Daily Gazette
St. James's murdered children:
Is a RITUAL VOODOO KILLER at work?

Sunday November 22nd, St. James Parish, Jamaica

Events are unfolding quickly in the Lily Martin case. Earlier today the police found a body matching her description, and Brandon Martin confirmed the girl was Lily; her throat had been cut and she'd been abandoned in a roadside shack. As we raced to get this information online, we received another report—Lily Martin, just like Amancia Higgins, was found with disturbing evidence of Obeah rituals on her person.

Experts suggested the bracelet found on Amancia Higgins was a protective talisman, and that her death might have been a regretted accident. However, Lily has now also been discovered with a bracelet that her family insists did not belong to her. It's impossible that both girls were killed by accident separately and days apart. In addition, our source claims strange symbols were found on the wall outside Lily's window the night she was kidnapped, further evidence that witchcraft is at work.

The police are calling this theory 'ludicrous and dangerous,' but Amancia's mother, Rayala Higgins, doesn't agree. "There is a killer out there using our girls in some sick ritual, and the police won't admit it. How many more will have to die before they listen?"

Why are the police so quick to ignore such obvious parallels? Although Obeah rituals have been illegal for centuries, those laws are very rarely enforced in modern times and many have called for their repeal. Are the police worried that if they acknowledge the truth, they will be faulted for not adequately protecting the people? Or are they afraid of retaliation from the practitioners themselves?

There may be an innocent explanation for these occurrences, but until the police investigate them, we can't know.

CHAPTER FORTY-ONE

Now

The couples wait under the watch of the two police officers, unable to leave the villa until the detectives arrive to talk to them. The villa, so welcoming and pleasant before, has turned into an endless purgatory they can't escape, but Rose's anger allows her a channel for her grief and desperation that keeps her from tottering over the brink of sanity. She clicks and scrolls, googling everything she can find about Obeah rituals as they wait for the police, and for Sheldon Howell, the Obeah expert Leo's colleagues track down.

Thankfully, Mr. Howell understands the urgency of the case; he arrives two hours later. A sixty-something black man with the bearing of a university professor, he has a kind smile and a compassionate manner, and Rose is drawn to him on sight.

"Thank you so much for coming, Mr. Howell," Rose says as Bree pours sorrel tea over ice for him. "We appreciate your help."

Mr. Howell takes her hands in his and meets her eyes. "Please call me Sheldon. I'm so sorry for your loss. I want to help bring the culprit to justice if I can."

"You're a practitioner of Obeah?" Brandon asks.

Sheldon's eyebrows rise. "That's a dangerous question. There are laws against practicing 'Obeah.'" His voice puts quotes around the words. "Even the word itself has a complicated, and racist, history."

Rose flushes.

He meets Rose's eyes again, and holds them. "But in my experience, it's important to differentiate ignorance from racism. And one way is that ignorant people are willing to learn and be corrected, while racists are not."

Rose nods.

"Many argue that the word 'Obeah' itself is a construct that White people applied to slave traditions they simply didn't understand. Laws have been passed against it and many other African traditions labeled 'witchcraft' in order to keep people of color powerless, enslaved, and jailed. Others use it to perpetuate fear and bias—as in *The Global Daily Gazette* news article Mr. Palser read to me on the phone. Words like 'Obeah,' 'Voodoo,' and 'witchcraft' have been used to stoke fear and rob people of their power for hundreds of years."

Rose nods again.

"But you asked me here to determine if Obeah was involved in your daughter's death. That may be difficult, because the laws that have forced the traditions to hide in darkness have also prevented formalized versions of the spiritual practices from being recorded. That means many people practice in different ways."

"So you can't tell what's real and what isn't?" Brandon asks.

Sheldon turns to him. "Intent is always difficult to determine. Please, tell me what the case is with your daughter."

Brandon takes Sheldon through a quick version of events, including the Amancia Higgins case, the bracelets found on the two girls, and the symbols drawn on the villa wall.

"I'm familiar with the Higgins case. Can you describe the bracelet found on Lily?" Sheldon asks.

"It was red, made with beads."

"And may I see the symbols on the wall?"

"The police tape is still up so you can't get close, but yes, you can see them," Brandon says.

Leo leads the way outside and through the gate, then points to the wall. Sheldon goes down on one knee so he's eye level with the writing. He examines the scribbles for a long moment, then pulls out his phone and spends several minutes on it before he stands back up with a scowl on his face.

"Does it tell you anything?" Brandon asks.

"Together, the story is very clear," Sheldon says, and points to Rose's pocket. "Google the phrase 'Obeah symbols' and click on images. Then scroll down a page, and show everyone what you find."

Rose follows his directions—and then gasps. She holds out the phone so the others can see.

The symbols on the wall are a jumbled mash of two images centered on the page.

CHAPTER FORTY-TWO

Now

Rose sits back in the Palsers' kitchen, arms wrapped around her abdomen, trying to process the implications of what she's just seen.

"And the bracelets?" she whispers.

"The bracelet found on Amancia may very well have been constructed as a talisman. But from your description, the one found on your daughter can be found in almost any tourist market on the island, it's not anything specific to Obeah. Of course, that doesn't mean it couldn't have been used for spell work. But in combination with the spurious symbols found on your wall…"

"You're saying someone faked it," Leo says.

"That's the most likely explanation." Sheldon pauses to sip his tea. "If they were symbols I'd just never seen before, I'd research them further to determine any way to find meaning from them. But the mishmash on your wall—it's like someone putting together a random string of words in a language they don't speak in an attempt to make what looks like a sentence. As though someone wants you to think they are conversant in the ways of Obeah, but they aren't."

"They're diverting attention," Bree says.

"I can't say that for certain. Perhaps it's someone who is mentally ill, or someone messing around with things they don't understand. But taken together, and given the timing after Amancia Higgins' death, there's one conclusion that seems far more likely than the others."

"A copycat," Leo says.

Sheldon's eyebrows rise. "Another possibility. But to me, what seems most likely is someone wants to tie this crime to the other one."

"Why do you say that's more likely?" Brandon asks.

Sheldon looks at each person around the table in turn as he answers. "I'm not a policeman, so take my opinion here with a large grain of salt. But my understanding of a copycat killer is that they would choose a similar victim, not a completely different type. Amancia Higgins was a Black Jamaican child. If this were a copycat, why would the killer choose a White American tourist, several years younger?"

"Opportunity?" Leo says.

"As I say, my expertise doesn't lie there." Sheldon rises. "All I can tell you with near certainty is that the talisman found with your daughter and the symbols on her wall are meant to confuse."

Once Sheldon leaves, Rose excuses herself and slips into her and Brandon's house. She sinks down onto the bed and lets the sobs take her over, like a creature in her chest is trying to rip its way out. After a time—she has no idea how long—Brandon checks on her, holds her in his arms and cries with her, and then goes back out to see about dinner for Jackson. She sobs until she feels like she has no more tears left, but they keep renewing somehow, and the emotion rips through her again and again, with no end in sight.

But the detectives still don't arrive and she can't continue crying indefinitely, because Jackson needs her. Brandon may be getting his dinner, but he needs his mother just the same, and she needs to pull herself together.

So she forces herself out of bed and back into the courtyard, where the silent group sits around the table mechanically doling out Chinese food the police allowed Leo to order for dinner. She sits and stares at the containers, which might as well be filled with sawdust.

"Rose, you need to at least *try* to eat something," Brandon says. "You didn't eat any lunch, but you said you'd try with Chinese food."

She blinks at him. "No I didn't."

He stares back at her, brow creased. "When I came to check on you. I told you we were thinking about soup, or Chinese food."

She nods. Her crying jag in the bedroom was mostly a blur—too much emotion and too much information to process, and while she remembers curling into the comfort of Brandon hugging her, she can't remember most of what they said to each other. She nods, and takes some fried rice from the container. "Sorry. I'll do my best."

Anabelle reaches over and grabs her hand. "I spent ten minutes after lunch looking for Michael's blue shorts when they were right on top of the pile in his drawer. It's a miracle any of us are functioning at all. But Brandon's right, you should try to eat a few bites at least."

Rose glances at Jackson in his playpen and nods. She needs to keep her strength up.

She forces a bite into her mouth. It tastes like shredded cardboard, and the hard ball in her stomach revolts. She swallows, then takes several more bites, swallowing each without chewing, then washes it all down with the Diet Coke Brandon puts next to her plate.

Her mind keeps returning to Lily. Maybe seeing what those animals did to her daughter will turn the police around, make them stop wasting time pointing fingers at the group. The men killed Lily and tried to cover their tracks, it was as simple as that—why couldn't they see that?

But it doesn't matter, because the evidence will make them see. There will be evidence at the shack, and evidence in the cars they took—or lack of evidence there. They'll see Lily wasn't in the car and something will point them in the right direction—

Unless they don't want to be pointed in the right direction.

The terrifying thought turns her entire body numb. Even in the United States dirty cops sometimes pervert the good work of a police department. And she's heard of countless stories of corrupt police overseas.

What's to stop these police from creating whatever evidence they need to convict one of the group for murder?

The slam of a car door jolts her out of her thoughts. She jumps up and rushes toward the gate to see who's there.

Keppler steps out of his car and hurries over, face grim.

Rose's heart races again. "What's wrong?"

"I have some news I thought I should deliver in person, as soon as possible." He turns to Brandon. "I just got off the phone with the detectives. The autopsy came back with some confusing results. It turns out that Lily's throat was cut after she was already dead."

CHAPTER FORTY-THREE

Now

"Her throat was cut postmortem?" Brandon asks.

"Yes. No bleeding, apparently, and something to do with how tense the muscles in her neck were if that makes any sense?" Keppler says.

Brandon nods, brow creased.

"So wait, I don't understand. If that didn't kill her, what—what did?" Rose stumbles over the words, and tears instantly overflow her eyes again as horrible possibilities flash through her mind.

"A broken neck. Which means, for whatever solace it gives you, her death was instantaneous."

"But that—" Rose struggles to put her thoughts into words, because who would do something like that? Who would break a little girl's neck and then slash it afterward? "That seems—I mean—why?"

"I asked the same thing. The doctor is having a hard time making a determination about what happened. She doesn't appear to have any other bruises, so it doesn't seem likely she fell or some such." He pauses, and puts a gentle edge on his tone. "And as far as he can tell, there wasn't any kind of fight or anything like that. If there were, she should have some defensive marks that should have developed by now."

"The kidnappers must have—mishandled her?" Leo asks, face white.

"Guys," Mateo says, shooting a significant glance at Rose. "Is this really the best time and place to talk about all this? Maybe we should—"

"No," Rose says in a strangled voice, louder than she intended, her eyes flicking from Mateo to Keppler. "I need to know what happened to my baby, and why. Tell me, now."

"The medical examiner said—" Keppler examines Rose's face, then hurries the rest of his words "—they said it's easier to break a child's neck than an adult's, but it's still not easy. Some sort of intentional force would have to be applied."

Bree grips the cup in front of her. "But it must have been an accident. Otherwise why attempt to make it look like an Obeah ritual, and cut—do the other things they did. They had to be diverting our attention."

"But if they knew she was dead, why not just leave her and run?" Leo says.

"There's something else I need to ask you before the police get here," Keppler says. "About the news report that just came out. They're going to want answers, and if I'm going to help you, I need to know what's in those sealed documents."

Rose's head spins. "What documents?"

"You haven't seen it?" He pulls out his phone, brings something up on the screen, and hands it to Rose. Brandon shifts to read it over her shoulder.

The Global Daily Gazette
A HIDDEN PAST

Sunday, November 22nd, St. James Parish, Jamaica

Information surrounding the Lily Martin murder continues to develop quickly. GDG has just discovered evidence that

Brandon Martin, respected surgeon and graduate of Stanford University, isn't quite what he seems.

Before marrying Rose Martin, Lily's mother, Brandon was married to Kayla Prentiss of San Jose, California. But when GDG tried to access the divorce records via computer today, we discovered the records are sealed. It's very difficult to get divorce proceedings sealed in California; even if both parties agree the action still requires a court order, and a determination must be made by the Department of Health. Such dramatic steps indicate some sort of volatile circumstance.

We spoke with Ms. Prentiss, who told us that she and Brandon Martin divorced because he wanted a family and she did not. However, while on the phone with Ms. Prentiss, we heard several children in the background; when we questioned her about them, she terminated the call. We confirmed from other sources that Ms. Prentiss has three biological children with her current husband. Further, irreconcilable differences regarding offspring would not be reason enough for divorce records to be sealed in the state of California.

So how does a woman who doesn't want children end up with three? And what was so potentially damaging that the court agreed to seal the divorce records? And whatever the answer is, is it relevant to Lily Martin's murder? GDG will continue to investigate.

Brandon yanks out his phone, tapping it as he paces toward the pool. "This is the last straw. It's character assassination. They're—"

A voice crackles out over speakerphone—Ray Madden's. "Brandon. What's up?"

"What the hell is going on? Have you seen this string of *Global Daily Gazette* reports?"

There's a pause before he answers. "I have."

"And?"

"And what? Rose called me in to get the press involved, and I did that. Why did you ask me to do it if you knew you had skeletons in your closet?"

"Everybody has skeletons in their closet. Millions of people get divorced every year. Countless people get fertility treatments, not just my sister. And how can a tragedy that happened when my wife was a child possibly be relevant? They're looking for anything they can spin."

"Of course they are, that's what tabloids do. You should have warned me about all of it so I could take control before they got their hands on it. I could have painted a beautiful picture that the press would have eaten up about how important Lily was to Rose after losing her own sister so young, and how Lily was even more valued in the family because your sister can't conceive. You would have had billions of people all over the world crying their eyes out, searching every nook and cranny for your daughter—"

"So get out there and do that now!"

Ray sighs. "I'll do my best. But now it'll look like you're covering up after the fact. The genie is out of the bottle and I'm not sure anything we can say now will help. You can't unring a bell."

Brandon swears loudly, and Jackson starts to cry. Rose rushes to comfort him.

"Can we threaten to sue, or send some sort of cease-and-desist order? Anything?" Brandon asks.

"Have they said anything factually untrue?"

"They've leapt from facts to vicious speculation."

"Speculation isn't illegal, and from what I've read, they've worded all of it very carefully."

"They're going to try to get my divorce records unsealed."

"Next to impossible."

"But they'll find someone who'll tell them something—"

"Tell them what? What's in the records?"

Brandon's face turns red. "I'm saying they'll find someone who'll make up something if they have to."

"And if they say something that isn't true, you can sue."

"So we have no recourse?"

"For what's happened so far? No. I'll do what I can, but that isn't much. So I'll stress again—the best thing you can do now is tell me if there are any other Bouncing Betties out there waiting to explode, in those court documents or otherwise."

Brandon's jaw sets. "I don't think so."

"You don't sound sure."

"That's because I don't exactly have a handle on this, Ray. I never thought my sister's fertility treatments and my wife's childhood trauma would be used against them when we're dealing with the murder of my daughter. I have no idea what might be next."

"Fair enough. But if you think of anything else, let me know immediately." Ray hangs up.

Brandon shoves the phone into his pocket and continues to pace. "I can't believe this, any of it."

Bree takes an audible deep breath. "You should have told him the truth."

Rose turns to examine her face. It's hard, like granite.

"There's no truth to tell, Bree." Brandon shoots her what's clearly a warning glare.

"Brandon? What's she talking about? Why are the records sealed?" Rose asks.

"If you pay enough money you can get anything sealed."

Rose narrows her eyes. "Then tell me what you needed to cover up so badly you bribed the court."

Brandon's jaw clenched.

"If you don't tell her," Bree said, "I will."

CHAPTER FORTY-FOUR

Now

Leo comes to stand behind Bree. "You said it yourself, Brandon. The reporters are going to find someone who knows. It's going to go public. You might as well come clean about it all."

Brandon's eyes flash between Leo and Bree. "You told him?"

"No," Bree says. "It's the only thing I've ever lied to my husband about. But you can't hide it any longer."

"It's not relevant," Brandon says. "It's no more relevant than your fertility treatments."

Keppler speaks up. "All the more reason to clear it up. Because even if the press don't manage to dig it up, I can promise you the JCF will. And if they don't hear it from you, they'll assume you're hiding it for a reason."

Brandon stares at him for a long moment, then slips into the closest chair. "I don't know where to start."

"Start with Kayla," Rose says, trying to keep her voice steady. "You told me the two of you divorced because she didn't want kids."

"And that's true," he says. "She didn't."

"She didn't want to have kids with *you*." Bree stares at the table in front of her.

Rose tenses. "Why?"

Brandon digs his front teeth into his bottom lip, and grimaces. He scans the courtyard, and when he doesn't find what he's looking for there, he answers. "She didn't think I'd make a fit father. She accused me of drinking too much."

Rose stares at the empty beer bottle next to him, and a pit in her stomach opens up. "You're an alcoholic?"

He meets her eye, angry. "No, I'm not."

Nobody speaks, and Rose takes in the pained expression on Bree's and Leo's faces.

Brandon also looks around. "You're kidding, right? I not only run my own practice successfully, but just took over Raymond Grist's so he could retire. I've never been late for an appointment. I'm an attentive father—and I even *volunteer on the weekends*." He jabs a finger in the air to stress the words.

"You went to rehab," Bree says. "I had to tell everyone we knew that you were spending three months in Doctors Without Borders."

Rose winces, and Mateo's jaw drops. Leo throws up his hands. "Unbelievable. And you have the nerve to judge *me*."

"Yes, I went to rehab, because Kayla said she'd divorce me if I didn't. But that doesn't mean I have a drinking problem."

"I'm pretty sure that's the exact definition of what it means," Leo says.

Brandon's hand slashes through his hair. "No. It means I went through a difficult time. The partners I was working with—they were at each other's throats and they wanted me to choose sides between them. Every day was like walking through a minefield waiting for my legs to be blown off. I started drinking a little more to ease the stress, and it snowballed."

"It wasn't just Kayla," Bree said, voice low. "Your partners asked you to leave the practice because of your drinking."

He gapes at her. "What the hell, Bree? The point is, it was all situational, and I've *never had an issue since*."

"No." Bree's hands are shaking and she won't look him in the eye. "You started again after you came back, and Kayla found out. That's when she divorced you. That's why you came back to Massachusetts, to start over."

Brandon's face turns so red it's almost purple. He swings around to Rose. "Tell them—do I walk around hung over? Do I ever not follow through on the things I say I'm going to do? Have I ever had a problem at work?"

Rose's mind instantly flies to the excuse he gave for cheating—that he'd been drunk. Drunk enough to do something that put their marriage at risk. Drunk enough to do something he'd supposedly never do if he'd been sober. And he's been drinking more lately…

When they first met, he rarely drank alcohol, but now he has at least a couple of glasses of wine every night. She assumed it was because of the stress of taking over his partner's practice. But—she glances at the empty Red Stripe bottle again—he's been drinking almost non-stop since they arrived in Jamaica, something she wrote off as well-earned relaxation. But is it? Does he have a problem?

She presses the tips of her fingers into her eyes and tries to think. She doesn't know—how is she supposed to know? Everyone gets drunk once in a while. And no, he hasn't had any problems at work, or dropped any balls at home.

Everyone's staring at her, demanding an answer, wanting her to pass judgment on the man she loves. She clears her throat. "No, not that I know of."

He points at her, then waves his hand. "See? I'm fine. I went through a hard time, and everybody overreacted. I fixed it, and dealt with the consequences. That's better than most people do." He storms off into the south house, slamming the door behind him.

Rose stares down at the table. It doesn't matter to her that he went to rehab before they met—she would never have held that against him. But he never told her about it, and neither had Bree, which meant he'd asked her to hide it. If it were really just a passing situational issue, why wouldn't you confide in the woman you love? Isn't that what marriage was, someone who loved you and stood by you despite your darkest secrets?

She'd told *him* about *her* darkest secret, admitted the fear to him that she hadn't even admitted to her therapist. She told him about the little voice that taunts her when she can't sleep at night, telling her there's a reason she can't remember going to the restroom that day in Children's Fairyland, because she did something horrific that her psyche couldn't allow her to remember. If she could tell him all that—how could he not tell her about a stint in rehab?

A bell rings though the courtyard—the police are at the gate.

"I didn't expect them to get here so quickly," Keppler says.

"I'll let them in," Bree says, voice grim.

CHAPTER FORTY-FIVE

Now

Rose watches as Bree returns with Detectives Williams and Shaw in tow.

"We'd like to speak to you all together again, if you don't mind." Detective Williams points toward the table at the center of the courtyard. Brandon and Leo pull out extra chairs from the kitchen. As during their last visit, Detective Williams sits at the head of the table while Detective Shaw takes the other end. He motions them all to sit.

So they can scan everyone's faces at once, Rose realizes. This isn't bad police procedure as she'd assumed last time—they already know the answers to the questions they're going to ask, that's not what they're interested in. They want to see who looks at whom, who speaks and who doesn't, what expression each has on their face. They're putting the group dynamic under the microscope, and they'll never get that by speaking to us separately.

Williams waits until they settle. "You're aware we've detained two men for questioning, men who were seen lingering down the road the night that Lily disappeared."

Everyone nods.

"As it turns out, these men have long histories. They've been arrested several times for a variety of offenses, most small, but they're known Fentanyl users. And when people addicted to opioids are kept away from their drugs, they become very, very cooperative." He pauses and watches the reactions.

Rose also scans the table, trying to see what Williams sees.

"They claim they were hired to kidnap Lily," he says, and again pauses to let the words sink in.

A complex stream of emotion rushes through Rose—anger at the men who did this, desperation for the loss of her little girl, relief to know the police have found the killers. "Who hired them?" she whispers.

"They don't know. They never got a name." Williams watches her.

"That's bullshit," Brandon says, leaning forward, his face mirroring Rose's rage. "You don't believe that?"

"We do," Williams responds. "They gave us the cell number of the person who hired them, and, not surprisingly, it belongs to a burner phone. We verified the times of the contact."

"Can't you track the phone back?" Mateo asks.

"We're working on that, but for now we haven't been able to find out who bought it," Williams says. "So we've come to ask you. Does anyone have reason to kidnap your child?"

"Absolutely not," Brandon says, voice taut.

"You said before that ransom kidnappings are common in Jamaica," Leo interjects. "We must have been at the wrong place at the wrong time."

Williams appraises him. "In such cases, the perpetrators don't hire other men to do the kidnapping for them. This is the first case that either Detective Shaw or I have ever dealt with where someone was hired to conduct a kidnapping. Because it makes no sense. Why take the extra risk of involving other people, of trusting them, just to have to split the ransom with them? Also, why did the ransom call never come?"

"Because they killed her in the process," Brandon chokes.

"Ah, that's another problem. We have seen *that* before," Williams says. "Kidnappers will try even more desperately to get their money if something has gone wrong."

Rose physically waves off the point. "You have them, that's what matters. They killed my baby, and they need to pay for that."

"We don't believe they killed her," Williams says. "You see, they say that while they were hired to kidnap the girl, they were not able to do so. When they approached the house to take her, two women and a man were running around the yard calling for her—and they correctly identified the three of you who did just that. They turned and hurried back to where they'd parked their car, then drove off the other way. They never touched Lily."

"That's ridiculous, of course they're gonna say that," Mateo says. "They probably had someone watching to see what happened, so they had a good story if they got caught."

"Under other circumstances, I'd agree with you," Williams says. "But in this case, a number of discrepancies lead us to believe they're telling the truth. For one, legitimate kidnappers rarely cut off part of a victim's nightgown and leave it purposefully behind."

"Purposefully?" Rose says.

"We told you someone cut Lily's nightgown with scissors or a knife, then tore off a piece and left it outside of a window. Why would a kidnapper do that?"

Rose stares mutely around the table, willing someone to come up with the answer.

"We also found wrapping for a medical-grade cotton swab that nobody will claim, and which makes no sense for a kidnapper to leave behind. And the symbols drawn on the wall. What purpose would that serve for them?"

Rose thinks back to the point Leo made earlier about the symbols—the only reason was to distract from Lily's death. But if Lily had already died in the process, why not just leave her and run?

"They're the ones you should be asking," Brandon says, and points to Rose. "Look at my wife's face. We're in pain, and you expect us to figure out why the men who killed our daughter did what they did?"

"We do," Williams says, voice even. "Because there's something else that worries us. These men were given insider information. They were told facts that matched what you told us. That you all checked on the children periodically, and that there would be music playing in the courtyard to cover any small noises they might make. They were given an approximate time to be ready to take Lily, and were told they'd receive a text when the coast was clear. But most importantly, they were told the window would be open for them."

"All that means is that someone was watching the house. They would have heard the music when they came to take Lily," Mateo says. "And they were the ones who opened the window, so that's how they know that."

Williams turns to look directly into his eyes, face still blank. "Except that somebody opened the window, as witnessed by both Dr. and Mrs. Martin, *before* Lily was taken."

A leaden silence falls over the group.

"There's an alternate explanation for everything you've mentioned," Leo finally objects.

"Not one that fits all of the facts together." Detective Williams leans forward ever so slightly in his chair. "Windows do not open themselves. Fabric doesn't have clean, unfrayed edges when it tears accidentally. Vomit doesn't appear in a toilet when nobody will admit to throwing up. Ersatz guzumba symbols and bracelets—yes, we also have expertise on these subjects—do not find themselves on walls and wrists." He tosses two pictures down onto the table.

Rose peers at them. One is of the markings on the wall, the other of a red bracelet on a tiny wrist. She pulls them closer.

Williams continues. "Two well-trained dogs do not follow the same path and alert to the same location if that site is wrong. And, hairs and fibers for a dead little girl do not miraculously appear in the spare-tire well of a car she's never been in—a car that the two men we've detained could not have driven."

The table is momentarily stunned. Bree breaks the silence. "You can't know if that hair is hers yet. Tests don't come back that fast."

"You're correct, we don't yet have a DNA determination. But the hairs and fibers have been compared microscopically to Lily's hair and her nightgown, and they match. It's only a matter of time before the DNA tests come back to confirm that." Detective Williams stands up, and Detective Shaw follows suit. "At this time, we must ask you not to leave Jamaica until our investigation is complete."

CHAPTER FORTY-SIX

The day of the disappearance

Rose

Jackson's cries woke Rose the morning after the trip to Dunn's River—not his normal cries, but the deeper, more woeful cries that signaled he wasn't well. She narrowed her eyes at Brandon's sleeping face. Of course Jackson's wailing hadn't woken *him*. She briefly considered jostling him awake, because it was his fault—after everything else, he'd insisted on staying for the fire show at the lagoon, where he chugged punch and tried to convince everyone he could spit fire, too, if they let him try.

She plodded off to change Jackson. His nose was running, and he coughed several times before the new diaper was secured. Lily was buried deep under her covers; Rose tried to wake her gently by planting a series of butterfly kisses on her face, but Lily screeched and smacked Rose's head in protest. When Rose finally managed to excavate her from the covers, Lily, too, had a runny nose.

An overtired, fussy set of kids didn't bode well for the day.

She corralled them both into the kitchen and was assembling breakfast when Brandon appeared, eyes bloodshot, hair sticking up, face pale and tinged slightly green.

"Oh, not you, too," Rose said.

He looked confused. "What?"

"The kids are sick."

He reached for the Ibuprofen bottle on the counter. "I just have a wicked headache. These'll kick in before I finish my shower."

As he shuffled off to the bathroom, Lily stabbed and flicked her spoon at the instant oatmeal in her bowl, speckling the table with oats.

"Stop that, now." Rose placed her hand on Lily's spoon to hold it steady. As soon as she let it go, Lily flung a spoonful of oatmeal across the room.

"Looks like you need a time out." Rose scooped Lily up into her arms.

"No!" Lily screeched into her ear, and instantly thrashed and squirmed like her bones had magically turned to rubber, one of her special talents.

But Rose had played the game far too many times, and pinned Lily's waist effectively to hers, neutralizing the effectiveness of the movements. As she dodged the flailing arms, she crossed to the empty kitchen corner and sat herself and Lily down. "Three minutes," Rose said.

As she waited for the minutes to count down, she tried not to think about keeping two fussy children away from the Caribbean sea all day long. She'd have to ask Leo to stop off and get the kids some cold medicine, at least.

CHAPTER FORTY-SEVEN

The day of the disappearance

Anabelle

Anabelle beamed as she peeked across the white sands and crystal waters of Doctor's Cave Beach. Such a great day, with a soft breeze through the palm trees dotting the beach, just enough to keep the warm, moist air dancing. The kind of day when all her problems went away and she got to hang out and enjoy being alive.

As much as she'd built up her hopes about investing in Sousie's farm, she was glad it was all off the table now. The whole thing had been like a rock in her shoe that dug into her with every step over the last few days, and no amount of money was worth bringing that back home with them. There was way too much drama going on with everyone, and she'd never been good with drama. Such a relief to be able to keep her nose clearly out of it all.

And, to top off the awesome day—Mateo had changed his mind that morning about putting Marcus in day care. Said she was right about the socialization, that it was time Marcus moved beyond play dates with Lily. It would be good for him to find some new friends, especially some boys, to hang out with. *So* sexist, but whatever, if that's what it took to get him to agree, that was fine with her.

The boys ran toward the water, excited and happy. Yep, she was one of the lucky few—gorgeous children, gorgeous husband, gorgeous life.

"How about here?" Rose asked, pointing a few yards away from one of the white wooden lifeguard towers, far back from the shore, nearly up against the covered cabanas.

"Looks good to me," Anabelle hurried to say before anyone could object. Because if it made Rose comfortable to put space between the water and the kids, why not? The water was only about twenty yards away anyhow, easy enough to soak it in. Rose looked completely wiped, and after her panic attack yesterday she deserved a break.

They pulled over some lounge chairs and umbrellas and stripped down to their swimsuits. Except Bree, who always did the redhead thing and hid as much of herself as possible, and slathered the rest with sunscreen. Anabelle set up two baby beach tents where the littler ones could hide and play with toys when they needed to get out of the sun, and Rose grabbed sunscreen out of her beach bag and covered the kids.

"I'm going to grab some drinks from the clubhouse," Brandon said. "Anybody want anything?"

"Do they do that bucket of beer thing like we had in Hawaii?" Mateo asked.

"I'm pretty sure they have some form of plastic-bottle beer," Leo said.

"I'd love a pina colada. Get one for Rose, too." Anabelle threw up her hand when Rose started to object.

"That's a lot to carry. I'll go with you," Leo said, and he and Brandon headed off, joking as they went.

Anabelle smiled again—thank God they'd put the tension behind them.

As soon as they were out of earshot, she turned to Rose. "I'm really feeling the sun today, and the boys want me to build a sand-castle with them. I think you should lay yourself right down, sip your pina colada, and relax while I watch the kids today. I'll make sure they stay out of the water unless they're holding onto me."

Rose's eyes bounced between the water and the kids, who were already digging into the nearby sand. "I can't let you do that—"

"Oh yes you can, because before we leave Jamaica I want to do that rafting thing on the Martha Brae River, and I want it to be all romantic with my husband, no kids allowed. Basically, I'm bribing you to watch my boys then."

Rose smiled so gratefully it was almost embarrassing. "Okay," she said. "But maybe just for an hour or two. I do have a book I'd love to finish."

"Get to it." Anabelle pointed to Rose's lounger, then helped the kids grab their shovels and buckets. From the corner of her eye she caught Mateo glaring at Rose, and turned to see Rose's face turn red. "Mateo, stop it! She deserves a break, and I want to play in the sand. What's your problem?"

Mateo's face shifted quickly. "Sorry, babe, you're right. I just want to make sure you get a break, too."

She rolled her eyes and blew him a kiss. "Love you."

Anabelle directed the kids as they gathered sand in buckets, periodically glancing back to make sure Rose wasn't stressing and Mateo was minding his own business. For the first few minutes it looked like Rose didn't know what to do with herself, but finally she leaned back in the lounger and cracked open her book. Bree did the same, but with earbuds. Mateo pulled out some dominoes and readied them on the table, and after Brandon and Leo returned and distributed the drinks, they played. Anabelle sipped her pina colada and watched the sandcastle grow while the clicking of tiles and the soft rolling of the waves lulled her.

The drink was stronger than she expected, and a little too much warmth hit her. "Michael, can you run and get me a bottle of water?"

He ran off and returned in a quick minute, and she took a long gulp. On second thought, she decided, she should toss the rest of the drink—she promised Rose she'd watch them, and she'd never forgive herself if something went wrong. She strode over to the water's edge, dumped out the rest of the pina colada, then washed out the sticky cup so the kids could use it to shape towers for the castle.

Finally the kids decided the castle was good enough, and it was time to dig out the moat. They had so much energy—after digging and digging and digging they were now literally bouncing for their turn to gather and carry heavy buckets of ocean water. She called them to the waves one at a time so she could watch each one fill their buckets safely, feeling silly to be so protective. The waves were so gentle they almost weren't waves, but she promised Rose, so that's what she was going to do.

They each waited for the others to finish, then she gave the signal to dump their water in—they were so excited they splashed each other like crazy and more water ended up on them than in the moat. They squealed and giggled and demanded to do it again, so she led them through it all a second time, soaking up their joy.

Once the moat was filled they turned their attention to repairing the damage they'd done to the castle during the first dump. The way Michael took over directing the others, he might just have a future in management, and Lily and Marcus worked together perfectly, like little fraternal twins. They really were adorable together—funny how since they were both three they were just about the same height and build, and although Marcus' skin was much darker since he was half Black, even the shape of their—

She freezes, and stares. Marcus and Lily have the same eyes.

Mateo's eyes.

She doesn't have to look up at Mateo's face to check because she's always adored their deep, soulful espresso color and the distinctive downturn at the outer corners that give him an adorable sad-puppy vulnerability. And she doesn't have to look at Rose's because she's always been jealous of their beautiful almond shape, and the milk-chocolate shade. But she stares at Brandon's because she needs to be sure.

Brandon's are blue and round, and perfectly centered under his brows. Not wide-set. Not turned-down.

Nothing like Lily's.

CHAPTER FORTY-EIGHT

Now

Leo shoots out of his seat in response to Detective Williams' proclamation. "You can't demand we stay in Jamaica if we aren't under arrest."

"You're correct," Detective Williams says. "We can make those arrests now, if you prefer."

Leo's jaw clamps shut.

"Our consulate will have something to say about that," Brandon says.

"They very well may. But please remember, Jamaica has an extradition treaty with the United States." Williams turns and leaves, with Shaw behind him.

Everyone sits in stunned silence, staring at one another.

"I apologize, Rose, you were right," Leo says after a long moment. "I have no idea what that was. This team is blatantly incompetent, or corrupt. I'm calling Keppler."

Rose stares down at the pictures on the table. "No. He wanted to set off a bomb. See what explodes and what doesn't."

"What do you mean?" Bree asks, her voice shaking.

Rose takes a moment to choose her words carefully. "Somebody here is involved in some way, and I need to know if—"

"But that's not possible," Leo cuts her off. "Williams is twisting the facts. Lying to us because he's desperate and needs to arrest someone. I'll bet all that nonsense about fibers and hair was just a bluff. Or he planted them."

"That might be, but he couldn't have faked the other things, like the scrap of fabric. We all saw most of it happen." Rose takes a deep breath and slides her hands onto the top of the table. "Too many confusing facts have been pulling at me as it is. I haven't wanted to believe it, but there's just too much now."

"No. Everyone here loved Lily," Mateo says. "There's something the police are missing."

Brandon rubs his eyes. "I agree. I just can't believe for a single second any one of us would have harmed her."

Rose continues to choose her words with care. "Maybe. But somebody's lying, and I need to know who."

"But there are a thousand reasons why someone might lie." Leo strides away from the table and gestures toward the street. "They might have misunderstood something, or made a mistake that was completely irrelevant and now they're afraid they'll look guilty if they admit it."

"Are you that person, Leo?" Rose asks quietly.

He whirls back around, and juts his head forward, face flushed. "No, I'm absolutely not."

Brandon stands up behind Rose. "Really? Because it seems strange to me that the dogs alerted to *your* car, and that—"

"My keys were on the coffee table in the central house. Anybody could have taken them at any time," he snaps. "And people can break into cars, it's not that hard. But if you're gonna come after me, let's talk about Rose's lapses in memory, and Rose's sister. How do we know *you* didn't open the window and just don't remember? Haven't we all been dancing around that since Brandon first told us at the water park?"

Rose flinches.

Anabelle slams her hand on the table. "Stop this, now! This is exactly what Williams wants, for us to eat each other alive, and we're playing right into it!"

Everyone stares at her, shocked into silence.

"You're right," Rose finally says. "He's planted the seeds of doubt. So what needs to happen now is, if anybody has something they've kept hidden or lied about for whatever reason, the time to come clean about it is now."

Rose stares around the room. Anabelle is the only one who meets her eyes.

Rose uses the silence as an excuse to leave without anyone following. She casts a glance at the crime-scene tape still plastered over the children's bedroom, then pulls out the picture she slipped off the table while everyone was distracted.

Because the bracelet in the picture, wrapped twice around Lily's little wrist—she recognizes it.

She crosses to the closet just off the living room space, where she's been gathering her souvenir purchases in their empty luggage. The contents are in disarray, but that's not conclusive—Lily might have dug into it when she wasn't looking. She dumps out the contents on the floor and sorts through it all. Postcards for her scrapbook. T-shirts. The truck she bought for Jackson and the doll she bought for Lily. Scads of jewelry.

But one of the bracelets is missing—the red one she hoped her mother would like.

A strange calm takes her over as she sits staring at the pile, her mind sifting through the events of the last week from this new vantage point. Both her theories about what might have happened are horrifying. As the police led them through everything, she clung to the hope that the police were wrong about one of them being involved, that maybe there was some strange explanation for the rest of it all.

But only the six of them could have known about that bracelet. And any one of them could have taken it—she and Anabelle looked through each other's purchases right out in the street while everyone looked on and talked about where to eat. And they'd all vacationed together before, had even shared rooms, multiple times. Everyone knew everyone else's habits, and it wouldn't have been hard for anyone to figure out where she stashed everything.

Except the level of premeditation involved in that just doesn't make sense, or coincide with the rest of the facts—especially the hired kidnappers. Try as she might, she can't make the bracelet fit into any of that.

That leaves only one possibility. She must have been the one to take the bracelet and put it on Lily's body. Something horrible happened, and she tried to cover it up after. The men who had tried to kidnap Lily must have been a nightmarish coincidence that she inadvertently foiled.

Every cell in her body rejects the idea—but the final piece of damning proof is in front of her. Or rather, is missing from in front of her.

Something else occurs to her. She stands, scans the room, then heads into the kitchen. On the table, partially obstructed by the detritus of the last few days, she spots what she's looking for. She snatches up the box of sidewalk chalk she bought that same day for the kids. She peers inside.

The red stick is missing.

CHAPTER FORTY-NINE

The day of the disappearance

Rose

"Mama, take it off." Lily pulled at her T-shirt as they walk back toward the car.

"No, bunny, leave it on. You're still a little wet and I don't want you getting cold when you're sick," Rose answered.

"I'm hot," Lily whined.

Then, out of nowhere, she screamed and fell to the ground, holding her foot.

Rose dropped the bags she was carrying and knelt down at her side to examine her, and Bree came back to her side. "Is she okay?"

"I'm not sure… It looks like she stepped on something… This seashell." Rose held up the culprit, which had a streak of Lily's blood on it. She looked up for Brandon, but he was striding purposefully to the car.

Bree bent over. "Oh, I see the cut. It's just a little one though, we won't have to cut off your leg or anything." She smiled and tried to tickle Lily's stomach.

Lily's eyes widened and her cries turned into full-on wails.

"Oh, no, no, my love, I was just joking!" Bree's face crumpled and she looked up to Rose for help.

"Shh, bunny, you're going to be just fine," Rose soothed, and put her hand on Lily's forehead. "She's starting to feel warm, that's why she's reacting that way. It's not you."

Bree gave her a grateful look. "I put a first-aid kit in the car."

Rose lifted Lily onto her hip, and Bree grabbed the bags she was carrying. Once back at the van, Bree pulled out the kit. "Brandon, Lily cut her foot. Do you want to bandage it?" she asked.

Brandon stared down at his phone, scrolling through something. "Does she need stitches?"

"No, it's not deep," Rose answered.

"Then I trust you."

Rose waved off the look Bree shot her. "I'll hold her and you do the Bactine."

Bree sprayed a healthy amount onto the foot, then dried off the excess with a tissue.

Rose put a sing-song in her voice. "And, here's the Band-Aid… and we're all done!"

Lily's crying calmed slightly, and she tucked her head into Rose's chest, still whimpering.

"Is it okay if we get the food to go?" Rose asked as she strapped Lily into her seat. "She's starting to feel warm, and Jackson does too. And can we stop by the pharmacy? Hopefully with a little NyQuil they'll both get a good night's sleep and be fine in the morning."

"I could use a trip to the pharmacy myself," Anabelle says without turning from the window.

"Okay, how about this," Leo said. "I'll drop off Matty and Brandon to order pizza and pasta, and while they wait for it, we'll go grab whatever you two need."

"Thank you, that's perfect," Rose said, and stroked Lily's hair.

When they got to the pharmacy, Anabelle ran in with Rose while Bree waited in the car.

"You'd think I'd learn by now," Anabelle said. "Every vacation I've ever been on, I get my cycle. I thought for sure not this time, so I didn't pack anything. But sure enough."

"I hate it when that happens," Rose said, distracted, as Anabelle broke off to a different part of the store.

Rose did a hurried search to find the cold medicines. Relieved to find familiar brands, she grabbed a bottle of Dimetapp for the day, then a bottle of NyQuil for the night—that would help them get more rest. She also grabbed an oral thermometer, then hurried to the front, where Anabelle had already finished her purchase.

Back in the car, Rose washed off the thermometer with a napkin and water from her bottle, then took Lily's temperature. A little high, but nothing to be too concerned about, and Jackson's turned out the same. Still, she needed to get them to bed as soon as possible.

Neither of the kids wanted to eat much. She made sure they each had a few bites, then shuffled them off to get ready for bed while Brandon helped clean up after the take-out.

Once they were changed for bed, she steered them toward the bathroom. Baths would take too much time, and they'd both had a dousing in the beach shower as they left—a quick wash would be enough. "Time to wash faces and brush teeth."

But as soon as she pulled the NyQuil out of the box, Lily started to fuss. "No, Mama!"

Rose did a quick calculation and came up with a bartering plan. "Tell you what. How about if you take the NyQuil, you don't have to brush your teeth?"

Lily started to object, but decided the deal was a good one. "Okay."

Rose pulled the bottle out of the box and stripped off the safety seals in record time. She double-checked the dosage amount and filled the cap to the line before Lily changed her mind. "Do you remember how to do it? Right up to the sink, take a big breath and hold your nose, okay?"

Lily breathed in, then pinched her little nose with her little fingers, squeezed her eyes shut, and opened her mouth. Rose poured in the medicine quickly but carefully. Lily gulped it down, then opened her mouth again to show she was done, her face screwed up in an accidentally hilarious grimace.

"Here's some water." Rose handed her the plastic cup, and Lily took a long drink.

Rose poured a smaller cupful for Jackson, set him on the edge of the sink, and poured it into his mouth. He sputtered and grimaced, and Rose quickly gave him some water, too.

Back in the bedroom, Rose read them a story, but by the end they were both still awake and fussy. She pulled Jackson out of the crib and cuddled him into her lap with one hand while she reached over to rub Lily's back. She narrated *Rupert the Rhinoceros* from memory—her favorite story from childhood, and one of the few she knew completely by heart. By the time she finished, Lily was snoring softly, and Jackson splayed out when she set him gently in his crib, sound asleep.

"That took forever," Mateo said when she reappeared. "You're already one drink behind."

Anabelle pointed to the rum punch in front of her chair. "Matty made them, so they'll peel your nail polish right off."

Rose laughed, and took a sip—Anabelle wasn't kidding. She'd have to be careful.

Except—*why?* Why did she have to be careful?

So far on this trip she'd had a total of two drinks, and even those she hadn't finished. She'd been taking care of the kids and making sure everything went as smoothly as possible, so she'd held off. And she'd managed to get through the falls and the lagoon, and even the beach today. Everything should be easier from this point on, and this was her vacation, too, right? And that was what

Brandon wanted, for them to have a chance to get away and relax. So—why shouldn't she enjoy herself for once?

She took a few more sips and savored them, letting the tingle warm her from the inside while the island breeze warmed her from the outside. She closed her eyes and one by one focused on allowing the tingle of the alcohol to release the tension from her muscles.

"What kind of music should I put on? Some dancehall, or something a little more relaxed and reggae?" Leo asked as he set his phone to sync with the sound system's Bluetooth.

"I'm in the mood for something mellow. Something that matches the ocean view," Rose answered.

"I have the perfect thing." Leo held up a hand, set the music to playing, then came back to the table.

Rose looked up to see Bree reappear from the center house, and did a double take—she was wearing the emerald sundress Rose had made for her.

Mateo smiled. "Bree, that looks so amazing on you! You should always, always wear green."

Bree blushed, and shot a look at both Anabelle and Rose. "Thanks."

They talked and chatted and played cards, and after the first hand Rose stopped even trying to focus on strategy. She pulled and discarded as they talked about everything and nothing, laughing and telling jokes, enjoying one another's company.

The alarm on her phone went off before she knew it—she'd set it to remind Brandon to check on the kids, she didn't like being out of earshot for long when they weren't feeling well. But it was his turn to deal the cards, so she slipped out in his place.

Jackson woke up when she came in. She lifted him out and rocked him back to sleep. She was just buzzed enough that the rocking soothed her, too, and she stared at the red batik curtains happily, wondering if jerk turkey might work for Thanksgiving.

By the time she returned to the courtyard, everyone had played several more hands, and Bree had put out cookies for dessert. Leo grabbed one as he and Bree pushed back from the table.

"We're beat. We're gonna head to bed," Leo said. "We just wanted to make sure to say goodnight to you before we headed off."

Mateo raised his eyebrows. Leo winked in return, and Bree blushed.

Anabelle turned toward Rose, and lowered her voice. "Do you have any Midol, by chance? I should have grabbed some at the store. Things are *not* going well."

"Ugh." She screwed up her face in solidarity. "I never leave home without it, it's in my toiletry bag on the shelf in the bathroom."

"Thanks." Anabelle padded off into the south house.

Mateo looked down at the drinks pitcher. "Empty. Time for another?"

"Oh, definitely." Brandon got up and followed him to the wet bar, then watched over him as he mixed the drinks.

Gathering up the cards waiting for her on the table with one hand, Rose considered another drink. She was feeling fairly tipsy as it was, and something told her Mateo'd make the second pitcher even stronger than the first. "Just half a glass for me," Rose said.

She took a gentle sip once Mateo poured the drink for her, and was instantly grateful—the batch was indeed even stronger than the last one, and the glow this one sent through her was even warmer.

They played two hands before Anabelle returned. Rose shook her head—before she had Lily she'd also had random, difficult cycles, and didn't miss them one bit.

Mateo watched her approach. "One of these nights before we leave, we should find a sitting service to watch the kids, and go check out the Hip Strip night scene. I've been wanting to since we got here."

Anabelle rolled her eyes, and Brandon waved him off.

"You're about fifteen years too old for that, buddy," Brandon said, with a joking tone.

Hurt pride flashed across Mateo's face. He hurried to cover it, but his tone was too casual. "Just to see what's changed and what hasn't. It'd be a laugh."

Rose studied Mateo's face. He couldn't seriously still see himself as part of that set, or really want to go rub among twenty-somethings to pounding music while paying for wildly overpriced drinks? No, she realized—he was veering into a mid-life crisis. That's why he'd suddenly hit on her again—he was trying to prove he was still attractive and virile. None of them, except maybe Anabelle, was getting any younger, and strange things happened when people started to feel they were closer to retirement than their high-school days.

"I'm so glad to be over that whole scene. But then, I hated everything about dating." She reached over to Brandon and rested her hand on his arm.

Anabelle shook her head. "I do miss the dancing."

"Maybe I'm getting old, but hanging out like this, with music at a reasonable volume and a calm game of cards that's really just an excuse for us to chat and spend time together—I'm actually, finally, relaxed." Rose turned to smile at Brandon.

He stared down, sorting his cards. "Good. I'm glad."

She took another sip of her drink and let the music seep farther into her soul.

Anabelle won the next hand, and Mateo won the following. When the timer went off again, it was Rose's turn to deal. "Brandon, will you go check on the kids?"

For a moment she thought he was going to object. But then he drained his glass and smiled. "Of course, my love. I'll be right back."

His shoes scuffled on the tiles as he went, and Rose turned to make sure he hadn't tripped.

"Careful, man," Mateo called after him, laughing. "The last thing we need is to have to rush you to the hospital because you break your leg or something."

"How strong did you make these?" Anabelle took a tentative sip of her drink, then pushed it away. "All I can taste is alcohol and sugar."

"You know me, if I'm not driving, I don't see the point in messing around." Mateo leaned over and buried his mouth on her neck.

Rose dropped her eyes to the cards she was shuffling. All the romance around her warmed her heart, especially because she wanted nothing more than for Mateo to put his attentions on Anabelle, exactly where they belonged. Maybe she'd send a few little flirty signals Brandon's way once he got back...

Anabelle laughed and pushed Mateo away. "You're just trying to distract me so I won't win another hand."

"I have a reputation to protect. I'm the gin rummy king." He threw his arms up over his head like a toreador about to strike.

"Then play, your majesty." Rose waved her hand over the stack of cards.

"Gotta go see a man about a horse," he said, and set off into the north house.

"Can you check on the boys when you're in there?" Anabelle asked.

He shot her a finger gun over his shoulder. As Rose dealt the cards, Anabelle jumped up and began to dance.

"I take it the Midol is kicking in?" Rose laughed, her shoulders bobbing back and forth to the steel-drum music as she organized her hand.

Anabelle nodded without answering, concentrating on her footwork.

When was the last time Rose had danced? She couldn't remember—which meant she needed to fix that, now. She jumped up, closed her eyes, and let the rhythm move her hips, her shoulders, her legs, her feet.

"Two beautiful women dancing—why do I need a club?" Mateo said when he returned.

Rose froze, then dropped back into her chair, laughing. "That was fun. I don't do that enough."

Brandon appeared out of the house. "Do what?"

"Dance." Anabelle turned toward him. "Can you bring me a bottle of water?"

Brandon paused at the wet bar and opened the mini-fridge. "You want one, too, Rose?"

"Yes. Thank you."

Brandon set a bottle in front of each woman, shaking his head. "Poor Jackson woke up again, and it took me forever to get him back down. At least Lily didn't wake up, that made it easier." He plopped into his chair, and turned to look at Rose, his face strained and apologetic. "You were right, honey, and I was wrong. We shouldn't have pushed them so hard yesterday. Maybe tomorrow we should just hang out here. Give them a chance to recover."

She leaned over to kiss him. "That sounds wonderful."

CHAPTER FIFTY

Now

Rose sits in a trance, staring down at the box of sidewalk chalk.

Jackson comes into the room, and throws his arms around her, Anabelle behind him. "Mama!"

"He was worried about you," Anabelle says.

Scooping him up, Rose turns and heads back into the courtyard, then she sets him down. "Go play with the boys."

As he toddles off, she sits back at the table. She slides the picture of Lily's wrist back out, and points to it. "I bought a bracelet like that when we were at the Hip Strip." She pauses and looks around at each of them. "And it's missing."

Anabelle looks up from where she's sitting on the ground putting together a puzzle with the boys. Mateo turns from where he's staring out at the ocean. Leo looks up from his phone, where he's furiously scrolling through something.

"Bree. Come out here, please," Leo calls, and she emerges from the center house.

Brandon's brow is knit. "Are you sure? Everything's been in disarray what with the police going through everything."

"That's probably it," Anabelle says. "You just misplaced it."

"The sidewalk chalk we bought? The red stick is also missing." Rose points to the other picture. "Chalk that's exactly this color."

"Oh, well, that's it then," Leo says. "The police probably took them both."

A burst of hope rushes through Rose, but dies quickly amid the chorus of insincere reactions that come from the others. Their voices are too fast and too high, and they're watching her like she might burst into flame. They're *handling* her, like she's a child. Or like they think she's insane.

Because she may very well *be* insane. And no matter how much she wants to believe otherwise, she can't deny that's where all the evidence points.

So she has to see this through, no matter where it leads. She has to be sure. So she picks up her phone. "That makes sense. I'll call them and verify. Or, wait, didn't they give us a sheet documenting everything they took?"

Leo stands and retrieves it without a word. Rose goes down the information carefully, and her heart drops further. "Neither is listed here."

Mateo shrugs. "They may have forgotten. I'm sure lots of things fall through the cracks."

"Right." She picks up the phone again. "I'll call."

Brandon's hand snakes out. "I'm not sure that's the best thing."

She stares up at him, confused. "Why?"

"Anabelle, can you take the kids in the house?" Brandon asks. She hesitates, but then goes.

He grabs both her hands in his, looks her in the eyes, and resumes. "I know what you're thinking, and I don't believe it for a second. There's simply no way anyone here—anyone—would harm Lily. That leaves only one other possibility: we can't trust these police. Like Leo said, they need an arrest, and they're going to do whatever they have to. For all we know, they took the bracelet from your belongings and planted it on Lily before we showed up to identify her. They've made their hostility clear, and they'll use anything else we give them to shore up whatever house of cards they're building. I think it's time for us to leave Jamaica."

Rose's head begins to fog—*was* it possible the police took both things with the intent to frame them? But why would they do that before they knew Lily was dead? She squeezes her eyes shut, trying to think it all through, struggling to keep hold of the clarity she had a moment ago.

She keeps getting confused when she looks at one or two facts too closely, keeps losing the forest for the trees. "No. There are too many things that they couldn't have manipulated. Like, how did the window get open before Lily even went missing?"

Brandon looks at the others. Leo and Mateo nod, and Leo speaks, his voice too calm. "You're right. There's no way they could have done that."

The glances they exchange stab at her. Part of her has been hoping her fears are just trying to sabotage her, that maybe she really didn't do this to her child. But if they all believe it, too... "You do think I'm responsible. You do think I hurt Lily," she whispers.

Leo raises both hands in front of him in a calm-down gesture. "I don't know. Not consciously, I don't think. But—well—it explains a lot, especially after what happened to Lillian Marie. Even Brandon was surprised by the article—"

She throws up a hand, and he stops talking. Time seems to slow, like everything's moving in slow motion. "You asked Brandon, not me. You've all been talking about it behind my back."

Brandon sits next to her and takes her hand. "Everyone has just been concerned. About Lily, and about you. We're not saying we think that's what happened, honey. But if something did happen, I'm sure it was an accident. Maybe Lily fell out of bed and hurt herself, and you found her that way and panicked, and it sent you into some sort of blackout. Maybe the same thing happened when you realized your sister was missing. We just don't know. We only know we have to protect you."

She stares off across the courtyard, overwhelmed and despondent, unable to speak.

"Honey, look at me."

She doesn't.

"Look at me, Rose, please."

She turns. His eyes are pleading. "The thing is, we'll never be able to convince the police it was an accident, so we're not safe here anymore. We need to get back to the States as soon as possible, because they'd have to put together a much more solid case to extradite you than they would to just put someone in jail temporarily here. And if there was some sort of accident and you've blocked it out, well, that means something isn't right, and we'll have a much easier time getting you help if you need it back home. God only knows what the mental health system is like here."

She stands and walks to the fence at the back of the courtyard, and stares out over the ocean. He's right, and she knows it—they all need to leave as soon as they can. The police are going to come for one of them, and of course she can't let anybody else take the fall for what she did. Not even the men who were hired to kidnap Lily, because they didn't actually, and even the person who hired them—

The police said whoever hired them gave them insider information. The kidnapping wasn't just some coincidence.

She whips back around and strides toward the table. "Those two men. The police said someone hired them to kidnap Lily—someone who gave them *inside information*. That doesn't fit with some accidental death I covered up, because they were hired *before* Lily went missing. Even if I'm suffering from some sort of memory fugue, *I couldn't have arranged that.* Not unless my blackout also gave me the miraculous ability to hire kidnappers in a country I've never been to before—and to *go back in time* to make that happen."

Panic flashes across Leo's face. Then, all vitality seems to drain out of him. He drops down into a chair and sags forward, bracing himself on the table with his elbows. "No, you're right. You didn't hire those men. I did."

CHAPTER FIFTY-ONE

Now

"What the fuck?" Brandon jumps up so fast his chair flies out from behind him. "You hired someone to kidnap my little girl? And now she's dead!"

Leo also leaps up, and circles around the table away from Brandon. "They didn't touch her, I swear. They didn't kill her and neither did I."

Mateo steps in front of Brandon, blocking his progress with a hand on his chest, but turns back to Leo, face twisted with rage. "You better explain. Quickly."

Rose shoots a glance at Bree—does she know about this?

But she looks as horrified as Rose feels. "He didn't tell me anything about it, I swear. Leo, tell them—"

Leo's head whips back and forth, trying to see everyone at once. "No, Bree didn't know. I knew she'd stop me if I told her about it. This was all me. But it's not how it sounds." He glances back at Mateo. "We need money. I made some bad investments and we've had some major expenses, and—well, it doesn't matter. We need money and—"

"So you kidnapped Lily?" Mateo cries. "Why didn't you just ask for help?"

Leo rubs his face, and barks a desperate laugh. "Ask who?" He turns to face Brandon. "You? You've said plenty to plenty of people, and not everybody is as loyal to you as you think. Told them how your sister, who you stress isn't *really* your sister, pissed away the inheritance she didn't deserve in the first place. And how your father's money should have come to you."

Rose glances again at Bree—red creeps up her neck as she looks down at the table. This part she knew about, how Brandon feels about her and the inheritance.

Leo continued. "So yeah, we get it, she's not your sister because to your mind the only thing that matters is blood—"

"I never said that, never even hinted that she doesn't matter because she's not my blood." Brandon's tone is icy. "And I never said she wasn't entitled to *any* inheritance from my father. But no, she sure as hell wasn't entitled to the *majority* of it."

"No, *you* were entitled to the majority, right?" Leo scoffs. "Never mind that you couldn't be bothered to work a day for your father, but that your sister helped manage his offices until the day he died. Never mind that when you liquidated the company on his deathbed, you took away the only thing that gave Bree's life meaning, especially since she was struggling to have a child. But you never realized that, because you never bothered to care, did you?"

Rose slams her hand down on the table. "What does this have to do with *my daughter*?"

Leo startles like he'd forgotten she was there, and his tone becomes whiny. "I'm saying he wouldn't have *given* us the money. He was so jealous and angry about it he couldn't see straight. So I figured when you were down here, I'd show him some solid, legitimate investment opportunities—"

Brandon snorts.

"—that would benefit both of us. A way for us to recoup enough money to get our dignity back while you walked away with a little extra pocket change. But I vastly underestimated just how bitter and vengeful your husband is."

Brandon pushes forward, stopped by Mateo's arm. "No, you underestimated how smart I am. A blind man could have seen your plot a mile away."

Leo shook his head. "I never expected you to *not see it*. I was trying to give you an excuse to be human. I hoped you'd want to help, especially since you knew how much Bree wanted a baby. Because family means so much to you, right? Or would nieces and nephews just be more competition for your father's money and memory?"

Brandon lunges at Leo, and Mateo needs to shove him with both arms to hold him back, and Brandon falls into a chair.

Leo continues. "But I wasn't surprised you didn't do the right thing. So I moved to plan B, a fake kidnapping—keyword, *fake*. I hired two guys I knew were desperate enough that they could use the money, but who weren't desperate enough to have their own agenda. Then, when you made it abundantly—and insultingly—clear that you'd never invest in anything I was involved in—and told Mateo not to, either—I gave them the green light. I knew your routine after a couple of nights, and knew we could get her out with almost no trouble or trauma. I've watched you carry Lily from the car—nothing wakes her up once she's asleep. With any luck, you'd have paid to recover her and she'd have been back in her bed before she woke up the next morning. But then the kids were sick and you were in there checking on them every five minutes."

Rose's arms and legs go numb as she stares at his face. "For money. You were willing to traumatize my daughter *for money*?"

"No." Leo's eyes plead with her. "I did it because the men I owe are going to kill me if I don't get it for them. And I have zero doubt they'll kill Bree, too."

"How much do you owe them?" Rose whispers.

"A hundred thousand dollars."

Rose tries to speak, but she can't. *A hundred thousand dollars?* That's all Lily's life was worth?

But Bree recovers her voice. "Why did they kill her?"

Leo whips toward her, pleading. "That's just it—they never got anywhere near her. What they told the police is true. I snuck into the room while you were playing cards and opened the window. But by the time they came to get her, she was already gone, and we were all out looking for her." He rubbed his face again, expression bewildered.

"You expect me to believe that?" Brandon yells. "Or is that what they told you, and you're stupid enough to believe it? But then, you have to be pretty damned stupid to think drug addicts could pull something like that off without anything going wrong!"

"Fuck you, Brandon. I *know* it's true because I never sent the message to them to come get her. I was supposed to text them when the coast was clear. When too much time passed, they started to get antsy so they came to see what was going on. When I drove out looking for Lily, I ran into them walking back to the car after they'd seen everyone running around."

"They'd probably already killed her and ditched her!" Brandon cries.

"They didn't have enough time. And why would they kill her, anyway? They knew if anything went wrong they wouldn't get their money. And if it was an accident, they'd have left her and taken off as fast and as far as they could get, they wouldn't have been strolling down the street."

"You're lying," Brandon says again. "You had my daughter kidnapped and you'll say anything now to get out of going to jail—"

Leo cuts him off. "The fibers and hairs are in *my* car, and they never had access to it—"

"How do we know they didn't? You could have given them a key—" Brandon says.

"You'd have heard it if the car started up right next to the gate, God knows the engine's not exactly quiet. That's why they had to walk down to get her, we'd have heard a car stop and the doors slam, even over the music. And you know the police have been over *their* car inside and out by now, and likely exposed the dogs to it, as well. If the police had found any evidence they'd been in contact with Lily, they'd be in jail right now and the police wouldn't be trying to turn us against each other."

Rose's head is spinning, trying to process everything Leo's saying—he's right, the idea that those men took Lily doesn't fit. If they had, that wouldn't explain the NyQuil on the floor, or the scrap of Lily's nightgown. Or the symbols on the wall, or the bracelet—

"The cadaver dog alerted *inside* the house, by Lily's bed," he continues. "She was dead before she was removed from the premises. Someone killed her and then covered it up. And yes, I need money, but I have no motive to want Lily dead."

"Nobody here does," Bree says.

Brandon sits back against the chair, head swinging back and forth. Mateo cautiously lets him go.

Leo runs a nervous hand through his hair. "I know what I did was despicable, and I know you'll never be able to forgive me. But the guys I hired didn't kill Lily. Brandon, you said it yourself. Whatever happened here, it must have been an accident."

Rose remains silent. Bree exchanges a look with Brandon, then looks out toward the ocean. Mateo stares down at the courtyard tile.

Leo turns to Rose. "We all love you, and we know whatever happened wasn't intentional. Brandon mentioned you started a new anxiety medicine right before you came, and you were drinking that night on top of it. You've been under a lot of stress, and maybe it all just got to be too much."

Brandon leans forward again, and Mateo's hand clamps back down.

"It doesn't make sense that those men took her, Brandon," Leo says. "You know it's true. We all do. Someone else is responsible."

Rose glances around to find everyone staring at her. The expressions are back—the judgment, but mixed with caution, pity, and concern.

Mateo expels a deep breath. "I think Brandon's right. I think we need to get out of here as soon as possible. At home we have options. Defense attorneys, psychiatric help. Whoever put Lily inside the trunk of Leo's car—" he pointedly doesn't meet Rose's eyes "—their hair or fibers or DNA will be there, too. It's only a matter of time before the police make an identification."

CHAPTER FIFTY-TWO

Now

As the certainty of what she's done sets in, desperation and panic engulf Rose like a tsunami that crashes, but won't recede. She can't catch her breath, like her chest is clasped in a vice. She dashes into the south house and grabs her emergency-panic-attack Xanax. She fishes out a pill and washes it down with a bottle of juice in the kitchen, then sinks to the floor and drops her head into her hands.

She can't deny it to herself anymore—the new prescription is the death knell. She forgot she changed it right before she came, far too short a period of time to have a real sense of how she was reacting to it, and even a little bit of alcohol could have reacted badly with it. There were always side effects of some sort, and whenever you change medications strange things can happen. The pharmacist always gave her an information sheet when she started a new prescription, but they all said pretty much the same thing so she'd stopped reading them long ago.

Stupid. Irresponsible. Unforgiveable.

She reaches for her phone, but it's out on the table in the courtyard. She spots Brandon's on the kitchen table and grabs it, enters his password, and searches Google. A list of side effects pops up: blurry vision, dizziness, drowsiness or fatigue, headaches. Loss of memory or concentration; confusion.

The phone slips from her hands and clatters to the floor.

Confusion. Loss of memory.

She forces herself through a series of deep breaths, as deep as she can manage when her chest refuses to expand, praying that the Xanax kicks in soon.

Confusion and loss of memory might be a long way from killing your own child and blacking it out—unless the medication is compounded by alcohol, and triggers a tendency that's been inside her all along.

She'd known this possibility was in her, and she'd been terrified of it since day one. Even more so after Lily was born because the moment the nurse handed that little bundle to her she fell into a desperate, all-encompassing love that made every emotion she'd ever felt pale in comparison. How has she allowed herself to be so irresponsible?

She leans back against the wall and closes her eyes. The pill is kicking in now—one benefit of taking them so rarely—and her breathing is calming down.

She also knows her brain wouldn't block something out unless it was truly horrific. She's researched it and knows that severe trauma interferes with how memories are recorded at the time, and then with how they're retrieved later. A black hole the size of this one must be due to something far, far beyond just traumatic.

But she can't believe she'd have *purposefully* hurt either Lily or Lillian Marie. Both must have been accidents. Lily loved to jump on the bed at home—maybe she'd woken up restless and done it here. When she'd gone to check on Lily, she must have found her dead, on the floor with a broken neck. And maybe that brought back the trauma of finding Lillian Marie missing, and triggered another blackout? Maybe that tapped into everything she'd read about Amancia Higgins, and terrified her so much she covered it all up?

But would she have done all that to cover up an accident that wasn't her fault? No, it was far more likely that she'd need to cover it up if she'd *caused* the accident. And if she caused an accident, covered it up, and blacked it all out—twice now—was Jackson safe with her?

Brandon was right. They needed to get out of Jamaica as soon as possible, back to the States. She could talk to her therapist there about checking herself into some sort of facility that could help her—maybe find a memory specialist to figure out what was going on. They know more about the brain now, more about memory—

She enters Brandon's password into the phone again and tries to Google memory and trauma and treatment. But she can't find anything relevant in the results, maybe it's the pill kicking in or maybe she's just not searching the right terms, but nothing even makes sense. After a few minutes, she gives up—the pill's definitely kicking in now and she's so very tired, she needs to lie down. She closes out the tab so Brandon won't see what she was searching—

And freezes as she sees the tab open behind it.

A website explaining how to have someone involuntarily committed for in-patient psychiatric treatment.

CHAPTER FIFTY-THREE

Now

Brandon's afraid of her. He thinks she's a danger to Jackson, or herself, or both. No matter how gently he put it outside, despite all his protestations about how it must have been an accident. And he's right. She stumbles into the bedroom and crawls under the covers, crying, and lets the Xanax pull her into oblivion.

The sun has gone down when she wakes to find Brandon standing over her.

"How are you feeling?" he asks.

The conversation in the yard comes rushing back to her, and tears fill her eyes again. "Not good. I had a panic attack, and I took a Xanax because I just—Lily—I—" Sobs seize her throat as she tries to say the words.

He pulls her into his arms and holds her. "I know. It's horrible to even think about. But there's no way you'd ever do anything to harm her on purpose. I'm absolutely certain about that."

"But… I used your phone to google memory problems, and I saw your search."

He gripped her tighter. "I was scared, Rose. When you were in here earlier, everybody came at me, about the meds and how you never wanted to have kids and that article about your sister's death, and Bree said keeping Jackson safe was the most important thing of all. But then the minute I googled it something snapped in my head, and I knew the whole idea was ridiculous. If you need it, we'll get help for you at home where you're comfortable, surrounded by the people who love you."

"I can't blame them. I don't trust *myself* to be around Jackson anymore."

"That's absolutely ridiculous. You didn't harm Lily on purpose and you'd never harm Jackson, either. Everything is going to be fine, we just need to get back home, to our regular lives. Away from this waking nightmare limbo. We all need some form of stability, especially Jackson, and then we can talk to your therapist and figure out what's going on. I left a message for Keppler to start making arrangements."

She clings to him and nods into his chest. "Can he get us out of here?"

He hands her a tissue. "Somehow, I'm sure. They can't hold us here indefinitely unless they're going to charge us. I'm sure they'll make some arrangement with the police back home to be sure we can't go anywhere, but we need to be where we understand the law and what our rights are."

She wipes her eyes. "You're right. There's nothing we can do here anyway, now that we know she's not…"

He strokes her hair. "Come eat. We got some of that curry soup, and you need to keep your strength up."

She shakes her head. "I can't face anybody, especially Leo after what he did. And I can't eat anything."

"I know." He stands, and holds out a hand to her. "But you have to, at least a little. And Jackson's been worried about you."

The thought of her little boy scared and confused, wondering if his mommy is okay, pulls her out of the bed. Despite the heat, she's chilly, and hugs her arms across her abdomen. He leads her out, hand on her lower back.

They all watch her cross the courtyard. "Are you feeling better?" Mateo asks.

"A little," Rose answers, and reaches down to scoop up Jackson from Bree's lap.

Bree doesn't release him.

"Thanks, Bree, but I can take him now," Rose says.

Bree stands and hands Jackson to Brandon. "You just said he's not safe with her."

Rose's eyes flash over to Brandon. "You said that?"

"That's not what I said." His face turns red and he glares at Bree. "I just said the police may try to argue that he's not, and that's dangerous. But I don't think it's a good idea for us to assume anything, or to make any judgments. We don't know what they're thinking, and they could be trying to make a case against any one of us, including you, so let's all stick together here."

Fear replaces the anger on Bree's face. "That's not—how can you—"

Brandon's jaw clenches and releases. "Come on, Bree. Do you think I haven't seen the nasty, jealous looks you've been shooting Rose since we arrived? The rolled eyes, dripping in contempt? You admitted yourself that article about you is true, and you've been walking a very fine line around the children you work with. You think the police aren't already considering whether you were the one who snapped? Maybe when you were *supposedly* in bed you crept in there and—"

"How fucking dare you!" Leo rushes out of the center house, where he'd apparently been listening. "After all your talk about Rose's memory, now you're gonna act like you think Bree did this?"

Brandon shoves Jackson into Rose's arms and flies toward Leo, fists raised. Leo's mouth slams shut and he screeches to a halt, fear blooming on his face. But it's too late.

"How dare *I*? After you hired men to kidnap my daughter, how dare *I*?" Brandon punches Leo directly in the eye, and Leo staggers back. "You're lucky I don't kill you right here, don't you ever dare say another word to me—"

Leo tries to block Brandon's second punch, but Brandon sidesteps the parry, then swings his left hand and connects an upper cut squarely with Leo's jaw.

Rose is horrified at how good it feels to watch Leo sink to the ground, and at how much she wants Brandon to hit him again.

"Brandon! Not in front of the kids!" Anabelle cries.

Brandon stares down at Leo, arms still raised, red-faced and panting. After a moment he drops his arms to his sides.

"The second we're all back in the States, I never want to lay eyes on you again." He turns to Bree. "Or you, as long as you're still married to *him*."

CHAPTER FIFTY-FOUR

Now

Brandon grabs Jackson and stalks off into the south house, cradling his fist. Rose starts to go after him, but decides to give him a moment alone to clean up the injured hand. And to process the fact that he didn't leave Jackson with her, despite defending her to Bree.

Bree helps Leo up and he examines his face. A bruise is already forming around his left eye; he wiggles his jaw back and forth to check that it's not broken.

"We need to get some ice on it." Bree leads him into the center house.

Mateo gathers Anabelle and the boys, who are sitting, scared and frozen, on the tile next to their Matchbox cars. "Come on, guys. We need to go pack up our stuff."

"Are we going home?" Michael asks, his voice low and afraid.

"Yes, baby. Hopefully we'll be on a plane tomorrow morning and you'll be able to sleep in your own bed soon." Anabelle stops for a moment as they head in, and turns back to Rose. "I don't think there's any way you harmed your daughter on purpose, and I'll testify to that in any court, in any country, anywhere in the world." She hefts Marcus on her hip and leads Michael across the courtyard.

Rose rips several sheets from the paper towel roll on the table and swipes at a puddle of soup someone spilled during the altercation. Her mind is clearer now—the initial impact of the Xanax has worn off enough that she's not sleepy, but still has enough residual effect to keep her calm. She tosses the sopping mess into a bowl, then gathers it with the others and carries it all over to the wet bar and washes everything.

When she's finished, she goes into the south house, hoping Brandon is calm enough to talk to now. He's at the kitchen table, on the phone, and Jackson is in his playpen, poking at his Turn-and-Learn Driver toy. A cheerful electronic tune ripples out of it, at odds with the tension suffusing the villa.

"No, they can't force you to stay here unless they press charges," Keppler's voice comes over speakerphone. "But I have to warn you, the optics of this will be horrible. It'll look like you're trying to run away."

"I don't give a damn how it looks." Brandon rakes his good hand nervously through his hair—it's shaking. "The police, the press, they've already decided one of us is guilty. We've waited here long enough. It needs to end. We need to grieve in peace."

Rose pulls one of the suitcases out of the closet and gestures to the master bedroom, indicating she's going to start packing. He nods, and she crosses to the bureau. She starts pulling out clothes and rolling them up the way Brandon prefers.

The work is mechanical, and her mind turns back to the mountain of confusion surrounding Lily's death. She's spent all of her life not knowing what happened to her sister, what exactly her role in it all was, and she's not sure she can go through that again with Lily. There has to be something, anything, that will give her insight into what she did that night, help her put the pieces together, and if she has any hope of holding on to any shred of sanity, she needs to find it.

The NyQuil still bothers her—she always gives the medicine over the sink, but if she were in some strange fugue there might be no sense to her actions. The chalk and the bracelet? She'd been reading more articles than she cared to admit about Obeah, so her subconscious surely had plenty to work with there. It must have all kicked in once she realized whatever it was she'd done.

What else had the police mentioned? They believe Lily was in the back of Leo's trunk. Could she have put her baby into a trunk like that? Maybe. But the car was strange, regardless. Leo was right that everybody on the patio would have heard the car if it started up. Sound would have traveled easily through the gate onto the patio, unlike sounds from inside the house that were blocked by layers of walls.

And how could she have driven the car when she hadn't ever driven on the left? Then again, on the quiet streets here, so late at night, she wouldn't actually have been forced to drive on one side or the other. Maybe she simply hadn't driven on the left, maybe she'd driven like she was at home, without thinking.

She sits down on the edge of the bed and closes her eyes. Maybe she's thinking about this the wrong way. She's been focusing on what the police told her and what the news reports said, and trying to think about the things she can't remember. Maybe it makes more sense to go back over what she *does* remember, see if anything becomes clearer that way, or triggers anything new.

She runs back over her memories of getting the kids ready for bed and putting them down. Of playing cards and drinking rum punch, and allowing herself to relax fully for the first time. Of checking the kids and changing Jackson and rocking him back to sleep. Of Bree and Leo excusing themselves because they were tired. Of Brandon going to check on the kids, and how he'd also had to rock Jackson back to sleep. And how she'd been taken over by one of her moments of pure love for Brandon, because he cared about his children so much and there's nothing sexier than a man who tries to be a good father, so she leaned over to kiss him—

The memory hits her like a slap to the face.

Vomit. Brandon had smelled vaguely of vomit.

She hadn't placed the odor at the time, had just noticed something a little sour and off. But there had been lots of new smells and foods over the last week, and it hadn't really even registered. But the police had asked about vomit, hadn't they? Asked if anyone had thrown up? And she and Brandon had both told them no.

Is her mind making this up? Revising the memory now to remember vomit when he'd really smelled like something else?

Rose grabs the hamper from the corner of the bedroom and empties it on the bed. She sorts through the clothes, looking for the ones Brandon was wearing that night. He changed into a blue polo shirt and beige cargo shorts when they returned from the beach.

She grabs the shirt, brings it up to her face, and sniffs.

Cologne. Rum.

And vomit.

CHAPTER FIFTY-FIVE

Now

Rose finds Brandon pouring himself a rum and Coke in the kitchen.

He turns when he hears her enter. "Hey, honey. I was just about to gather everyone together. I just finished with Keppler."

She nods and lifts Jackson from his playpen. "You get Mateo and Anabelle. I'll get Bree and Leo."

He returns from the north house with Mateo. "Anabelle's still packing with the boys."

As soon as Leo appears, Brandon's face tightens, like his mouth is filled with something bitter. "I meant what I said. I can't ever forgive you for what you've done. But for now, we all have to present a unified front and get ourselves back home safely."

Leo nods, and everyone sits.

"Keppler's making the calls right now." Brandon takes a big swig from his drink. "We can leave, but he says it'll go easier if we all agree to a few things. Mainly that the police back home be made aware of the situation, and that we agree not to leave Massachusetts without notifying them until this is all cleared up. He thinks if we agree, they'll be less likely to arrest one or more of us in an attempt to keep us all here."

"If that's what it takes," Leo says. "Bree and I will go tonight and pick up what we need from the other house. The house came fully furnished, so there isn't much. Just clothes and a few personal items."

Bree looks down at her hands.

Mateo pulls out his phone. "So we need to book flights. I say the first one out, we're on it."

Brandon shakes his head. "I already made the arrangements. There's a flight out to Logan at five in the morning. We should leave around three to be sure we get there on time."

"Sounds good," Mateo says.

"Great. Let's finish packing." Brandon starts to get up.

Rose clears her throat and watches his face closely. "I have something I need to ask you."

A micro-flash of something—annoyance? Fear?—crosses his face before he smiles reassuringly. "What is it?"

She almost loses her nerve. No matter what, he's going to be very, *very* angry. But if there's a good explanation for it, she needs to know. "The night Lily disappeared. Did you throw up?"

His brow creases. "Of course not."

"You're sure? Everything happened so fast."

"I think I'd remember something like that. Why?"

"Well." She shifts in her chair. "I've been going over everything in my mind, and I remembered the police said something about vomit in the toilet."

"Right. And I told them then I hadn't. My best guess is one of the kids threw up during the time you can't remember."

She looks down at the table. "Except the kids are too small, I never have them stand over the toilet. And Dr. Shultz said never to have them hold it until I can get them to the bathroom, they can choke to death on it that way. So I give them a pan or mixing bowl if I can get there in time, and if not, I let them vomit where they are, and clean it up."

The table's completely still. Everyone stares at Brandon, unmoving.

He puts on an exasperated smile. "That must be what happened, then. You had them vomit in a bowl and tossed it into the toilet when they were done."

Her heart sinks, and the light that's been shining on her life for the past five years goes out.

She's been hoping, more than she even realized, that he has a good explanation. But he doesn't, he's making it up as he goes along. And he's trying to put the blame on her.

She looks down at the table for a moment, gathering courage. Then she nods and looks back up. "Except I just pulled out the shirt you were wearing that night, and it smells like vomit."

He pauses for just a beat too long, then shrugs. "Maybe Jackson spit up while I was rocking him, and I didn't notice."

"The bottom part of the sleeve. The forearm. Like if you were to wipe your mouth after vomiting."

He tries for a charmingly exasperated expression. "I guess he spit up *there* then, when I picked him up or put him down, and I didn't notice."

That was it, then. He was lying, and there was only one possible reason for that.

Her courage wavered. If she dropped the issue now, everything would be fine. They could all go home to their normal lives. Pretend the vomit and all the other anomalies aren't relevant. Pretend the whole horrific vacation had never happened.

Except that wasn't fair to Lily—because her beautiful daughter would never get to go home again. Never get to have another play date, or another plate of Thanksgiving turkey, or open another Christmas present. Never graduate high school or college, or fall in love, or have a baby of her own.

The statue she'd seen in Montego Bay flashed through her mind. She couldn't do what was easy. She needed to do what was right. Lily deserved to have someone, especially her mother, fight for her truth.

A tear slid down Rose's cheek. "When you came back from checking on the kids, I kissed you. I smelled it on your breath."

The exasperated charm dropped from his face. "You're lying. You're trying to blame what you did on me. Otherwise you would have mentioned it before."

"I only put the pieces together completely when I checked your shirt just now." She took a deep breath, and forced the rest out in a rush. "The police mentioned it, which means they took a sample of the vomit. And I just googled it—you can test vomit for DNA. They'll know whose it is soon."

Silence envelops the courtyard. Brandon's face cycles through several expressions, like someone flipping through a catalog of emotions, choosing which one to put on.

He settles on rage, and slams a fist into the table. "I'm a doctor. Don't you think I fucking know that? And I also know that my DNA is all over that toilet, and any defense attorney in the *US system* will be able to cast all sorts of reasonable doubt on whatever swab they took, even if mine is the only profile that comes out of it. But the longer we stay here, the more pieces they'll put together, and it's only a matter of time before they build a case I can't get out of."

"Brandon, no." Bree's hands flutter to her face. "No. I need you to look me in the eye and tell me you didn't kill Lily."

Brandon turns, looks her in the eye, and speaks.

CHAPTER FIFTY-SIX

The day of the disappearance

Brandon

"Brandon, will you go check on the kids?" Rose asked him.

That irritated him. He turned his sip of punch into a gulp, draining the rest to hide his reaction. The ice clanked against his teeth and he set the glass down, fake smile affixed in place. "Of course, my love. I'll be right back."

He crossed the portico, stumbling slightly over the cracks in the tile as he went.

"Careful, man," Mateo called after him, laughing. "The last thing we need is to have to rush you to the hospital because you break your leg or something."

"How strong did you make these?" Anabelle's annoying cackle made him twitch. "All I can taste is alcohol and sugar."

"You know me, if I'm not driving, I don't see the point in messing around," Mateo said.

Brandon shook his head as he entered the house. Anabelle wouldn't know a strong drink if it bit her in the ass. He'd barely been able to taste the alcohol. He'd had to add extra to his glass when Rose had gone to check on the kids.

Soft crying greeted him as he neared their bedroom. "Mama… Mama…"

Lily's voice. He pushed open the door to find her lying on the bed, covers kicked off, whimpering. She turned her head to look at him, brown eyes red with tears, and cranked it up a notch. "Daddy, I don't feel good!"

Jackson woke up and joined in on the crying.

Daddy. Brandon's jaw snapped tight with anger at the word, and at the sight of Mateo's wide brown eyes staring up at him.

He'd realized it earlier that day at the beach, and couldn't believe he'd never noticed it before. Although, he might not have noticed it *then* if it hadn't been for Anabelle. He looked up to see her frozen, a shocked look on her face, and for a moment he thought she was having some sort of episode. He'd followed her eyes to Lily building the castle with Michael and Marcus, laughing and smiling and helping each other. Nothing she could possibly be upset about—it was a charming scene, like a shot of a frolicking family from a television commercial, especially Lily and Marcus, who, despite the difference in skin tone, looked almost like twins.

Then it hit him like a seven forty seven.

He peered closer, studying Lily with a new attention. He always thought she took after Rose, but he was wrong. Rose's eyes were the color of coffee with milk, while Lily's were the same near-black as the boys'. And while Rose's eyes turned up at the corner like a cat's, Lily's turned down, just like Michael's and Marcus'.

And Mateo's.

He tried to tell himself he was imagining it. That he was on his third Red Stripe, so he was probably a little impaired even if he *felt* just fine. But he worked on faces for a living, made decisions every day about eye shape and nose shape and the overall composition of the face. He could be blind, stinking drunk and he wouldn't have been able to mistake it.

He tried to put his focus back on the dominoes he was playing, but every time he looked at Mateo he wanted to knock his teeth out. This man smiling at him, vacationing with him on the fumes of his father's money, drinking his alcohol and pretending to be his friend—this man had fucked his wife and tried to pass off his child as Brandon's.

When they finished the game, he pretended to take a nap to give himself time to think it through. If he confronted Rose or Mateo, they'd deny it, and that would get him nowhere. His father's cutthroat skills with stock analysis might have missed him in many ways, but his business instincts hadn't: a smart man negotiated any situation from a position of power, not weakness. You don't ask questions you don't already know the answer to, and don't make accusations you can't back up. Reality was a bank of shifting sand that people would manipulate if they were able, so you never, ever gave them forewarning about what was coming.

What he needed was a paternity test.

A few strands of Mateo's hair if he could manage it, and a few strands of Lily's. Or maybe he could find a way to get Mateo to let him take a swab—tell him some story about a preemptive genetic test for prostate cancer or some such, Mateo would buy that no problem. It would take a few weeks to get the results, and then he'd get both of them in the same room and blow up their worlds the way they'd blown up his.

"Daddy," Lily's voice bleated from the bed. "I don't feel well."

Brandon turned his back on her and picked up Jackson, who instantly stuck his thumb in his mouth and cradled his head in Brandon's shoulder. "Hey, buddy. You feeling sick?"

Jackson sniffled, pulling in the drop of snot that had snaked most of the way to his mouth. Some sort of cold, Brandon thought. Rose was right about that. He needed more medicine—he looked around the room, which swayed when he turned his head. Where had the cheating bitch put the NyQuil? The bathroom?

"Daddy!" Lily called, her voice accusatory.

"You have to wait. You woke your brother," he snapped, then turned away from the shocked look on her face. She wasn't used to anger from him, he normally spoiled her and fussed over her. A small pang tugged at him momentarily, but almost instantly his own weakness sickened him. Because she was *not* his daughter.

She had *no right* to expect anything from him. She was manipulating him. Expecting to get what she wanted, trying to put herself ahead of her brother, the same way Bree always did. With *his* father, not hers. But she manipulated Reginald Martin and made him love her more and he, the king of *legacy*, fell for it every time, even down to the inheritance that *should have been Brandon's*.

He stumbled over the threshold and nearly dropped Jackson, but managed to catch him just in time. He leaned against the wall for a moment to pull himself together. He was too buzzed, the rum was hitting him hard, maybe it wasn't smart to walk with the baby. Safer to leave him in the crib. Bring the NyQuil to him.

When he returned from the bathroom with the bottle, Lily was whimpering louder than ever, and the sound drilled into his skull. "Can't you shut up for just one damned minute?"

Lily's mouth clamped shut in surprise.

He filled the cap to the upper line and told Jackson to open his mouth. He was a good boy, he always did what he was told, but now he didn't for some reason, but that was okay. He held open Jackson's mouth so he wouldn't be able to move it because Jackson didn't like medicine—who did—and he poured the cap in. Jackson swallowed and sputtered and Brandon swiped a tissue across his face to clean up what he'd spit out. Then he gave Jackson a kiss and laid him down in the crib, and rubbed his belly until his eyes slowly closed. "Back to sleep, now."

Then he turned to Lily. She was apparently over her shock, because she stared up at him with an angry, petulant face.

How dare *she* be angry at *him*? She was the one masquerading as his daughter, worming her way in like a parasite stealing his love from *his real child*.

He shook his head to clear it, and picked up the NyQuil. He filled the cup to the line again, and set the bottle down. "Open up."

Mateo's brown eyes glared up at him. "No. Don't like it," she said, and clamped her mouth shut, lips pushed in.

"Don't care if you like it," he imitated her tone and stepped toward her. "Open up, Bree."

She shook her head.

He grabbed her mouth and squeezed it open. But she was stronger than Jackson and he underestimated her, and she twisted at the last moment and smacked the cap out of his hand. It flew back, splashing onto the floor.

"Damned brat!" He grabbed the bottle and filled the cap again and set it on the nightstand next to her bed. Her face changed from defiance to fear as he sat next to her and pinned her to the wall, then tucked her into his side. He wrapped his arm around her head this time, grabbing her mouth again with her hand.

As he reached up for the cap, she squirmed violently, trying to escape his grasp.

"Cut it out, Bree. I tried to do it the easy way but you wouldn't let me, so we're gonna do it the hard way. It's your own fault." He squeezed her mouth until it opened, and she cried out. She pushed sharply against him, and almost got away—but he clenched her head hard and fast, muscles turning to steel, wrenching her back in place against the wall.

He poured the noxious liquid into her mouth then slammed it shut so she couldn't spit it back again, then waited a long moment and finally dropped his hand. "There. You're done. Was that really worth all that fuss?"

She didn't answer. Her mouth dropped open, eyes wide, and NyQuil dribbled down her face and neck.

He pulled his arm away, expecting her to wriggle from his grasp. But she collapsed back onto the bed, unmoving, eyes still wide.

Head twisted at an impossible angle.

CHAPTER FIFTY-SEVEN

The day of the disappearance

Brandon

Adrenaline suddenly coursed through him like a giant bolt of electricity, counteracting his alcohol fog. She wasn't being difficult—something was very wrong.

"Oh God. Oh, God. No, no, no—Lily, answer me." He grabbed her shoulders and shook her.

Her head lolled to the other side, and her eyes stared off to the floor, unmoving. He stuck two fingers over her carotid artery, searching for a pulse. Nothing. He leaned his ear next to her mouth—she wasn't breathing. He palpated her neck.

Cervical fracture.

Oh God—what had he done? Terror and desperation ripped through him—there was no point trying CPR, no point in trying to get an ambulance, this wasn't something she could come back from. She'd died instantly—and he'd killed her.

Nausea bubbled up inside him. He dashed to the bathroom, pulled up the lid to the toilet, and vomited the contents of his stomach into the bowl. When he finished, he wiped his mouth with his sleeve, and flushed.

He rubbed his eyes and tried to think. The police would come. They'd never believe it was an accident, especially with how drunk he was, and at the very least he'd be charged for negligent manslaughter. It was only a matter of time before his trip to rehab came to light—Kayla would scream it from the rooftops as soon as she heard Lily was dead, that was what she'd been afraid of the entire time and why she wouldn't have children with him.

Even if he managed to avoid jail, his career would be over—nobody would trust an alcoholic who'd killed a child. And who knew if he'd even be allowed to go home to be prosecuted, the Jamaican officials might insist on trying him and he had no idea what the laws were here—

What was that story Rose had gone on and on about? A kidnapped girl whose body had been discovered nearby, something like that. He pulled his cell out of his pocket and googled it. Yes, that was right, several little girls had been kidnapped in the last year. One of them found, with an Obeah bracelet wrapped up in the blanket.

He could do the same thing. Get her away from the house, make the police think someone had snatched her and killed her? He was her father, of course his DNA and whatever would be on her, they couldn't use that to prove anything. So he just had to get her body as far away as possible. And he needed to act fast—Rose would assume one of the kids needed to be put back to sleep, but if he took too long, she'd come check on him.

He snatched up the toenail clippers from Rose's bag and hurried back into the kids' bedroom to open the window. It was already open—how had he not noticed? He clipped the edge of her nightgown so he could rip off a strip of the fabric. He tossed Lily and the fabric out of the window, then kicked off his sandals and ran as silently as he could manage through the wing of the house into the central living area where Leo kept the keys to the cars. He grabbed the key ring, dashed back to his part of the house trying to think as he ran—he needed something to make it look like Obeah. The girl in the story had a bracelet—hadn't Rose picked up some bracelets at that store where he'd done the haggling?

He ran to the living room closet, pawed through the bag of trinkets, and grabbed the first bracelet he came to.

What else did he need to worry about? Fingerprints? No, there was a reason for his prints to be on everything. Except he had to be careful about where he put his hands on the windowsill.

As he ran back to the kids' bedroom, he spotted the sidewalk chalk they'd pulled out for Lily. He snatched it up—he could write something on the outside of the wall that would be even more convincing than just the bracelet.

Placing his hands carefully, he climbed out of the window. Then he quickly googled Obeah symbols, scrolled down enough to avoid the obvious, and picked several to scrawl onto the wall. When he finished, he threw the chalk over the property fence, into the greenery that sloped down the mountain. They'd never find it there. Then he picked up Lily and carried her to the minivan.

And immediately recognized several huge holes in his plan.

He'd never be able to start the car without everyone hearing. And, he had no idea how far he'd have to drive to find a place to leave her. How long had he been gone? Rose might come looking for him any minute, and he'd never be able to explain it if he were gone when she did. Shit. Shit, shit, shit, shit.

He set Lily down next to the van and dropped into a squat, forcing his brain to work. He'd just have to hide her in the vehicle and find a way to get rid of her later. When Rose realized she was missing, there would be confusion and craziness—he'd find some way to take the car out to search for her and get rid of her then. He didn't have a choice, he'd have to figure it out—he'd have time, hopefully at least an hour before Rose went to check on Lily again. He'd come up with something.

He opened the minivan as quietly as he could and looked for a place to hide her out of sight. Nothing was big enough. The spare-tire compartment? He searched for it but couldn't find it, then realized it was under the vehicle. That wouldn't work.

He opened the trunk of Leo's car. There was a spare-tire compartment, but was it big enough? He pulled out the tire and shoved Lily inside. He had to curl her arms and legs around her and she still barely fit, but he made it work—thank God she was small. He dropped the cover over her and laid the tire on top of the compartment.

Back through the window into the bedroom. Sandals back on, NyQuil put away in the bathroom. He tossed the chalk box back on the crowded table where he'd found it.

He stood for a minute recovering his composure before returning outside, and used the time to think everything through once more. The adrenaline had sharpened his thinking but there was still an undercurrent of fog from the rum punch, and he had a nagging feeling he'd forgotten something. Probably several somethings.

Still, he'd done well, not bad at all for a plan he had to come up with on the spur of the moment. And between the vomiting and the adrenaline, by the time Rose did the next check on the kids, he'd practically be sober, and in the chaos he could fix any mistakes he'd made. And hadn't Rose spent the last month telling him how the Jamaican police here were understaffed and overburdened? They wouldn't look deeply into any of it, anyway.

It would work. It had to.

He took a final deep breath, composed his face, then went back outside, covering any residual air of confusion or fear with an exasperated shake of the head. "Poor Jackson woke up again, and it took me forever to get him back down. At least Lily didn't wake up, that made it easier." He dropped into the chair. "You were right, honey, and I was wrong. We shouldn't have pushed them so hard yesterday. Maybe tomorrow we should just hang out here. Give them a chance to recover."

She smiled, and leaned over to kiss him. "That sounds wonderful."

CHAPTER FIFTY-EIGHT

Now

Brandon finishes his story and collapses forward onto the table, sobbing, head on his arms. A stunned silence fills the courtyard.

Contradictory emotions churn through Rose—she wants to fling herself at him, fists flying, and tear him apart for killing her baby girl. Not just for killing her, but for covering it up—to the point of slicing open her throat, for God's sake—how could he bring himself to do something so heinous?

But his wrenching sobs rip at her heart—this was an accident, and he's as heartbroken as she is. And she's made plenty of mistakes while learning how to care for the kids, dangerous ones like when she'd turned her back when Lily was a baby, just for a moment, and Lily had rolled off the couch and onto the floor. Lily had been fine, but what if she hadn't been? Would Rose have deserved to go to jail for it?

You weren't drunk, a voice whispers in her head. *And you didn't try to blame someone else for it.*

But no, that isn't fair, he hasn't *exactly* blamed her for it—it isn't like he's turned her in or something. He just glommed onto it as a convenient excuse to get everyone to look the other way.

Is there a difference?

She can't let herself think about all that right now. Now she has to deal with the current situation.

She reaches across the table and lays her hand on his. "It was an accident. You didn't hurt her on purpose. We all know you'd never do that."

He sits up and blows his nose on a paper towel. "No. I didn't do it on purpose."

"And it's going to be okay," she says. "We'll get back home and you'll tell the police what happened, and you'll go to rehab. It won't be fun, but—"

He stiffens. "No way in hell. You think they're going to just pat me on the head and say 'everybody makes mistakes?' This is negligent homicide. Maybe manslaughter if I can get the right attorney, but even then, there's no way I'm not going to jail. Especially not after I tried to cover up what I did."

"We'll hire the best attorneys and you'll tell the court you're going to rehab. I've seen it on episodes of *Intervention*, if the person is willing to get help, they don't have to go to jail—"

"You're not getting this. I'm not going to tell the truth to anybody. Not the police, not the attorneys, nobody." He glances around at everyone. "And neither are any of you. We're gonna get on that plane in the morning and get back to the States, and our attorneys are going to shut this down, and we'll put it all behind us."

Mateo shoots Rose a look. It says *are you okay with this?*, but there's something else to it. Heartbreak, she realizes—his daughter has been ripped away from him, too, even if he's only known Lily was his for a few days.

Bree speaks before she can. "No, Brandon. You may not have done this on purpose, but you still have to take responsibility for it."

"This isn't your choice to make, Brianna," Brandon says, leaning slightly toward her.

"Yes, it is. Not only did you kill my niece, you tried to blame Rose for it. You sat here this afternoon and convinced us all she had some sort of memory fugue, and even that she'd killed her sister." She stands up. "If you don't tell the police, I will."

"Sit down, little *sister*," Brandon spits. "We're all in this together now, whether you like it or not. If you go to the police, I'll be forced to tell them Leo hired men to kidnap my daughter. I wonder, if it comes down to proof you hired kidnappers versus a little bit of mystery vomit in a toilet—which evidence do you think a jury will find more convincing?"

Bree flinches, and Leo goes pale.

"And, I have to wonder. You've been so attentive to Lily and so upset about your inability to have your own children—I really only have Leo's word for the fact that the kidnapping *was* fake. Maybe you intended to disappear with her, never to be seen again. You've got goons hunting you down in the middle of Sam Sharpe Square—oh yes, Leo, I'm not an idiot, I saw what was happening there—and nothing to lose by running off to Venezuela or God knows where."

"That's enough, Brandon. You're talking to your sister," Mateo says.

"Right. The *stepsister* who took my father's legacy from me. I'm not going to let her take the rest of my life, too."

"You're headed to a dark place with these threats," Mateo continues, keeping his voice steady and even, like he's trying to lull an angry bull. "And there's no reason for it. Like Rosie said, your attorney will be able to get you a deal. Are you really willing to turn on the people who love you just to avoid going to rehab?"

"I know you're not that stupid, Matty. Do you really think I can have any type of career after two stints in rehab and killing my own child? Most of my business is elective surgery for rich women with more money than brains. Do you think the soccer moms of Marblehead are gonna line up to trust their faces to a drunken child killer?"

"I don't know about that," Mateo says. "But there are a few things I do know. One—those men who admitted they were hired to kill Lily? They'll be charged at least with kidnapping, and possibly even murder. And I know I'm not willing to be party to that, to sending innocent men to jail for the rest of their lives."

"Innocent? They were going to kidnap my daughter!"

"But they didn't," Mateo says, still keeping his voice steady.

"That's splitting hairs. Even if they'd only taken her for a few hours and we got her right back, she'd have been traumatized for life. That's far from innocent."

"You can't put men away for an act they only thought about committing, Brandon." Mateo holds up a hand in a *stop* gesture. "But it doesn't matter. Your conscience may allow you to live with that, but mine won't."

"Oh, right, I forgot. You're so righteous, with such a strong moral compass. It's not like you fucked my wife or anything like that."

Bree looks confused, and Leo leans forward. Mateo sends a questioning look to Rose—*did you tell him?*—and she shakes her head, stunned.

"If I tell the police *you're* actually Lily's biological father, maybe they won't care." Brandon juts his head toward the north house where Anabelle is packing with the kids. "But your wife sure as hell will."

Bree gasps and stares at Rose. Leo's eyes ping-pong between everyone's faces.

"And," Brandon's voice slices through the taut air, "if Rose decides she just can't live with hiding the truth, well, I've already talked to an attorney about my concerns that my wife may be having dangerous breaks from reality."

Rose tenses. Part of her knew this was coming, has known since she realized the truth about the vomit. But she wanted to believe he wouldn't stoop that low.

"You'd have your wife put away to avoid embarrassment," Leo says. "The woman you love."

"You mean the woman who cheated on me and passed off another man's child as mine? No. I'd get her the help she badly needs. The entire time I've known her she's been on antidepressants or anti-anxiety meds or both. She's also been in therapy the entire time, but obviously none of that has been able to help her successfully deal with the past—she still can't even remember what role she played in her sister's disappearance. And if she'd be willing to turn me in for something she knows is accidental, well, then, she's clearly unstable." Brandon reaches over and strokes his son's hair. "And I can't have someone who's unstable around my son. He's my legacy. And my father's."

That she doesn't see coming—that he'd threaten to take her son away from her. She has no doubt he can do it—he'll be able to put enough doubt into any judge or child protective service agent to get custody, especially when paired with whatever high-powered attorney he's retained.

"I honestly don't understand why this is even an issue." Brandon makes eye contact with each person in turn. "You know this was an accident. And you know those horrible men were willing to take money to kidnap my daughter, and deserve to be punished for that. There is no miscarriage of justice here."

"What do I tell Anabelle?" Mateo asks quietly.

Brandon scratches the side of his jaw, managing to infuse the gesture with menace. "I'm sure you'll think of something. It seems to me you're pretty good at keeping her in the dark."

Rose meets Bree's eyes, expecting judgment and disgust. Instead she finds concern, and fear. Mateo looks angry, but trapped. Leo's expression is desperate but resigned, even slightly relieved—but then, why wouldn't it be? He gets off the hook this way, too.

She stares at her husband, the man she's loved so much for so long. She doesn't recognize him—this man who would go to such horrific extremes to cover up a mistake, then threaten all of the people who love him. Has she ever known who he really is?

She stands. "It sounds like the only thing left for us to do is pack."

CHAPTER FIFTY-NINE

Now

The evening passes in somber silence as everyone packs, cleans, and finalizes arrangements. Brandon plays with Jackson while Rose does most of the work, and Rose sees her future—she'll be a prisoner in a marriage that isn't just loveless, but is now actively hostile. She'll be a glorified nanny and trophy wife, there to show up to the parties when Brandon needs her, to host dinners, to care for his son. And if she does anything he doesn't like, he'll have her committed or take away her son.

She wants to believe he couldn't get away with it, but she's not certain. He's persuasive, and he has standing in the community. She has a huge stain on her history that will work against her, and nobody's going to believe her if push comes to shove. They never have.

But that's not what she's really afraid of. What really matters is Jackson. What will happen to him if he's raised in such a twisted environment? There's nothing but potential in his beautiful eyes—he's sweet and he's smart and he's fascinated by fire trucks. He's quick to laughter and loves to cuddle and shares his food and toys with joy.

But what will happen to him if he's raised by an untreated alcoholic? By someone who rages and abuses and slowly, one day at a time, saps all the joy and spirit out of him? Will he become sullen and introverted, the sort of teenager who cuts himself? Or the sort of angry man who lashes out and harms others, continuing the cycle of abuse?

Either way, she can't bear to see his shining light extinguished. She tickles his stomach and he giggles; she bends her forehead to touch his, and he reaches his hands up around her neck. She lifts him into a hug and cuddles him for a moment, fighting back the tears in her eyes.

She's done all she can do. Her only hope now is that the police intercept them before they can get to the United States. If they don't, she'll never get out from under Brandon.

Her hands shake as she packs the suitcases and she loses focus, opening drawers she's already opened before, looking for items she's already found. After checking the refrigerator three times, she pauses and considers taking another Xanax. No, she decides. She needs every bit of her wits about her for the next twenty-four hours, and Jackson needs her, too.

She sets out clothes for each of them, along with the toiletries they'll need to get ready.

"Don't worry about that." Brandon's voice startles her from behind. "We won't have time to shower. Just get up and go—I want to be there and board the plane as early as possible."

"Okay. That makes sense." She tries not to shudder.

His hand startles her as he turns her to face him. "It's going to be okay, Rose. We're both heartbroken over Lily, and it's going to take time. But before you know it, we'll have another baby on the way, and we'll have something to be happy about again. Just tell me you forgive me."

She hides the revulsion that washes over her. Is that really what he thinks—that another baby can replace Lily? That after what he's said and done and threatened anything can ever be alright again? "It was an accident. Of course I forgive you."

He leans in to kiss her, and the disgust intensifies.

He opens the freezer and clinks ice into a glass. She winces as he fills it with rum.

But then—maybe it's a good thing. Let him get drunk. It'll be easier for everyone.

He lifts his drink in a toast. "And there's a silver lining to every cloud—I'll know for sure the new baby is mine."

CHAPTER SIXTY

Now

In the morning, Rose slips Jackson into jeans and her favorite of his shirts, red with a yellow truck in the middle. He yawns and smiles up at her, and she hugs him close and tries not to start crying again, because if she starts, she may never stop.

They all load up the new rental car in near silence. Bree casts worried looks at Rose. Anabelle seems confused. Leo and Mateo avoid eye contact with Brandon.

As Leo drives to the airport, Rose stares out the window, willing the police cars to appear.

They don't.

After they return the rental car, they head into the airport. Then check-in, security, gleaming white terminals of shops filled with duty-free alcohol, gifts, overpriced food. As they navigate through it all, Rose glances back periodically, praying to see officers striding toward them with purpose. With each step closer to the gate, her hope fades a little more.

Then they sit in a group of empty gray chairs waiting to board, the only conversation among them the strangely muted chatter of Anabelle and Mateo's boys. They know something's wrong, and instinctively tread lightly.

Rose continues to scan the terminal, double-taking on every uniform.

The gate agent welcomes families with children to pre-board. Rose ushers Jackson on, with Anabelle and the boys following closely behind. They settle into the first-class seats, the only ones available last minute. The flight attendants bring orange juice for her and Jackson and champagne for Brandon. Rose scans every passenger as they slowly file past, on their way to stuffing luggage into overhead compartments and locating seats.

The flight attendants close the doors and start their announcements. The plane shifts, and rolls backwards.

The police aren't coming to save them.

CHAPTER SIXTY-ONE

Now

Brandon sleeps during the flight, and Jackson alternates between napping and playing with his stacking cups. Rose entertains him as needed, and spends the rest of the time staring out the window.

The plane lands at Logan Airport, and taxis to the gate. As the plane continues to roll, roll, roll, Rose feels like she's caught in a strange purgatory, at once both needing the torturous ride to end, and desperately clinging to her last moments of freedom. Finally, the plane shudders to a stop, and the seat belt light goes off. With the same stifling silence they've had since leaving the villa, they gather their belongings and exit down the jetway. As they spew into the terminal, Rose looks for the baggage claim sign.

Four uniformed officers wait at the far end of the gate.

Rose's heart leaps for a moment—but falls instantly. This is wrong. Why would the *American* police be waiting?

"Brandon Martin?" One of the officers, a tall, thin, pasty-white blond man steps forward, blocking their path.

"I'm Brandon Martin." Brandon extends his hand. "I'm the one who called about the fifty-one-fifty situation. That's my wife, there, she's the one that needs the psychiatric hold."

The officer doesn't move. "We'd like to speak to you, please, over here, so we aren't in the way of the other passengers."

Brandon follows the police officer to the side of space. "I don't think she'll resist, but that's probably smart either way."

Fear paralyzes Rose—it never occurred to her he'd do something like this before they even left the airport. Her eyes squeeze shut and she hugs Jackson close, inhaling a long, deep breath to memorize his talcum-power-and-baby-shampoo scent. Then she turns to hand him off to Bree.

For once, Bree doesn't take him. She's staring at Brandon with fury in her eyes. She steps forward. "Don't you dare even think about touching her. Whatever he told you about her, it's not true. She's not crazy and she didn't touch a hair on her daughter's head."

Rose stares at Bree, frozen by shock.

"Who are you, ma'am?" the officer asks.

"I'm Brianna Palser, Brandon Martin's sister. *Stepsister*," she adds with deliberate sarcasm.

"Bree, it's okay, don't—" Rose grabs Bree's arm.

Two of the other officers shift toward Bree.

"This isn't about Mrs. Martin." The blond officer glances at Leo, who stands behind Bree. "But would that make you Leo Palser?"

He goes pale. "Yes."

One of the other officers reaches for his arm. "Please come with me."

Bree glances at each of the officers and steps back. Rose stays at her side as the second officer leads Leo out of earshot.

The officer with Brandon continues, tone formal. "Dr. Martin, the Jamaica Constabulary Force has been in contact with us, and we have some questions to ask you about your daughter's death. We'd like you to accompany us back to the station."

"There's been a misunderstanding. I'm not the one responsible for my daughter's death. My wife is. Rose, there." He turns and points at her. "I called—"

"We received your call, sir. The Jamaican police alerted us that you'd likely try to confuse the issue by implicating your wife."

Brandon's face turns purple-red as he scans each of their faces, trying to figure out how this happened. He abandons the attempt as the officers reach for him. "Rose, get Audrey to call me as soon as possible."

Rose nods. The officer gestures Brandon forward, and the phalanx of police surround him. They join up with the officer detaining Leo and continue down the terminal.

Relief floods her, so completely she's sure her knees will buckle out from under her—then Bree's hand reaches out to steady her. Anabelle steps over to her other side.

She sends up a silent prayer of thanks. The detectives received her message after all—and the voice recording she made of Brandon's confession on her phone must have been clear enough, at least in the right places.

CHAPTER SIXTY-TWO

Now

Mateo waits until the small group of curious passengers moves on before turning to Rose. "What the hell just happened?"

"Are you okay?" Bree asks, examining her face closely.

"I'm not, but I will be." She turns to Mateo. "I found a search about involuntary psychiatric commitment on his phone before we left. When I first saw it, I thought he was worried about Jackson's safety with me. But when I remembered about the vomit, I realized his intentions might not be good, and I needed to protect myself. So I used the voice recorder on my phone to capture our conversation when I confronted him. I thought he might say something useful, but never expected a full confession. He never left me alone after that, so I wasn't able to call the police directly. All I could do was upload the recording and send them the link, and I didn't know until right now if they'd even received it."

"Is that legal?" Anabelle asks.

"I don't know." Rose stares at the ground. "I didn't have time to find out. I'm guessing it is or that they won't need to use it in court, otherwise they wouldn't have acted on it. Maybe because the American police got a tip from the Jamaican police, that's all that matters?"

"I can't believe it." Mateo looks like he's just been greeted by a UFO. "He actually arranged a psychiatric hold for you?"

Rose nods again, still trying to process it herself. "I guess he figured it was only a matter of time before I'd try to get away from him once we were back in the States."

"I just—I can't believe he'd do that," Mateo says.

Bree looks at him like he's an idiot. "After he blackmailed all of us last night, you can't believe it?"

Anabelle's eyes widen, but she doesn't speak.

Mateo's eyes flick manically over the terminal. "I mean—we were doing what he asked. I thought he really did just want to put it all behind us."

Bree laughed, a bitter, harsh noise like sandpaper on a tree. "When have you ever known Brandon to let a vendetta go?"

Mateo didn't respond.

"Exactly," Bree says. "He just never had an issue with *you*. It's far easier to excuse behavior when you've never been in the cross hairs. Now, we need to get Rose and Jackson out of here."

The trip home passes in a blur. Baggage claim, customs, all through the obscenely busy Thanksgiving-travel congestion of the airport. Rose clings to Jackson and keeps her head down, feeling like she's careening through a tunnel whose walls are trying to swallow her. Then the relative calm of the SUV, which Bree drives while Rose and Jackson sit in the back, one hand intermittently reaching back to grasp Rose's. Mateo and Anabelle take their own car and promise to bring dinner after they unpack and the boys nap.

"Take whichever bedroom you want," Rose says as she and Bree unload the baggage. "When does your tenant's lease run out?"

"Not until March," Bree answers. "But don't worry, I'll find a place as soon as I can."

"No." Rose turns to her. "When you thought the police were there for me, you told the truth to save me."

"I couldn't let you rot away in some psychiatric facility." Bree looks at the floor. "Even if it meant that Leo had to go to jail. Although I guess they were coming for him anyway. I just couldn't let Brandon victimize you, not like—" She stops short.

Rose pulls her into a hug. "He hurt you when you were children, didn't he?"

"Not physically, but—" She starts to cry softly.

Rose holds her for a long moment, then pulls back and looks into her eyes. "My house is your house as long as you need it. I won't allow you to rent a place you can't afford when I have two spare bedrooms. Not only are you my family by marriage, but you were just willing to sacrifice yourself to save my life, and my son's."

Bree nods, tears lining her face. "I've spent so much time feeling defensive and sorry for myself because Brandon treated me like I wasn't *real* family, and then I couldn't have a family of my own. I channeled all of that into resenting you because you had everything I wanted. And because it was easier than being angry with Brandon, and with my father, who created the dynamic in the first place. You've never hurt me, and I've been awful to you, especially lately. Standing up in that moment was the least I owed you."

Rose hugs Bree again. A tear slides down her cheek as she whispers, "You'll always have a family. Jackson and me."

CHAPTER SIXTY-THREE

Now

The Global Daily Gazette
BRANDON MARTIN CONVICTED OF
DAUGHTER'S HOMICIDE

October 25th, Marblehead, Massachusetts, USA

Brandon Martin was convicted today of the criminally negligent homicide of his daughter, Lily Martin, 3, in Jamaica last November.

According to court reports, Dr. Martin, who was intoxicated at the time, accidentally broke Lily's neck while trying to force her to take a dose of NyQuil. He then attempted to cover up his role in her death by staging a kidnapping and desecrating his daughter's corpse.

After a relatively short two-week trial, the jury returned a verdict in under six hours. Dr. Martin's sentencing hearing has been set, and the district attorney is expected to request the maximum sentence, not only because of the attempts to cover up the crime, but also to blame the death on his wife, Rose Martin, and to have her committed to involuntary psychiatric care.

"We're pleased with the jury's decision, and the speed with which they delivered it," said Assistant District Attorney

Plunkett. *"While Lily's death was not premeditated, the devious actions undertaken by Dr. Martin to hide his role in that death are despicable. We hope Judge Mallory will send a clear message during sentencing that such behavior will not be tolerated by the Commonwealth of Massachusetts."*

Meanwhile, Leo Palser, Brandon Martin's brother-in-law, pleaded guilty to conspiracy to kidnap in a foreign country. Palser claimed that the planned kidnapping was never intended to harm Lily, and his conspirators confirmed details of the plan. His ex-wife, Brianna Palser, and Rose Martin both testified that they believe he never meant Lily harm, and asked the judge to take that into consideration. He sentenced Mr. Palser to five years in prison. He'll be eligible for parole after twenty months.

GDG was unable to reach either Rose Martin or Brianna Palser for comment.

CHAPTER SIXTY-FOUR

Now

Rose

"Mama! Watch me!"

Rose smiles and watches Jackson slide down the plastic chute, tracking the top of his head as he twists through the corkscrew turn. He reaches the bottom and stands, wobbly, then runs through the tanbark to her.

She reaches down and rubs his head. "Good job!"

"Go again!" he says, and runs off toward the steps.

She watches him go, amazed at how much he's changed in the year since they returned from Jamaica. How much bigger he is and how much more coordinated. A pang hits her as she considers how his baby face has shifted into something still baby-ish, but undeniably older, the line of his cheekbones ever-so-slightly closer to Brandon's.

She has ten years until Brandon is released. Nine now, actually, because of time served. Then he'll be out, and she'll have to make a decision about how to handle custody. Brandon will have a right to seek it, and the court will decide. The question is, what does she hope that decision will be?

She wants what's best for Jackson, but what is that? Jackson needs a father, and deserves *his* father if possible. And doesn't

Brandon deserve to be in his son's life? He made a mistake, fueled by alcohol, but he's paying for that mistake. And by the time he's out, he'll have been sober for ten years. Surely that will make a difference?

But she's not sure. The qualities she took for strength in him turned out to be pride, arrogance, and insecurity. She hadn't realized the depths of his resentment against Bree and his father, or that his obsessive need for children was really just ego validation. His drinking was a consequence of those issues, not the cause of them. So will he still be the same man when he gets out of jail, and will he pass those values on to Jackson?

She sighs. Part of her wants to run from the decision, to take Jackson and move back to California. She has family there, and could easily transition her design line to a new location. It would take time to build a new network of sources and clients, but it would be possible, and her reputation has been taking off—morbidly curious people are drawn to the woman who saved her son from his murderous father. Now that the divorce is final she could date again, maybe find a partner who'd be an excellent father to Jackson.

But her feelings aren't the only ones that matter.

Jackson twirls around the corkscrew again, then almost crashes into a little girl with brown hair and dark eyes. He pauses for a second to stare at her, and Rose waits for the tears—the resemblance to Lily is astonishing—but he breaks into a big smile, then runs past Rose to the steps again.

Rose wipes away her own tears, and turns her back to the little girl. The people who say time heals all wounds are wrong. The wound was still there, she'd only gotten better at distracting herself from it. But when something reminds her, like this sweet little girl, she plunges right back into the center of it, like her heart has just been ripped out for the first time.

But Jackson is young, and the memory of his sister is already fading for him. That gives her hope. She has nine years to lay a solid foundation of morals and self-esteem to guide him through whatever he needs. Can she do enough? Can any parent?

For now, all she can do is focus on recovering from the trauma of losing Lily, so she can be the best mother possible for him.

CHAPTER SIXTY-FIVE

Now

Bree

Bree gathers up her handouts and her laptop, then hurries out of the applied child development classroom. The professor's lecture has gone over time and she needs to meet up with Rose at the park so she can take Jackson for the afternoon.

When the police officially arrested Leo, Bree nearly had a breakdown, right in the middle of making jerk chicken for Rose and Jackson. She had no money, no children, and no way to support herself. Yes, she had a liberal arts degree from Wellesley, twenty years old and never used because she'd assumed she'd always have a role to play in her father's company, and the only other thing she'd ever wanted to be was a mother.

Rose had pulled the burning rice off of the stove and poured them each a large glass of red wine. Then, while they waited for the chicken to finish in the oven, Rose convinced Bree that her life was just beginning. They spent the evening finishing that bottle of wine while Bree talked out her options.

"What am I going to do?" she'd wailed.

Rose was quiet for a moment, searching the room for answers. "I'll tell you what you're going to do. You loved teaching those kids, right? So you'll go back to school and get your teaching certification."

The idea had been a revelation. Working with the kids in Jamaica had been just something to do to give back to the community while she waited for her life as a mother to start, but she loved it far more than she expected to. As soon as Rose planted the seed into her mind, it began to sprout. "But, that's, what, at least two years of school? It's a master's degree, right?"

"I'm not sure, but so what?" Rose said. "Two years will pass whether you go back to school or not. The only question is whether you have your certification at the end of it."

"But who knows if I can get into a program? And I don't have the money to pay for it, even if I do."

Rose grabbed her hand. "We'll figure out what you have to do to get in, and I'll pay your tuition."

"I can't let you do that," Bree objected.

Rose waved her off. "Of course you can. But if you insist, you can pay me back in babysitting. I'm the breadwinner now, and I'm gonna need help with Jackson while I work. So you'll go back to school, and I'll work around your class schedule."

Bree had stared at her across the table, speechless and grateful. "I don't know what to say."

"Say, 'let's get started researching those programs.'" Rose jumped up and retrieved her laptop from her office.

Bree had come a hair's breadth from confessing the full truth to her at that moment.

About how the idea to kidnap Lily had really been hers.

How it had first come to her as she sat in the courtyard of the villa waiting for everyone to arrive from the airport, reading the article about Amancia Higgins, caught up in her jealousy and resentment about mothers who didn't deserve the children they'd been blessed with. A fake kidnapping would serve two purposes: get the money from Brandon she and Leo needed so badly, and teach Rose a lesson about how much she should treasure her children.

Leo hadn't realized it was Bree's idea, of course. She'd never overtly mentioned it to him—if she had, he would have suspected her motive had just as much to do with punishing Rose as anything else, and would have recoiled from her. But she knew her husband as well as she knew herself, and she knew how to manipulate him. She left the paper folded to the right section out on the bureau, and made exactly the right comments when he saw it. She put the idea in his head as surely as if she'd said it outright, and she hadn't even felt badly about it.

Until she realized how completely wrong she'd been about Rose's love for her children. The day in the water park was a jolt of reality about what it meant to be a mother, the good and the bad of what it really required of you, and about all the cues she'd misread from Rose. And when she found out about Lillian Marie's death and realized that Rose's hesitation about children had stemmed from the fear she'd be a bad mother—well, Bree had never loathed herself as much as she had in that moment. And still did.

But Rose would never understand any of that, and would never be able to forgive her. If Bree came clean, she'd lose the only family she had left. So she said nothing, and they spent the rest of that evening researching academic programs.

Now, going as quickly as she safely can, Bree pulls up to the sidewalk surrounding the park and trots to the jungle gym. As she approaches, she stares at Rose's profile. Even as Rose smiles at Jackson climbing up the slide, there's a deep sadness to her face. Bree's miscarriages were enough to nearly destroy her—she can't imagine how much more painful it is to lose a child you've protected and loved for over three years. How had she failed to see how much Rose loved her children? How could she have treated Rose like an enemy for so long?

Jealousy—pure and simple. Envy for what Rose had, and what Bree felt she was entitled to.

Rose is a far better sister-in-law than she deserves. And she's deeply grateful to have realized that, and for the chance to mend as much of their relationship as she's able. She'll spend the rest of her life making amends to Rose and Jackson for the horrible choice she made.

CHAPTER SIXTY-SIX

Now

Rose

From the corner of her eye, Rose sees Bree power walking across the grass. She checks her phone. "Okay, Jackson, Aunty Bree is here. Time for you to go home and get some lunch."

"Already?"

Bree reaches them. "Yep, already. I'm actually a few minutes late, so you got extra time to play."

He slides down one final time, then runs over to them. "I have fish sticks?"

Bree laughs. "Of course you can have fish sticks."

Jackson reaches up and grabs Rose's hand in one of his, and Bree's in the other. They start walking toward the cars.

"Mama? Aunty Bree?" He looks up at them.

Rose looks down. "Yes, sweetheart?"

"I love you." He starts jumping as he walks.

"I love you, too, sweetie," Rose says, and Bree echoes her.

A text buzzes onto Rose's phone. She pulls it out and reads. "It's from Anabelle."

Bree leans over to see.

Hey, it's been a while. First, I need to admit something to you. The swab wrapper that the police found with Lily was mine.

I figured out Lily was probably Mateo's daughter that day on the beach, and bought a paternity test at the pharmacy. I swabbed her cheek when I pretended to borrow your Midol. I should have told the police the truth, but I was worried they would think I was the one who hurt her.

Second, Mateo told me he came on to you again while we were in Jamaica, but you shut it down. That tells me something important. I can't see us ever being close friends again, but for the sake of the boys and Bree, I'd like to see if we can move forward. Are you free for lunch?

Bree squeezes Rose's arm. "See, I told you. You just had to give her time."

Rose does a quick calculation. She's supposed to meet up with one of her vendors, but the time is flexible. She makes a decision and sends her response.

1 p.m. at my house?

Anabelle responds almost immediately.

I'll bring Marcus.

Rose wipes away another tear.

See you soon.

EPILOGUE

The Global Daily Gazette
NOTORIOUS SERIAL KILLER TED BAINES DIES

December 13th, San Quentin, California

Ted Baines died today of metastatic pancreatic cancer at the age of 61.

Baines had been serving several life sentences in San Quentin prison for the murder of three children between 1990 and 2010.

Several years into his prison stay, Baines reconnected with his Catholic faith. When faced with the prognosis for his cancer, he made a full confession to a priest, and to authorities, about three other children he murdered in order to "Meet his maker with a clean soul, and give whatever closure is possible to their families." After carefully vetting the confession to be sure Baines' details matched up with the unsolved cases, the police contacted the families and today released the children's names to the public. Amanda Reyes, 6, was found strangled and buried in a shallow grave outside of Petaluma in 1990; Lillian Marie MacGavin, 5, was found drowned in Oakland's Lake Merritt in 1995; Bella Anderson, 6, was found drowned in San Jose's Guadalupe river in 2002.

The cities of Petaluma, Oakland, and San Jose will be holding candlelight vigil remembrance ceremonies simul-

taneously for the three girls; the families ask that in lieu of bringing and leaving flowers, donations may be made to The Polly Klaas Foundation, a non-profit that helps with the recovery of missing children.

A LETTER FROM
M.M. CHOUINARD

Thank you so much for reading *The Vacation*. If you enjoyed the book and have time to leave me a short, honest review on Amazon, Goodreads, or wherever you purchased the book, I'd really appreciate it. Reviews help me reach new readers, and that means I get to bring you more books! Also, if you know of friends or family who would enjoy the book, I'd love your recommendation there, too. And if you have a moment to say hi on social media, please do—I love hearing from you!

If you'd like to keep up to date with any of my new releases, please click the link below to sign up for Bookouture's newsletter; your email will never be shared, and they'll only contact you when they have news about a new Bookouture release.

www.bookouture.com/mm-chouinard

You can also sign up for my personal newsletter at www.mmchouinard.com for news directly from me about all my activities; I also will never share your email. And you can connect with me via my website, Facebook, Goodreads, and Twitter. I'd love to hear from you.

*

Children are particularly vulnerable beings. According to the National Center for Missing & Exploited Children, 421,394 children were reported missing in 2019 to the FBI's National Crime Information Center (NCIC). According to the International Center for Missing & Exploited Children estimates (most based on 2015 numbers), the number that go missing in Australia each year is 20,000; in Canada, 45,288; in Germany, 100,000; in India, 96,000; in Russia, 45,000; in Spain, 20,000; in the UK, 112,853, and in 2015, 1,984 children were reported missing in Jamaica. Some of these children are abducted or harmed by strangers; some by the people they trust and love. But one thing is true in all cases: resources can make all the difference in recovering a missing child and returning them to their family, or at least in providing that family with closure. At the end of this book, I mention an organization close to my heart, The Polly Klaas Foundation; they help recover missing children, educate the public, and advocate for public policies that protect children. They'd surely appreciate your support, as would any other organization devoted to recovering missing children.

Thank you again, so very much, for your support of my books. It means the world to me!

M.

www.mmchouinard.com

mmchouinardauthor

author/show/5998529.M_M_Chouinard

@m_m_chouinard

ACKNOWLEDGMENTS

Thank you so, so much to everyone who takes a chance on my books—I'm deeply grateful! And to everyone who takes the time to review them, blog about them, or tell a friend about them—your support means the world to me.

I am also deeply grateful for the amazing team of people at Bookouture whose time and talent works so much magic on my words. Leodora Darlington's input helped shape the book, and Maisie Lawrence's amazing editing helped work out the kinks. Alexandra Holmes, Martina Arzu, Jane Eastgate and Ramesh Kumar all helped edit and produce it; Kim Nash, Noelle Holten, and Sarah Hardy tirelessly promoted it; Hannah Deuce and Alex Crow helped market it; Rhianna Louise and Alba Proko made the audiobook a reality; and Jenny Geras, Laura Deacon and Natalie Butlin oversaw it all. You are all amazing!

Thank you very much to John's Hall All Age School and to Oakland's Children's Fairyland for patiently answering my strange questions. Any errors/inaccuracies that exist are my fault entirely.

Thanks also to my writing tribe, who help me in more ways than I have space to list. This includes especially Shelly Jackson Buffington, Jon Robson, Erika Anderson-Bolden, Dianna Fernandez-Nichols, Christina Flores, D.K. Dailey, Sharon Alva, Karen McCoy, and my fellow Bookouture authors.

Thanks also to my furbabies—my happy place is puzzling out plot holes with two cats in my lap, another behind my head, and my dog pressed against my side.

But my deepest debt of gratitude is to my husband; his unflagging faith in me has allowed me to believe in myself, and his ability to eat leftovers multiple days in a row has allowed me to meet more than one deadline.